Fixing up homes can be tricky.
Finding true love can be even trickier.
But finding a killer can be plain old deadly . . .

Twin sister divorcees Sunny Taylor and Eve Vaughn have had their fill of both heartaches and headaches. So when they settle down in the small Louisiana town of Sugar Ledge and open a remodeling and repair company, they think they've finally found some peace—even though Eve is still open for romance while Sunny considers her own heart out-of-business.

Then their newest customer ends up face-down in a pond, and his widow is found dead soon after. Unfortunately, Sunny was witnessed having an unpleasant moment with the distraught woman, and suspicion falls on the twins. And when an attempt is made on Eve's life, they find themselves pulled into a murder mystery neither knows how to navigate.

With a town of prying eyes on them, and an unknown culprit out to stop them, Sunny and Eve will have to depend on each other like never before if they're going to clip a killer in the bud.

Books by June Shaw

Twin Sisters Mysteries
A Fatal Romance

Published by Kensington Publishing Corporation

A Fatal Romance

A Twin Sisters Mystery

June Shaw

LYRICAL PRESS
Kensington Publishing Corp.
www.kensingtonbooks.com

Lyrical Press books are published by
Kensington Publishing Corp. 119 West 40th Street New York, NY 10018

First Electronic Edition: January 2017
eISBN-13: 978-1-5161-0092-7
eISBN-10: 1-5161-0092-1

First Print Edition: January 2017
ISBN-13: 978-1-5161-0095-8
ISBN-10: 1-5161-0095-6

Printed in the United States of America

Acknowledgements

Thank you to my children, grandchildren, and Bob, for your generous belief and support through all of my writing endeavors.

My writers' groups Mystery Writers of America, Sisters in Crime, Guppies, and Romance Writers of America—especially SOLA, our South Louisiana chapter of RWA, you continue to give me tremendous inspiration and generously share the vast scope of your knowledge.

I truly appreciate the many individuals who helped edit my work, especially Vicki Mchenry.

Marci Clark, I can't thank you enough for your help.

To my readers—I adore you! Thanks for following my work and telling others about it. I love hearing from you at jushaw@bellsouth.net and also seeing your reviews of my books!

Chapter 1

I stood in a rear pew as a petite woman in red stepped into the church carrying an urn and stumbled. She fell forward. Her urn bounced. Its top popped open, and ashes flew. A man's remains were escaping.

"Oh, no!" people cried.

"Jingle bells," I hummed and tried to control my disorder but could not. Words from the song spewed out of my mouth.

"Not now," my twin Eve said at my ear while ashes sprinkled around us like falling gray snow. She pointed to my jacket's sleeve and open pocket. "Uh-oh. Parts of him fell in there."

I saw a few drops like dust on the sleeve and jerked my pocket wider open. Powdery bits lay across the tissue I'd blotted my beige lipstick with right before coming inside St. Gertrude's. "I think that's tissue residue," I said, wanting to convince myself. I grabbed the pocket to turn it inside out.

"Don't dump that." Eve shoved on my pocket. "It might be his leg. Or bits of his private parts."

"Here comes Santa Claus," I sang.

She slapped a hand over my mouth. "Hush, Sunny."

The dead man's wife shoved up from her stomach to her knees, head spinning toward me so fast I feared she'd get whiplash.

"Sorry," Eve told her. "My sister can't help it."

Beyond the wife a sixtyish priest, younger one, and other people appeared squeamish scooping coarse ashes off seats of the rough-hewn pews. An older version of the wife used a broom and dustpan to sweep ash from the floor. People dumped their findings back into the urn. Other mourners scooted from the church through side doors. A boiled crayfish scent teased my nostrils. Someone must have peeled a few crustaceans for a breakfast omelet and didn't soap her hands well enough.

Ashes scattered along the worn green carpet like a seed trail to entice birds.

"Look, there's more of him. I'll go find a vacuum," I said.

The widow faced me. "No! Get out."

"But she's my sister," Eve said.

"As if I can't tell. You leave with her. Go away." The petite woman wobbled on shiny stilettos, aiming a finger toward the front door.

I sympathized with her before this minute. Now she was ticking me off. I'd been kicked out of places before, but never a funeral. "I didn't really know your husband, but Eve did. I stopped to see if she wanted to go out for lunch, and she asked me to come here first. She said y'all were nice people."

"We are!" The roots of the wife's pecan-brown hair were black, I saw, standing toe-to-toe with her, although my toes were much bigger inside my size ten pumps. I was five eight and a half. She was barely five feet. Five feisty feet. "But you're not going to suck up parts of my husband's body in a vacuum bag." She whipped her pointed finger toward me like a weapon. "And you need to stop singing."

I wanted to stop but imagined parts of the man that might be sucked into a vacuum cleaner and ripped out a loud chorus, my face burning. Nearby mourners appeared shocked. Mouths dropped open.

"You don't know my sister," Eve told the little woman who'd just lost a spouse. Actually, lost him twice. "Sunny can't help singing when she's afraid. And that includes anything dealing with sex, courtesy of her ex-husband."

"What does sex have to do with Zane?" The wife's cheeks flamed.

Should I tell her about his privates possibly being in my pocket? Second thoughts said not to. "Who knows? But you don't need to worry. I certainly wasn't having an affair with your husband," I said, quieting my song to a hum.

"Just the thought of sex makes her sing," my sister explained. "Maybe it's a good thing she doesn't think of it often."

The widow shook her finger. "Zane was always faithful to me."

"I'm sure he was," I said, working to get my singing instincts under control. Nodding toward the carpet, I spoke without a hint of a tune. "I'd really like to help you get those pieces of him out of the rug. If we can just find an empty vacuum bag, I'll—"

"Go! Get away!"

I stomped out of the church into muggy spring air. Eve clopped behind me toward her Lexus in the parking lot.

"You told me they were fine people," I said.

"They are. At least he is. Or was." Eve shook her head, making sunshine spread golden highlights over her flame-red waves. Her clear blue eyes sparkled. I was glad few people could tell us apart. "I only met his wife that day I laid their pavers, and Zane stayed and helped a little. When she got home, he introduced us. She seemed pleasant."

"I guess you never know."

"Good grief, Sunny. You kept singing after she spilled her husband."

I lowered my face toward the chipped sidewalk.

Eve touched my arm. "I know, but maybe you can try harder."

I nodded. She knew how long I'd fought to stop the songs that began when a major tragedy threw my life into an unending tailspin. Junior high had been especially painful.

At the next corner, we waited for a truck to pass. I checked my sleeve in the sunshine, relieved that if any ashes had been there, the breeze had blown them off to a better place. "There weren't many people in church."

Eve frowned. She started across the street. "They've lived here less than three years and don't have much family. Zane's job kept him out of town a lot. When he joined our line-dance class, he said his wife was shy and didn't like to dance anyway."

"I don't think she's shy. I think she was involved in his death."

"What?" Eve stopped. "The man drowned. It was an accident."

I spread my hands. "In his own yard? Why didn't he fall in that pond before now?"

"Because this week he tripped on a cypress knee near the job we did in their yard and knocked his head on the tree and fell in. He couldn't swim. And you don't even know his wife."

No, neither she nor her husband had been home when we created that seating area in their yard. I tugged on Eve's arm to get her across the street so oncoming cars waiting for us could turn.

She kept talking. "Darn it, Daria Snelling might not be the sweetest person right after her husband's ashes flew to the heavens, but that doesn't make her a killer."

"Eve, you know I have good instincts about people. And covers on burial urns are sealed. They aren't supposed to come off." I created a mental picture of what happened. "Besides, she was walking along carpet. There weren't any bumps for her to trip over."

My twin's face pinched up. Not a pretty picture. "How do you know that?"

"Her shoes. When the organ music started and everyone turned to look back, I noticed her shoes."

"I can't believe this, Sunny. You aren't usually that shallow." She stomped off ahead of me.

I strolled faster behind. "You know I can't even pronounce the brands of expensive shoes. I saw she was tiny but looked extra tall, so I glanced at her shoes. Her heels must be four inches. That's really showy for a grieving widow."

"Wearing stilettos make her a murderer?"

"And a bright red dress. Red?" I caught up with Eve. "I think she wanted to dump her husband so his remains couldn't all be buried together."

She threw up her palms. "You are so sick. The man was my friend."

"Geez, you worked for him briefly and saw him a couple of times in dance class."

"That doesn't give you the right to cut down his family."

"And if you hadn't made that dig about my unhappiness with sex, his wife wouldn't have gotten so upset."

Eve knew my limited experience with sex had come with Kev soon after our marriage. If I'd known how unpleasant one man could make the quick chore, I would have started chuckling in bed much sooner. Eve and I were both divorced—she, three times, her choice—and her admiring exes still showered her with gifts. Kevin left me with little and did so after my spontaneous laughter about frightening things escalated to include sex. But he made the intimacy so unpleasant I had begun to dread it.

Watching my sister, I saw myself a little slimmer, wearing dressier clothes and an unpleasant grimace. At thirty-eight, she was fairly attractive in a black knit top and skirt, emerald green jacket, and spike heels. I wore low heels and tan slacks with a white shirt and my favorite jacket, a rust-colored silk. With a pocket that now held parts of Zane Snelling.

"Sis," I said, "do you see any ashes in my hair? Or on my sleeve or other places on my clothes?"

She did a quick inspection of my hair and looked longer at my clothes, while I did the same to her. "I don't see anything anymore." She checked inside my pocket. "Except in there."

"You're clean," I said, voice dull from knowing I still wore parts of a man. I slid my jacket off and carefully folded it, not letting anything escape.

Eve wrenched her car door open and flung herself inside. I slid onto the passenger seat. "Buckle up." She waited until I did before pulling onto the street.

"Do you want to go out for lunch?" I asked.

"My stomach's too upset. I'm going to change clothes and hit the gym."

Positive news came to mind. "Anna Tabor wants us to give her a price to replace the picture window in her den with a glass block one." It wasn't much of a job, but we were still pleased with every one that came in.

"Why does she want that?"

"She said it would be unusual and attractive. I'll do the estimate this evening."

"Okay. I'll check your work tomorrow, and we'll schedule her in."

I nodded. Our deceased father had been an excellent carpenter who made us enjoy working with our hands. We'd done quite a bit of work with him and liked changing the design of some of his jobs. Ever since I convinced Eve to join me to start Twin Sisters Remodeling & Repairs months ago, we were gradually building up our name and earning people's trust. We were both strong and knew how to use subcontractors and power tools. So far my estimates all turned out correct. Still, being dyslexic made me want all written work and numbers double-checked. Early struggles and some teachers' hurtful comments made me still doubt myself.

Most of the sugar cane stalks in fields Eve drove past stood three feet tall. On the opposite side of the highway, the brown bayou lazed along, shielding gators, turtles, catfish, and other water creatures. We sped by shotgun houses dotted between brick homes in our small town of Sugar Ledge and entered our subdivision. Houses were brick and stucco and most of the lawns well-tended, especially on Eve's street. She reached her house, remoted the garage door, and pulled in.

"I shouldn't have snapped at you. I'm sorry," she said.

I leaned over and kissed her forehead like Mom used to do to let us know anytime we were forgiven. "To make amends, can I see what you're working on?"

She considered a minute, then led the way through her picture-book house. The lingering fragrance from vanilla triple-scented candles made me want yellow cake. The spacious den held large windows and pale neutral shades, its main color from Mexican floor tile and Eve's muted-tone abstracts, which I determined she painted when she was between dating or marriage.

She kept most of her home with a colorless feel like a blank canvas, letting her imagination soar. Pulling a key from the second drawer of an end table beside the white marshmallow-leather sofa, she unlocked a door off the den.

Shell-shocked. Her studio made me feel that way even more so than usual. While the rest of her house gave off a bland feel, this room was infused with color, especially on a huge canvas on an easel in the center of the room. Splashes of color and bright dots of varying sizes filled almost every inch of the canvas.

"Intriguing," I said. "Who does it represent?"

"Dave Price. That man is terrific."

"I can tell. Y'all must have an explosive relationship."

"I only know him casually. Of course I'm planning to change that." Her grin widened. "This is how I'm expecting our relationship to become."

"Impressive."

The other dozen or so paintings on easels and standing on the floor represented men she'd dated or married. Some wore drab shades. A couple of canvases showed small vases. Others held crudely-drawn flowers or apples. She wasn't a proficient artist, but while our business grew, this gave her something to do with extra time besides line dancing once a week and working out at the gym. She didn't get to see her daughter in Houston often enough. A sex therapist would enjoy analyzing what she did in here.

"Thanks for letting me see your latest work. Sorry about the funeral ruckus."

"You didn't cause it." The fair skin between her eyes creased. "I'd like to know what happened after we left the church."

I'd prefer to know what really happened to the dead man before we went there. "Maybe you'll find out. See you later." I locked the stained-glass front door on my way out.

Ambling alongside her taupe stucco house, I paused in back to admire the fountain burbling on her patio. Inside it, a stone angel poured bleach-scented water. Again, I wished the fountain held live fish instead of the almost real-looking plastic gold ones. Angling through the little grass path between the yards behind her house, I passed a dog-eared cedar fence on the right and white solid vinyl fence panels on the left. Then I stepped across the next street, which was mine. Yards and cars here were less fancy than on hers. A couple of clunkers sat in circular drives. Even the air smelled less pure.

"Your petunias still look good," I told Miss Hawthorne, kneeling beside the purple blossoms lining the concrete path to her front stoop.

"Thank you. Oh, Sunny, look. The girdle you sold me still works great. Two years old and still holding me in." She struggled up to her feet. Miss Hawthorne was probably older than my mother and didn't like help. She'd insisted on a girdle, not that newer stuff she said was smaller than her gloves, and bought it from me while I still worked at Fancy Ladies, our town's only upscale dress shop. I'd needed to quit that job since I had developed excruciating heel spurs that wouldn't get better until I stopped standing all day every day, and surgery wouldn't correct them.

The top of Miss Hawthorne's plump face hid beneath the wide floppy brim of her straw hat, which didn't hide her pleasant smile. Dirt tumbled off the knees of her slacks. The girdle pushed her stomach up and made the thick roll above her waist more pronounced through her knit shirt. I'd learned to notice details while I fitted ladies with undergarments and determined she had gained fifteen pounds since I sold her that girdle.

"You look good, Miss Hawthorne. But next time you're at Fancy Ladies, you might check out the newer styles. You could find a control panty or shaper that's more comfortable."

"Oh no, hon, this works just fine."

"Good. I'll see you later." I strolled off, pleased to know her smile finally returned after her misery because a relative's pet she had been keeping escaped from her fenced backyard.

A couple of houses to the left, I reached mine, a gray brick with a darker gray stucco entrance. I entered, experiencing the same stir of unpleasant emotions as every other time I returned from Eve's. My place was pleasant, yet now felt like it held too much clutter, even if there wasn't much extra. The house even smelled dull. I plugged in a vanilla-scented air freshener.

Standing beneath the foyer light, I yanked my jacket pocket wide open. Course grayish bits of a man lay inside. I strode to my kitchen trashcan and stepped on the pedal to pop it open, ready to turn my pocket inside out.

No, that wouldn't be right. I let the can's top close. Where else might I put these powdery flakes? I couldn't dump them in my yard or even think of flushing them.

This was part of a person that needed to be treated with respect. I hung the jacket in the foyer, grabbed a phonebook, and looked up a number, relieved to find the person listed. I punched in numerals and listened to the phone ring. A click sounded.

"Snelling residence," a woman said. "We can't get to the phone now, but we will return your call as soon as we're home if you leave your number." Daria Snelling sounded much more pleasant on the machine than she had in church.

I hitched up my chin and tried to sound cheerful. "Hello, Mrs. Snelling. This is the tall redhead who blurted a song this morning at St. Gertrude's. I'm sorry I sang and really sorry about your husband." I cleared my throat. "I called to tell you I have something of his. I'm sure it's something you'll want." I gave my number in case she didn't have caller I.D. and hung up.

My stomach rumbled, reminding me of why I'd stopped at Eve's in the first place. I considered eating leftover red beans and sausage, but instead yanked rice from the fridge, heated a pile of it in a bowl, and squirted my initials over it with ketchup. I munched on this entrée with a chunk of lettuce topped with a few raisins, fat-free ranch dressing, and crunchy chow mein noodles.

In my bedroom, I peeled off church clothes and struggled to snap my jeans, then yanked on a purple T-shirt with gold letters in front that said TWIN SISTERS. Small letters on its back said Remodeling & Repairs.

I slipped into my backyard, where flats of flowers waited. Sunshine and temperatures in the mid-sixties made the spring afternoon appealing. A cool breeze pushed off earlier mugginess that reminded us soon south Louisiana would treat us all to steam baths.

Digging up scraggly plants, I tossed them aside, noting sirens in the distance. A harsh memory trying to erupt froze me in place. I fought the remembrance from my youth and forced it away.

I stabbed soil with my shovel, knowing something was definitely not right with Daria Snelling. Years of working in close contact with women at Fancy Ladies let me learn much more than I wanted to about their private lives so that now my initial instincts were normally correct. Dragging topsoil to the flowerbeds, I mentally weighed the probability of what police decided happened to Zane Snelling and shook my head. Why had he tripped and slid into the deep water in their backyard near the seating area Eve and I recently completed?

Uneasy about his drowning, I added weed preventer to my beds and topped the mounds with cypress mulch. Next came tall coneflowers as a nice backdrop. I set daylilies in front and filled in the closest section with coreopsis.

When the sun was dipping behind rooftops, my riot of color pleased me. I watered everything and kicked off my dirty shoes near the backdoor. Walking into the kitchen, I was ready to develop a bid for Anna Tabor's window that would add to our other pending jobs. A flashing red light on the answering machine caught my attention. I pressed the button, expecting Mrs. Snelling.

"Sunny! Where are you?" Eve yelled.

My heart slammed against my ribs. Something happened to Mom?

I played the next message. "Sunny, it's Eve. I need you!"

My quivering finger pressed her number in Memory on my phone.

"Where have you been?" she asked with a sob. "I've been calling."

"Planting flowers. Is it Mom?"

"Somebody broke into my house!"

"What? Are you okay?"

"No. Come over."

"I'm there!" I raced toward my sister.

Chapter 2

Swallowing a song, I rushed beyond the plywood plastered across the sliding glass door leading to Eve's art room. I sped across the patio to her locked kitchen door and shoved on the bell. She didn't answer soon enough, so I beat on her door. It swung open.

"Oh, Sunny!" She flew into my arms, her intense trembles matching mine.

I gripped her as though my strength could protect her. "Are you hurt? I'll get an ambulance." I stepped back, scanning her head, arms, and torso.

"I'm fine. I wasn't home."

"What happened?"

Shrugging off my attempt to inspect her more, she drew me inside and locked her door. She guided me to the den and pointed to her studio's shut door. "They got in there."

"Did they take anything?"

"It's awful." She shoved the door open to the room where she painted.

My knees locked while I stared at massive red X's spray painted across every one of her paintings now tossed like trash by the roadside.

"And look at this." She stepped behind a cluster of her ruined art. On the wall, painted words looked like dripping blood: *WHERE IS WHAT'S HIS?*

"What does this mean? What do you have? Who does it belong to?"

"I don't have a thing." She wore an annoyed expression.

"But you must." I stared at the words.

"Sunny, I have no idea what that's about. The police just left. They asked enough questions and didn't seem to believe everything I told them, but I sure thought you would."

"I do." I gripped her hands and shivered from the possibility of what could have happened to her.

"Thank goodness I was gone." She walked toward the shattered sliding door that 3/8 inch plywood shielded. "The police think the burglar saw me leaving for the gym and then broke in. The intruder searched this room but didn't find what he was looking for and tried to reach the rest of the house. Look." Deep scrapes sliced into wood around the door's locking mechanism. The double-keyed lock she'd installed prevented that person from going any farther inside the house.

Eve stared at the art, her face rumpled with sadness. "Those weren't Rembrandts, but they were important to me."

"Maybe you can paint more."

She looked barely energetic enough for a shrug.

"Who boarded the door?"

She shuffled from her studio and tilted her head toward the left. "Jake Angelette brought over some of the wood he keeps in his garage and helped me nail it up."

"He just moved there. I could have done it with you."

"But I couldn't reach you. And slamming a hammer against something felt good."

I understood why she hadn't wanted to use her power tools. I nudged my chin toward the ruined paintings. "Which one of those men would the intruder be talking about?"

She dropped to the sofa that released a soft *whoosh*. "I don't know. The police asked what I had that belonged to a man. I don't have a thing. They wanted to know why anybody would break in there and smash everything and write those words on my wall if it wasn't true."

I sat with her. "What did you tell them?"

She threw out her hands. "They were taking the word of a crook instead of me."

"What about all the men your paintings represented?"

She shoved up to her feet, eyes wider. "You don't think I told the police *that*?"

"If you don't, how will they have any clue as to what this is about?"

She bent to look me in the eye. "Sunny, the meaning of those paintings is private. Art is a personal thing."

"One of the guys you dated must have left something here."

"Don't you think I've checked? I went over every room. There's nothing."

I walked back to her studio and stared at *WHERE IS WHAT'S HIS?* Gooseflesh erupted on my arms. "This is my fault."

"How could it possibly be your fault? Did you do it?"

"Of course not, but maybe I did something stupid that caused someone to come and create this mess. I left a message on Daria Snelling's answering machine saying I have something important of her husband's. You know, those parts of him in my jacket. She probably came for what I have and did this."

Eve narrowed her eyes. "What else did you say in your message?"

"I gave her my number."

"Then why would she break in here? All she'd have to do is pick up the phone and call you."

"I know. I didn't give my address or my name, just said I was the tall redhead who sang. Maybe since she'd met you once, she thought I was you and found out where you live."

Eve tightened her lips. "I can't believe she would do this."

I blew out a sigh, not reminding her of what I thought of the woman. "But I don't understand why she hasn't called yet."

My sister ambled to the den. "Maybe she didn't get home from the church. Who knows how long it takes to do everything she needed to do there and afterward?"

"Well, you can't stay in this house. The burglar might return. Come stay with me."

Eyes stern, she shook her head. "The police suggested I stay someplace else, especially tonight, but nobody's going to run me out of my house." She was always the braver twin, the one who peeked into dark spaces first. "Anyway, he or she wouldn't come back right away while police are checking so closely. And tonight I'm having company." Her lips tilted up a little at the edges.

Ah, a date. "Does your company carry a gun?"

"Yes."

"Good. And will this be Dave, the exciting guy from your last painting?"

"Don't I wish? No, my second ex is in town and needs a place to stay."

My mind took a quick mental scroll. "Stan? You're going to make him sleep in a guest bedroom, right?"

"That's none of your business." She glanced at the frameless wall clock, large black numbers circling a small center. "Time for you to leave. I wanted you to know what happened."

"Call if you change your mind. Or if you need me."

She nodded. "Thanks. I don't think I'll need anyone else tonight. The police should be driving by my house often."

I hummed, afraid for her and figuring she could become intimate with that man, her second ex, which frightened me while I imagined myself wrapped up in a sexual interlude. I didn't understand how she could enjoy romance so much but couldn't judge anyone's actions. Stan currently lived in Shreveport and always seemed nice enough. I hadn't seen him in a while.

I departed through the front door and heard Eve throw the bolt. Inspecting outside the doorway, I found no sign of tampering. I checked around the windows in front. Nobody tried to get in that I could see. Creeping beside the house, I rubbed my hand over the stucco and tried to see inside the windows like a burglar might.

Normally Eve left the drapes in her dining room and spare bedrooms open. Tonight they were shut with only white backing visible. I stepped close to those windows, trying to peer through the sides or middles, pleased that the drapes fit snugly. I could tell there was light in those rooms but saw nothing else. On tiptoes, I tried to peek into her bathroom window.

Curtains inside ruffled and parted, making me stumble backward. A face against the window stared down at me. It resembled mine. Eve held her cell phone away from her ear. Unhooking her window, she slid it up an inch. "My neighbor said somebody's looking in my windows, and I should call the police to come back."

"Good for her." I turned to the house on the right. Busybody Mrs. Wilburn might finally have a positive purpose. Maybe she'd help protect my sister.

"Wait a sec," Eve said. "Let me tell her it's just you so she won't get the cavalry out here." She placed her phone close to her mouth and spoke.

I waved at Mrs. Wilburn, the frightfully pale woman whose mean dark eyes stared at me from a window in a brightly lit room. Royce stood behind her, watching me. He'd come for a rare visit to his mother?

She dropped her drapes without either of them returning my greeting.

"She's not happy to see me," I called to Eve.

"She's worried. Maybe the guy will come back and grab her. Okay, I need to get ready. And my neck's twisted with me up on the ledge of the hot tub bending down to talk to you."

I gave her a one finger wave. "Have fun."

"I always do." My sister flashed the most beautiful smile. "And, Sunny, the police already did what you're doing out there."

"Maybe I can catch something they missed."

"Right." She smirked. "You might be messing up and covering shoeprints with yours."

"I hadn't thought about that." Not surprised that I'd mess up, I scooted back from her house.

"Later." Eve dropped her curtains.

I trotted back to my house without noting anything unusual along the way. Inside, I worried about my sister. Then decided the man with her tonight should provide safety, at least letting a would-be thief see his car or truck out front. I hoped Stan drove a large truck. A mean-looking black one.

Needing to eat before doing paperwork but not too hungry, I fixed a couple of ham and cracker sandwiches and spread jelly between crackers for dessert. Afterward I worked on an estimate for Anna's window, concern for Eve foremost in my mind. Since my worry wouldn't help her, I focused on the small job.

We would need to pull Anna Tabor's existing window out of her bathroom. We'd never installed glass block before, but it had to be similar to laying floor tile, which we had done often. We'd just finished a job like that in a young couple's kitchen. I phoned Badeaux Lumber, which stayed open late, and spoke to Luke about what we needed. They didn't keep glass blocks in stock but would order them. He gave me prices and assured me my plan for the job was correct. We'd build from both jambs toward the center and use flat spacers between the blocks. Of course we'd plumb and level them while we worked. Putting my glasses on, I developed an estimate for Anna.

In the morning, I phoned Eve. She didn't answer immediately, scattering jitters through me like sprayed fire ants. Should I rush over?

"Umm?" she answered, voice groggy.

"Sorry if I woke you, but I wanted to make sure you're all right."

"No, that's okay. It's my sister," she said to someone.

"Y'all go back to sleep," I said. "Or whatever."

With a laugh, she hung up.

At least this morning she was safe. I wanted to stay around her, or especially to get her to come and spend time at my house, away from hers. Maybe if I fixed some of her favorite foods, I could bribe her here and then get her to stay until the police arrested whoever broke into her house.

My phone rang. "Hello. This is Twin Sisters," I said, making my voice cheerful.

"Hey, Sunny, it's Mona at Fancy Ladies. I hate to call at the last minute, but the last woman we hired developed kidney stones. Could you possibly come in for us?"

Today? After someone broke into Eve's house yesterday? "Sorry, I can't."

"We'd need help for at least a week."

I did have free time the next few days. The business Eve and I started was growing slowly, and we hadn't managed to snag any large jobs yet. Women in town knew me as a person who'd sold them their undergarments and sleepwear, while men knew me as a tall redhead. Now that Eve lived here, who knew what her status was, but neither of our reputations so far led people to believe we'd be expert craftsmen. We had been showing them gradually. I was grateful that I was thrifty and had put money aside. Anna wasn't in a rush for her project, and my heel spurs had been feeling better the last week or so. But Eve needed me available to help keep her safe now. "Sorry, I can't. Maybe some other time?"

A sigh. "Okay, thanks. Maybe so."

I really hated to turn down that simple task of selling undies since I would soon need my roof replaced, and I could use the extra income.

On the way to the grocery store, I swung in front of Eve's place. I'd spoken to her moments ago, but wanted to make certain she was still all right. I dug in my purse and found my eyeglass case empty. I'd probably left my glasses near the pad with estimates.

Even so, I couldn't miss the black Hummer squatting in the circular drive out front like an army tank. Stan's business must be doing well. No sign of any new break-ins. I probably shouldn't tiptoe around her windows to make sure. Making a decision, I drove on.

Who could have broken into Eve's house, wanting something of a man's? I had met some of the guys she dated since her last divorce, but after a while they looked alike. Their dark hair held touches of gray, and they appeared to work out in gyms. Energetic men, they kept their white smiles aimed at my sister, who resembled me—but she put out, and I didn't. She gave them that bit of information right when they met me, which I felt was unnecessary.

The store's parking lot was almost empty. I marched inside and inspected bananas and homegrown tomatoes as well as I could without my glasses.

"Sunny," a deep voice called. Eve's first husband, Jacques Thibodaux, stepped near and kissed my cheek. "How nice to see you."

"You, too, Jacques." Was there a convention of my sister's exes in town? Her most recent ex-husband lived forty miles away, but we never saw him. Jacques lived in Houston. His hair was thinner and grayer since I'd last laid eyes on him. He'd thickened in the waist. I glanced behind him, hoping to see the daughter he and Sunny had produced. "Where's the little one?"

His smile widened at my suggestion that their grown offspring was little. "She's teaching those preschoolers. My wife Melanie came down with me a couple of days for my friend's funeral."

A wretchedly thin high-heeled blonde sashayed near and flopped out her long hand. "Melanie," she said with a Texas twang.

Clasping her frigid hand made me want an overcoat. "I'm Sunny."

"The *little one* wanted to come but needs to save time off for when she has the baby," Jacques said.

That baby would make my sister a grandmother. Hard to believe, even though Eve's daughter had gotten pregnant and married young, just like Eve did the first time around.

"I saw you at Zane Snelling's funeral," I told Melanie. "You were using a broom."

"I was there, too," Jacques said. "But I went out after his wife tripped. There was no way I could sweep up my buddy. Zane and I used to work together in the oilfield."

"I didn't know him," Melanie said, "but I wanted to help."

I smiled tight-lipped and wondered what Jacques might think if he knew I had parts of his friend at home in my pocket.

He wrapped an arm around his wife. "This here's a good woman. She doesn't even mind those things I give your sister."

"I have you," she said with a smile she froze in place and faced me. "I know Jacques pays your twin a nice alimony, even though he wouldn't have to. And I've learned about the cars." Those would be the Lexuses he sends Eve every couple of years.

"We can still afford them," Jacques said.

"Jacques can give your sister anything he wants." Melanie planted a kiss on his lips. "Except his heart."

Ugh, mush. "Please give my niece a big hug for me," I told Jacques.

"I sure will."

Melanie's gaze raked me from head to toe. "I know his first wife is your twin. Does she still look like you?"

I offered a bright smile. "Yes, she does."

Melanie pursed her lips. I waited for her to say something complimentary. Instead, she moved away and picked through cantaloupes.

Jacques leaned near my ear. "Tell my gal I still miss her."

Stunned, I returned a wave to his wife when she came back to Jacques. Gripping his hand, she took him and her cantaloupe toward the checkout.

Did he really still miss Eve? He had sent her those cars hoping to get her back and let her know how important she'd been to him, he'd always said. Eventually he gave up, met someone else, and remarried.

And did his wife really mean she didn't mind the cars and jewelry he sent my sister?

My legs tensed. Jacques and Melanie were only in town a few days. Could she have broken into Eve's house? But if she did, what might this young woman want? Eve's latest car? She should figure it would be locked in the garage. Besides, she couldn't just drive the thing away. Jacques would notice she had that beauty.

Of course she could destroy it.

What about Eve's other two exes? As far as I knew, they only gave her nice gifts after their divorces to mimic what Jacques did. At least that's what Eve determined. Neither of those men had remarried, but they might be in relationships with women who'd want ... what?

I grabbed cans of whole tomatoes and tomato paste. Stared at them in my hands. A large can, the whole tomatoes, like a large man. Or the small can—like a petite woman. Could she smash a sliding glass door until she got inside?

Absolutely. A woman could also do all of that damage to the paintings.

"I would have liked it," a woman said from the end of the canned vegetable aisle. Her voice sounded somewhat familiar, so I paid closer attention. Daria Snelling walked past with an empty buggy. Again this morning she wore crimson—a short sheath with matching heels.

She didn't glance my way. A man on the other side of her wore a navy shirt, wide sunglasses, and a baseball cap, and didn't appear to have a buggy. I may have seen him before, but wasn't certain.

I moved closer. Peeking into the rear aisle, I could see only their backsides. I sensed they were talking pleasantly. They didn't pick up anything or seem to care about groceries. Understandable for her with just losing a husband. But why had she come into the store today? Only to amble? To talk to this person?

I yanked up a couple more items and rushed to show up at the checkout when they arrived.

Daria headed toward me, her buggy still empty. Had she even noticed? I shoved over to a checkout counter three away from hers, considering what to do next. The man with the cap stood behind her, a hefty teen cashier blocking most of his face. The man's hand gripped a loaf of white bread. Not a diet person. Probably without a dieting wife. I didn't spot a ring.

I considered lining up behind him, but Daria might still be furious with me, and having her yell at me in a store couldn't produce anything positive. I did want to know why she hadn't responded to my message on her answering machine. Why wouldn't a wife rush to call an unfamiliar woman who claimed to own something of her deceased husband's?

Plucking my groceries out of the cart, I set them in front of the cashier who asked if I found everything I needed.

"I sure did." I glanced again at Daria's checkout.

She headed for the exit. No buggy. Only a purse on her arm. The man striding behind her.

I paid for my groceries, tossed them in plastic bags before the cashier could, and rushed outside. In the busy parking lot, I found no sign of her or the fellow who'd followed her. Disappointment sucked down my spirit. I didn't care what she did. What I did care about was properly disposing of her husband's remains that I unwillingly possessed.

Along the highway, I made a quick stop at a squat building that formerly sold ice. Now two signs out front read *Shrimp* and *Welding Supplies*. I chose shrimp. Buying a couple pounds of medium peeled ones, I then swung down my sister's street, hating that I did. I didn't want to start checking on her, but this day was different. This was the day after somebody broke into her house.

A few houses before hers, I stomped the brakes. My mouth went dry.

The Hummer was gone from Eve's driveway. A large truck took its place. A midnight blue truck. Why would another man be there right after Stan left? The person who drove it might have been the one who broke into her house. He may have just been waiting for Stan to leave.

I hadn't been able to save one sister. I needed to save this one.

Chapter 3

Knowing I could do whatever was necessary if Eve was in trouble, I mentally rummaged through my vehicle. I couldn't reach the tire jack fast enough. The tool was in the truck bed beneath boxes of ceramic tile we would soon use in a customer's bathroom. The toolbox behind my cab held hammers and crowbars I could reach in a minute.

Envisioning my plan to grab one of each and rush in yelling and wielding them, I was almost at Eve's. Her front door opened. A man stepped out, followed by my sister. She wore spiky heels and a sky blue dress and wasn't screaming for help or even looking unhappy. In fact, she nudged up to the guy and didn't pay attention to the street.

From what I could see of him as I passed, he appeared slightly younger than some men she normally dated. Of course Stan had just left her house from his overnighter while I grocery shopped. And a new guy was already there?

I checked my rearview mirror. He stood a bit taller than Eve and looked thick in the shoulders and trim in the waist. The man pointed toward the front of her house while she smiled and kept nodding, looking at him, not where he indicated.

I drove around the block to my own place, hauled groceries inside, and phoned her.

"Hello," she said like a happy sparrow.

"Who is he?"

"Who?"

"The guy standing beside you. Or that you're standing against. Who is he?"

She took a minute in which I imagined she backed away from him and glanced around, expecting to see me. "Where are you?" she asked much softer.

"In my house. Just like you should be since yours was broken into yesterday. You should have your doors bolted against guys like the ones you have streaming in and out of your place." She didn't respond, so I kept going. "You probably don't even know the name of this new one who stopped by right after your other guy left."

What was wrong with me? I was being ugly and didn't normally preach or pass judgment.

But when I was a child, I'd watched our other sister murdered. Now I was grown. I couldn't let anything happen to Eve.

"I'll talk to you tomorrow," she said, tone snippy.

"I'm fixing shrimp creole for lunch today," I got in before she disconnected. I stomped through my kitchen, wanting to dash to her house and protect her, but she sounded okay, at least for the moment. Eve might not have replied when I told her the dish I'd planned, but she would come over. Shrimp creole was one of her favorites. She didn't eat it often since she didn't cook much, but if someone served her the dish, she almost kissed the preparer's feet.

With barely enough time to get everything ready, I filled a pot of water with a pinch of salt and turned the fire high. I chopped and smothered onions, bell pepper, and garlic—the trinity of southern cooking. When the salty water came to a rolling boil, I went for the rice and saw I hadn't bought any.

Why not? I mused and recalled I'd been heading for the aisle with rice when I spied Daria and went after her. Since returning to the store would take too long, I called a couple of my neighbors.

At 11:59 a.m. my doorbell rang. One dong at a time. The front door. Eve wasn't using her key and wanted to let me know she was still annoyed.

"So glad you came," I said, letting her in.

She trotted past me, nose in the air. "If I hadn't come here, you probably would have staked out my house. I figured this would be better."

Her sarcasm made me grit my teeth. I told myself everything would be fine. The money I'd missed out on at Fancy Ladies this week didn't matter. Taking the time to shop this morning and prepare her special dish wasn't important, either. I followed her to my kitchen.

"You were pretty sure of yourself, believing I'd come." She stood, fists on hips, and surveyed the table set for two.

"Maybe I have a date planned."

"More likely you'd planned yourself a libido memorial."

Her smart remark made me almost sorry I'd cooked for her. She stepped near the stove, checking the largest pot. "I thought you'd have shrimp creole. These are noodles."

"I wanted to try something different." And the only one of my neighbors who'd been home was also out of rice. "I know you like variety in your life."

She flitted her eyes at me. Eve spooned some of the shrimp dish over the pasta. She took sweet peas from a smaller pot, set her plate on the table, and grabbed soft drinks from the fridge—Diet Coke for me, Sprite for her.

"Okay, I'm sorry." She tasted the noodles coated with red sauce. "This isn't bad."

"You're forgiven." I tried the shrimp dish, also deciding it was tasty. My secret ingredient for any tomato dish was a couple of heaping tablespoons of sugar. I normally cooked the sauce longer, but hadn't had time today. "Why were two men at your house this morning?"

"If you really must know, Stan left for his meeting in New Orleans. And no, we didn't sleep together. After he was gone, Dave Price came over. He owns a burglar alarm company."

"So that's why he was pointing, showing where you needed alarms installed."

She grinned, her empty fork aimed at me. "You really were in front of my house."

"I drove by. And I'm glad you're finally getting an alarm."

"I didn't say I would. I just had him come over and check things out. At the same time, I was checking him out." She rolled her eyes expressively. "A good-looking guy, huh?"

"Who notices?" I asked with a shrug. Picturing him, I found it difficult to keep from smiling. "Oh, something strange happened at the supermarket. I saw Daria with a man."

"What's so strange about that?"

"First, she never returned my phone call from yesterday. And she didn't have a thing in her buggy. She looked happy with that guy."

"Who was he?"

"I don't know. I couldn't see much of his face."

Eve dabbed her lips with her napkin. "She might have just wanted mints or to get out of the house. And looking happy with a guy isn't strange, you know. I look happy with guys all the time."

"Exactly my point."

"Hmm." She considered a moment, nibbling on a shrimp.

We ate more in silence, minds maybe working in sync.

"You could be the poster girl for women who never get happy around a guy," she said.

I ignored her comment. "Besides all that, Daria doesn't even care about what I have of her husband's? She must have heard my message by now, but she still hasn't called." I shoved my chair back and stood. "I think we need to go talk to your widow friend."

Eve carried her plate to the sink. "She isn't my friend. I was only introduced to her."

"Right. Let's go see what she's made of." I headed for the foyer. "I'll wear the jacket and give her the rest of her husband."

My sister waited in her car she had driven over. The leather seats made a soft *swish* and caressed my hips. She glanced toward my jacket's pocket. "How do you think she'll get him out of there?"

Unconsciously, I'd slid my hand in and instantly jerked it away, checking to make sure no trace of him lodged under my nails. "She can pour his ashes back in her urn." I pulled my pocket open without touching anything inside, hoping by some magic turn of events, he would have evaporated.

No such luck. Over the white tissue, ashy bits of a man resembled Eve's abstracts. I'd found this pricey silk jacket at an end-of-season sale at Fancy Ladies. It was my favorite, lightweight with the rust color brightening some of my other outfits. I couldn't afford another one anytime soon. Daria needed to remove her husband from it.

"Eve, you might not want to think this of your dead friend's wife, but she could have a lover, maybe that guy with her in the store. I hope when we get to her house, he isn't with her in a compromising situation."

She drove, eyes toward the street. "That would be bad, but worse things have happened."

"Yes, she could have killed her husband to be with that man."

Eve pushed out a sigh. "You read too many novels—people killing for romance. He was probably just someone who didn't get to go to the funeral."

"Oh," I said, remembering. "I talked to your first ex and his wife buying groceries."

"I noticed them across from us in the church. I've heard Jacques's new wife doesn't like me."

"Can you blame her? He's sends you much more than he needs to."

"I knew they were coming to the funeral, but Nicole wasn't." She flashed a lovely smile. "I can't wait for my daughter to have a baby."

"Maw Maw," I called her as many in this area called their elderly grandmas.

She pushed her tight lips forward in a pout. "Let's think of something nicer for the child to call me."

We'd passed only a few other houses that trickled along this barren stretch of woods and grasses beside winding Felicity Bayou. The early afternoon felt like deepening dusk when we reached the Snelling home. The house was red brick with a black mansard roof, a rarity around here. The property sank into a thicket of trees shrouded with moss as though hiding from spying eyes. The scene, much darker than the area leading to it, emitted a sense of gloom. Daria had yelled at me the only time she saw me. How would she react now?

Eve gave me a quick glance. "Apprehensive?"

"A little."

"We don't have to stop."

I glanced at my pocket. "Yes, we do."

A windowless sliding door for the attached garage was shut. Its red bricks brighter than the rest of the house told me someone enclosed the double carport awhile after the house was built. Eve parked in front of the garage.

The minute I stepped along the slim path to the front entry, the tangy scent of pine trees and pungent swamp water activated my sinuses, making me sniffle. No one had planted flowers or shrubs to add a feeling of life to the grass out front. No music or noise came from inside. Drapes were shut.

"Can't tell if anyone's home," Eve said.

I rang the doorbell. Maybe Daria was in her house. Possibly not alone. I shoved the bell once again. No sound or ruffled curtains. In case the bell didn't work, I pounded on the door. We waited. Not even the whisper of a footstep.

"Let's check the windows," I said.

Eve followed to the left. A picture window in front of the house may have led to a den, but the drapes remained tight. Other windows with closed curtains would probably lead to bathrooms and bedrooms.

"Maybe we should go home," Eve said. "We really shouldn't intrude."

Was she thinking this recently-widowed woman might really be in a sexual situation?

"But she might have killed him."

Eve wrinkled reddish-brown eyebrows and shook her head. Still, she didn't look certain. We'd both always enjoyed adventure with a little anxiety added to the mix.

A thicket of wild swamp vines and hackberry and cypress trees hemmed in the backyard, enclosing the large pond twenty feet behind the house that took Zane Snelling's life. I felt a tug at my heart while I stared at the brown water where two geese decoys floated, knowing a man died in its depths. If Zane and his wife lived here almost three years, why would he fall into the pond this week, when no one was near? She supposedly shopped at the mall forty miles away, returned, and found him floating face down.

"Nice job with the pavers." I nodded to the left of the pond. "Sorry I couldn't finish them with you."

"When you had achy joints and high fever?"

I shrugged. We'd dug the grass from that space and laid sand and crushed stone. I'd been using a pipe to screed the sand when chills and a hundred-and-two-degree fever struck. She sent me home. Eve returned the next morning while I shivered in bed, waiting for pain relievers to make my body feel half normal. My flu lasted six days.

"Those red-charcoal pavers were a good choice."

"I think it came out all right. Except he fell right there." The skin outside Eve's eyes crinkled, and her eyes misted. She looked ready to cry, which I never ever would do again. She stared at the hard knees of the cypress trees that grew beside the seating area we created. Smooth ground around it sloped to the water.

I gripped her hand. "You told him a clearer spot would be better. He wanted it right there. It wasn't your fault. Or mine."

She turned her head away as though unable to stand seeing where he died any longer. "Look, a light's on in the house."

I moved close and peeked in a window. The refrigerator and square table with four chairs sat inside a brightly-lit kitchen.

"She could have gone out and left a light on," Eve said, a sad touch of guilt remaining in her eye.

"You want an excuse to leave." Seeing the site where he died surely made her uncomfortable, as it did me. "The woman might have killed her husband, who was your friend. Let's just check," I whispered.

"But suppose she did kill him. She could kill us."

"She wouldn't have a reason to. We won't say anything that would let her know we considered she might be a killer. The police can check that. I just want to give her what's rightfully hers." I tapped my pocket. "The final remains of her husband."

Eve shook her head. "But what if she had the urn buried? What's she supposed to do with those other parts of him? Sprinkle them around his grave?"

"That will be up to her." I rushed to the backdoor and rang the bell. We waited and looked at each other. Nobody answered. A small stack of leftover pavers stood near the door. I rang the bell again, knocked, and tried the knob. The door opened.

"Bells Will Be Ringing" ripped up my throat.

"What's wrong?" Eve rushed behind.

The mistress of the house was right inside, blood covering her floor and head.

Chapter 4

Daria's open eyes stared. She didn't flinch or do a thing but lie still.

"Get away from here." Eve held her phone to her ear and shoved against my arm. "The 9-1-1 woman can't hear me with you singing so loud."

Sucking in breaths, I stomped from the door and slunk around the water, struggling to squelch my violent trembles. The bloody body of the woman lying inside the doorway tried to jerk me back to the most horrible day when my life violently changed. Shaky, soft lyrics spewed from my throat.

I tried to stop thinking of death and blocked out approaching sirens. I stepped across the pavers Eve had laid near the pond, lowered myself to the oak bench Zane had probably bought from a craftsman, and submerged myself in right now.

Even if the pavers occupied a fairly large area, two people wouldn't fit on his bench. He'd told Eve he wanted this space to sit alone and drink beer. No shed, no barn, barbecue pit, or table back here. If he worked for an oilfield company, his job might have kept him inside. Most southerners enjoyed their yards, especially those with ponds, and stocked them with fish. No small swirl indicated bream or bass near the surface. No tiny head of a turtle poking up, either. The geese on the water turned with the strong breeze that pushed against my back as it swept in from the east. Long strings of algae snagged small branches along the water's edge. Some tendrils may have captured Zane Snelling after he fell in.

What surprised me were tiny green balls growing on tips of some of the cypress branches. I'd never noticed them on cypresses before. Standing, I broke the end of a small branch. I sat again and forced my mind to study it. A slight pleasant bark scent. Pale green feathery leaves. Ridged balls that could decorate a little Christmas tree.

Sound forced itself to my mind. Sirens stopped blaring, letting a mourning dove's coo touch the air. A car door slammed, keys jangled, and what may have been a leather holster slapped a runner's legs. This young man in uniform flashed a badge at me. "I'm Officer Legendre. You called about a possible homicide?"

I pointed to the door. He dashed there, looked at Eve and back at me, his face registering that we are identical. His attention riveted on Daria, lying right inside her kitchen door.

"You found her like this?" he asked Eve.

"We did. This is awful." Eve stepped away to let him do his business. She came and stood next to me, clutching my hand. "You okay?"

"No."

She squeezed onto the seat beside me, snaked an arm around my shoulder, and held tight.

More sirens came. They silenced, and people with and without uniforms rushed near, glanced at us, seemed to decide we weren't threats, and dashed toward the mistress of the house.

An older cop with lips most women would kill for walked toward us. His tree-trunk legs stepped so firmly his shoes sank into grass, slowing him. I'd seen him in town. Read his name in the paper.

"I'm Detective Wilet with the Landry Parish Sheriff's Department." He showed his I.D. and whipped out a pen and pad. "And you are?"

"Sunny Taylor," I said.

"You can see that I'm her twin. Eve Vaughn."

"Yvonne who?"

She shook her head. "It's two words. My last name is Vaughn. The first is Eve. Actually, that's short for Evening. She's Sunny, and I'm Evening. That was our mother's attempt at being clever, naming us after the weather and time of day we were born."

"Wasn't your house just broken into?" the detective asked with a distinctly darker expression.

"I'm afraid so."

The detective's eyes shifted toward the backdoor. He focused on his paper and jotted notes. "Did you know the victim?"

"I met her. That's all," Eve said.

"I didn't." Having Daria yell at me did not constitute a meet and greet. I peered at the doorway. Couldn't see her and didn't want to. "Is she dead?"

"It appears so. Would you tell me what happened?"

I swallowed. Someone snuffed out this woman's life. How awful. We told the circumstances of finding her. No, we hadn't touched her, hadn't gone inside, hadn't touched the doorframe or anything near it. Didn't see or hear anyone else.

"Did you say she was your friend?" Wilet asked Eve.

Was he trying to put words in her mouth?

"No. I did some work back here, but her husband was the only one around. She came home, and he introduced us, and she went inside."

Our questioner asked more, causing us to say Daria's husband Zane just died. He drowned back here. The detective knew of his death. The intensity of his eyes and his chin's firmness said he knew much more than he was telling us.

"Why did you come here today?" He aimed his question at me and then Eve.

She faced me, the ESP we sometimes shared evident in her stony expression.

I pressed my arms against my sides like I could hide her former friend in my pocket. If I mentioned the ashes, the detective might confiscate my jacket. I wanted to keep it. But mainly, Zane didn't do anything wrong. I wouldn't want part of him in some musty evidence room where he'd probably never get out.

"Eve wanted to show me the job she finished here," I said. "I'd started the work with her, but got sick, and she had to finish alone. Nobody answered the doorbell out front, so we walked back here, thinking no one was home." I looked at Eve. "You did a nice job completing the project. Just maybe you could have tapped those pavers a sixteenth of an inch farther down on that edge." I tilted my head toward the opposite side from where we'd walked.

Her eyes went all squinty. She wanted to tell me off.

I told the officer about knocking on the backdoor and then kind of trying the knob in case she was inside and unable to get to the door and we would have called out her name.

"But we didn't need to call her." I swallowed, trying not to mentally see what we'd discovered inside. Across the yard people gathered around the doorway and beyond, marking their spaces, inspecting Daria and her house, taking pictures, taking measurements.

Fear tightened my chest. What happened to this attractive woman who just lost her husband? Had someone killed him—and now her? A carol sought to escape. I forced my throat tight to stifle the song and covered my mouth with a hand to further stop the words, some still erupting like a muffled cry.

The detective stared at me, his forehead creased, while he surely waited for an explanation for my outburst. Getting none, he said, "I'll want to speak with you two another day." He speared me with his gaze as though daring me to open my mouth again, then tromped off toward the others.

Eve didn't glance at the pond before returning to her car. "I can't believe this happened," she said once I got in, and we were riding off.

"I know. He died, and then we found *her*. That's horrific. And it sure shoots holes in my theory about her being his killer."

My twin gave her head a brief turn and narrowed her eyes at me.

"Sorry. I don't mean to be insensitive. You looked closer at her than I did. Were there any signs of what happened? Was she shot?"

"I didn't look that closely. And I wouldn't know a gunshot wound from any other wound, would you?"

I swallowed, felt my back tremble. "No."

"I'm sorry." She reached out and squeezed my hand. Her ringing phone made me grateful for anything to get my thoughts away from murder. She also needed distraction.

"Hello," she said, tone bland. "Oh, hi." Her arm holding the cell phone lifted along with her attitude. "I would like that information. No, I'm not home right now. Tomorrow? Great. I'll see you then." She clicked off, dropped her phone in her purse, and kept gazing ahead.

"A girlfriend?" I asked.

"No."

"From your enthusiasm, I should have figured."

She raised her chin and aimed her face at the road, heading toward our neighborhood. "That was Dave Price."

"Ah, the charming Mr. Price." I watched a grin brighten her face, then changed the subject. "You need to come and stay at my house."

Keeping her lips tight, she shook her head and turned down my street. "My place is being watched now more than ever. And as you heard, I have plans for tomorrow morning." Without giving me a chance to protest, she pulled up at my house and kept her motor running.

"You'll call if you need me? And if you change your mind, just come over. I'll be home."

Her nod and back-of-the-hand wave as though she were shooing a sand fly told me to leave.

Sleep didn't come easily. I was certain it didn't for her either, although she'd put on that show of bravado. I kept my phone next to my pillow and checked it often to see if she'd texted me, or maybe she'd called and I had drifted off and hadn't heard it.

Morning brought me back to thoughts from the previous evening. During the last days, somebody broke into Eve's house. A woman I'd encountered turned up dead, probably murdered. Her husband drowned. Accidental? Unlikely, although I wasn't as certain since she'd also died. Police would surely look into Zane's death more now that it appeared somebody killed his wife. An image of my sister Crystal slammed into my mind. I sang through my shower and while I dressed in jeans and another work T-shirt, knowing I couldn't dwell on death.

Shortly after I forced breakfast down my throat so I wouldn't get weak, Eve called.

"You're doing okay?" I asked.

"Yep, excellent."

"Wonderful. I kept wanting to call you all night and this morning or drive over there to make sure."

She released a small laugh. "I figured you might have passed by a few hundred times already." A small hesitation. "Can you come over now?"

"You know it." We disconnected, and I scurried across the street and between fences to reach her house, briefly noting the dismal morning before she let me in her backdoor and gave me a hug.

"You are so good," she said.

The warm body contact felt especially soothing after my gloomy thoughts. "Thanks, Sis. So are you."

Once we backed out of the hug, she gripped my fingers. "I'm glad you think so." Her deep breath and glance to the side gave me pause about her purpose for wanting me here.

"You're really all right?" I asked. "Do you want to come to my house or just get away from this place?"

"Actually, no." She faced me. "That good-looking Dave Price is about to come over to discuss a possible alarm system."

"Good." I grinned. He would give her a nice distraction from worry. "And you're sure you want me here?"

"No." She frowned. "Yes, I do."

Confusion swamped my brain. I nodded, wondering where this was going. "Okay."

"I'm attracted to him but the tiniest pinch concerned. When he stopped by yesterday morning, he needed to hurry to get to a job, so he walked around the house fast and saw the broken sliding glass door. He asked if the glass was going to be replaced, and I told him probably. I said he should come back and find out."

"So what's the problem?"

"He didn't ask what happened to the sliding door. And I'm thinking—could he be the person who broke in here?"

"You're kidding." Now she really had me confused. "You believe he could be? Hadn't you called him to come over?"

She spread her hands. "Yes, but that was right before Stan left. He got here just minutes after Stan drove away. Dave told me he'd been in the neighborhood. Had he been scouting my house? Besides, he would have been able to tell beforehand that I didn't have an alarm in place."

"Really?" None of what she suggested made total sense. "So cancel the call."

Her pinched expression suggested I was off kilter. "Are you kidding me? He could be the one."

I nodded. I'd seen her painting that suggested her intense attraction to this man. Yes, it would be wonderful if she could meet the perfect one for her. She had tried. Being settled with a man she could share equal love with had been her goal for years. I wanted her to reach that goal.

She swept through the room, shaking her head as though mentally trying to sort things. "I saw him a couple of times since his shop opened last year and wanted to meet him, but wasn't sure about getting an alarm system. Now I can have him right here for a while." Her pacing halted in front of me.

"And you want me to be your backup here just in case, right?"

She grabbed my fingers, leaned her forehead against mine, and looked me in the eye, a sure sign of trouble. "Sunny, I really like him, and I don't really believe he's a bad guy. But with all the strange things that've just happened, the thought occurred."

"That's definitely not enough to call the police."

"Correct. And I do want to check him out, you know. See if he might care about me." She offered a warm smile.

"So...?" By the time she finished telling me her idea, the man might come over and leave.

"That wouldn't be possible if you and I are both here."

"Okay."

She squeezed my hands. "So I need you to be me."

Chapter 5

"Uh-uh, no way."

We'd had fun tricking others when we were little. I hadn't played the part of Eve since high school, that day she didn't show up to take her final exam in science. Most people couldn't tell us apart unless we were together, and then they might notice slight differences, mainly that she was slimmer. I hadn't been great in science but understood that subject a little more than she did. She needed a passing grade on that test, or she would have flunked the course. I only took the exam because she'd begged.

Maybe I should have let her fail so she would've learned a lesson. But she was my sister. *My sister.*

Now that I thought about it, the reason she hadn't studied back then was also her interest in a cute guy who found her attractive, too. Who knows where they went off to?

"Sunny, there is no way I'd let you get hurt. I really don't believe he's a bad guy, but I need to be one hundred percent certain, and you can be much more objective about people, especially male ones." She gave me her sad eyed, lower-lip-out hopeless look. "I truly believe he could be my soul mate."

"Oh, Eve."

"I mean it. He seems real nice, and I think he likes me. But you are a great judge of men, and you know I am not."

I hummed, considering the possibility of looting or sex.

She set her index finger on the tip of my nose. "You meet with him."

"Excuse me?"

"You have a clear head. You can judge him, and he wouldn't behave the same if we were both here. I'll be right across the street watching to make sure everything's okay."

"Wow, what protection." I stepped to the door of her art room. "If a man tries to hurt me in your house, you'll do what? Throw a rock at the door to scare him?"

"I'm sure he's not a bad person. He surely isn't a killer."

"Eve, this time—"

"I'll be right out there, and I'll call you as soon as he gets inside. Then you can tell him I'm coming over—of course you'll say I'm you. And tell him the police will be following to do more inspecting in the house. Besides, Stan left me a pistol. It's loaded."

My stomach clenched like a fist ready to punch. "A loaded gun? You're kidding."

She yanked open the top drawer of the end table to the right of the sofa and lifted a pistol. Black, silver top. Metallic smell. "There, it's off safety. This is easy to use. You just point and pull."

I backed away, shaking my head. "No, Eve."

She kept nodding. "I'm just kidding about having to use a gun. But you can stay close to the table after he comes inside. If he wanted to do anything bad, he'd probably try it right away. You'll be fine, Sunny. You know I wouldn't ask you to do this if I believed he'd hurt you." She smiled, looking pleased with her plan.

"This isn't a good idea."

"Just do this one favor for me, please. Stay here. Be nice to him— unless he tries to hurt you." She smiled wider. "Kidding. I'm just jittery. And I really, *really* like him."

The shadow of a truck crossed the sheer curtains in front of her den.

She returned the pistol to the drawer. "I've gotten close to Dave, so he expects that of me—*you*. Just be nice. You'll be safe. Promise." She swiped her fingers across her heart. "I'll be right out there."

She waited, purse on her arm, letting me make up my mind. She looked so much like me, except for her better clothes and more confident attitude. This idea of performing was rather intriguing and pulled my mind away from death scenes. She had no real reason to think the man would hurt anyone, and my current purpose in life was keeping her safe.

I shivered and hummed. "I'll do it."

"You won't regret it. I owe you. Big time."

I forced a cheerful laugh. "Right. This will be a breeze. Go on."

She hugged me and dashed toward the door to the garage. My mind screamed *Are you crazy?* while my stomach squeezed into a knot no Boy Scout could ever untie.

Chimes from the front door rang out.

Anxiety swelled through my chest. I had to go through with our plan. Eve needed the man checked out. If he wasn't okay, he wouldn't have stayed in business long. A call to the BBB should tell if complaints were registered, like had he bludgeoned any customers? With an unsteady step, I moved to the peephole.

Dave Price stood away from the door. A tiny image showed him waiting patiently. He didn't keep ringing the doorbell like I would have. I sucked in a breath and unlocked the door.

"Hello." I thrust my hand out.

He took it with a broad hand that was warm, his grip firm. "Hello, Eve. You asked me to come back."

His greeting brought me to fully recall I was playing a role. My sister would have told this fine-looking businessman to call her by her first name.

"Yes, Dave, please come in."

Dave stood taller than me and wore a nice dress shirt and slacks. He carried a briefcase with a new leather smell and stepped into the foyer. Eve would stand close to him. I probably should do that. I took steps much farther into his space than I normally would with a stranger, especially a male. His gaze held on my face with eyes the comforting color of hot chocolate on a cold day. I felt his nearness. He didn't shift away or move closer.

"Come sit down." I led him into the den, and he lowered himself to the sofa, not far from the right end. I started to protest. Second thoughts made me keep my lips tight. I couldn't tell him not to sit there because I needed to be near my sister's weapon.

"I'm sorry I didn't wait for you to sit first," he said. "Sometimes I'm not much of a gentleman."

Remembering to be Eve, I said, "I don't always want a man to be a gentleman." I winced, especially when his lips turned up at one edge. "I'll just...sit, too." I nodded toward the tiny space to the right of him, where I could grab that gun if I needed it. He adjusted, sliding away a little so I could squeeze in. The pulse in my temple counted off seconds. He carried a light scent of spearmint, maybe toothpaste or a mint. And an enticing smell of male.

Enticing? Where did that come from?

The phone on the end table rang. I yanked it up. "Yes?"

"Is everything okay?" Eve asked.

I glanced at the person I'd thought I might fear. "Things here are fine."

"Good. His truck was parked in front when I pulled out of the garage, but he was already going in the house. I don't guess he noticed me, and I'm sure he doesn't know we're twins."

"Excuse me. I'll just be a minute," I told Dave, who nodded and shifted farther away on the seat. With more space, I stood and carried the phone to the kitchen.

"Sunny," Eve said, "are you sure you're all right?"

"Yes. I'm just moving so I can talk without him hearing. Do you think there's a chance he knows it's me and not you?"

"He doesn't know I have a twin. Have you gotten close to him?"

"Yes, on the sofa."

"Then scoot even closer. I've done that. Dave doesn't seem to mind."

I considered how close I would need to scoot. My hip would squash his.

"You aren't scared of him," my twin pointed out.

"What makes you think that?"

"You haven't even hummed."

She was right. In fact I'd felt fairly comfortable with the man. "I haven't decided on my feelings yet."

"Okay, just don't get too confident. Go and tell him what we said about your sister coming over with police who'll have information about the break-in. I'll stay right here. Keep the phone close."

"So you think—"

"He's fine. Go join him."

Once she hung up, I considered her confusing comments: Get closer to him; don't get too confident. I marched back to the den. "That was my sister. She's coming over with the police." When he nodded, seeming unconcerned, I added, "Somebody broke the backdoor. They're going to find out who it was."

He didn't flinch or show any sign of fearing the law. "Then that's why there's wood instead of glass on the sliding door frame. Nobody ran into it or batted a ball."

"Right. So the police will come over soon with my sister E—" I cut off the rest of her name once I realized what I was doing.

"E?"

I shrugged. "A nickname." Remembering to be Eve, I wedged my behind between the arm of the sofa and him. My hip rubbed his thigh, making heat spread across mine.

"Have you decided yet?" he asked.

I stared at him, thoughts scrambled.

"Do you know whether you want a burglar alarm installed? That's why you asked me to come back here, right?"

"Yes. Absolutely. That's why." What would Eve want? She didn't say for sure. I lifted the phone I still gripped.

Dave watched me. Oh great, what was I thinking? I couldn't call her and ask. I set the phone on the end table that held a pistol she had suggested I might need to point at this person. Was he a threat? I didn't think so, but didn't know threatening people, so I could barely judge one. Maybe I even knew Daria's killer.

Dave's gaze gripped me in place, making me excited, afraid.

I forced myself to break eye contact. "Tell you what. Let me think about it a little longer. I'll let you know tomorrow."

"Of course." He pushed up to his feet. "But then I won't be able to schedule you in for a couple of months. We have a full slate coming up. A job we were supposed to start tomorrow got postponed, so I was going to be able to work you in this week." His boyish grin softened my heart.

I stood, my chest inches from his. "Yes, do it." A chill scrambled through me.

"Great. I think it would be good for you."

I nodded and closed my eyes, experiencing my breaths and his warmth.

"I'll call my office and get started," he said, walking away.

I wanted him close again. I jerked my head back. *Good grief, Sunny, what's going on?* But I was supposed to be Eve, I told myself. *She* liked him. A lot, it seemed. Still, I found myself wanting to go with Dave. I should watch him and make certain he wouldn't do anything wrong.

He stepped toward the shut door leading to Eve's studio.

"Not in there," I said, voice suddenly quivering.

He shoved the door open and stared at the ruined paintings and writing on the wall. Dave turned to me, his dark gaze piercing. Fear skittered through my chest, catching a tune in my throat. This stranger could be the person who broke into that room but hadn't been able to get to what he wanted.

Yet.

Chapter 6

"Sorry," he said. "I shoved on the door before I heard you say not to."

Was that true? Being around him was supposed to make me forget death. It wasn't happening. He stepped into Eve's studio, scanned the damaged paintings and wall, and turned to me. "The glass can be changed, of course, but a sliding glass door won't keep out a person who's determined to get in."

"I know, but neither will most windows or doors. One day I might close in that space."

"Good because even our best system will only give a warning. It won't stop a smart thief or worse." He allowed me a minute to contemplate his words. "So you'll want us to install the system we talked about?"

He and Eve must have discussed a certain one. "Yes." I thrust out my hand, letting him know he should go first. He stepped into the den. I didn't invite him to sit but mentally saw the pistol Eve set in the drawer and remembered how easy she said it was to shoot. Was he a bad guy or great one? I hadn't decided.

"I'll check the windows and exterior doors and the wiring in the attic," he said.

I nodded. "Can you check the windows and doors from outside?"

He gave me a hard stare. With a brief nod, he proceeded out the front door. My breath relaxed. I would keep him in open spaces where other people would be near.

The phone rang, and I grabbed it.

"You're okay," Eve said.

"I am never switching roles again."

"Fine. I saw him come out the front looking unhappy. I was afraid he hurt you and then searched for what was written on the wall but couldn't find it and stormed outside."

"Oh, terrific. Yep, I could be here in your house bleeding to death, and you'd be sitting in your plush car across the street."

"Sunny, I'm sorry. He didn't try to hurt you, did he?"

"No, but thanks for asking." I calmed a pinch. "I'm still not totally comfortable about him."

"But it is kind of exciting to have a man with a dark edge. It makes him rather mysterious." Her tone hinted of a grin.

My anger flared. "How about if you come here with his dark edge?"

"Come on, Sis. He shouldn't be there much longer."

"I ordered the alarm system and asked him to go outside to check all the openings to your house."

She didn't respond right away. "Did you know it was drizzling when he got there?"

No, I hadn't noticed. Maybe that was what made him annoyed. I opened the door and peeked at Eve parked across the street under a mossy branch of an oak. And saw the falling water had intensified beyond the range of a drizzle. "I'd better go," I said and pressed the off button.

Dave was measuring the window on a spare bedroom and making notes when I hustled out to him. "Hi," I said, cell phone in hand. "My sister just called again. She'll be here soon. Would you like to come in until it stops raining?"

Fierce eyes peered at mine. "No, thank you. This is obviously where you'd prefer to have me." He moved off to the next window.

I couldn't deny his statement. Running inside, I stashed the phone in my pocket, grabbed an umbrella from a stand in the foyer, and ran back out. He stood near a bathroom window and shifted his pad under the soffit, trying to keep his paper dry.

I thrust the open umbrella over him. Within seconds, rain soaked me. I realized he was already drenched. Giving him a weak smile, I offered the umbrella.

He looked at it. At me. At my breasts, outlined through my wet T-shirt. With a sigh, he stamped off to the next window.

Shivering from his gaze or a chill, I wasn't sure what to do but spied his black dress shoes in what was now a mud puddle. If any shoeprints had remained around Eve's house, his shoes would cover them. Somebody broke into this house and wanted more from it.

Him?

I snagged a sane thought. I was the one who urged him outside. He was a great-looking guy—a terrific combination of little boy and rugged male—quite possibly my sister's soul mate, the one she's been looking for all along.

Rushing behind him, I thrust myself under the roof's overhang and held the umbrella over his head. He threw me a solemn glance. When he stepped father along the house, I followed with my raised umbrella. At the plywood-covered sliding door, he stopped. "Do you want to wait on this one? Or if you have the glass changed soon, we can install a sensor for it."

"That would be fine."

"I don't want the umbrella, thanks. I'm already wet." He did look nice with his shirt and slacks clinging to that body with well-defined muscles. "If you want to stay out here to check on what I'm doing, that's okay, but keep the umbrella to yourself."

"Check on you? I'm sure you're doing everything right. I'll go back inside and get out of your way."

"I'll let you know when I'm finished."

I rushed in the house. Even wet and chilled I felt a warm blush. Okay, I told myself, the only reason I cared about the man was to make sure he wouldn't try to harm Eve. I got her on the phone. "Are you watching your guy get soaked?"

"I can't believe he's out there like that. Why didn't you make him stay inside?"

"Grrr." I wandered through rooms, scanning almost-bare closets in guest bedrooms and opening drawers. What might an intruder have wanted?

"He's moving to the window on the side of my bedroom," she reported, keeping me up on his whereabouts. "Maybe he'll go in there and stay."

"Sis, I hate to interrupt your musing about a man, but you do remember someone murdered a woman across town? And you recall that somebody broke into your house?"

"Yes, Sunny." She used her stern voice.

"The man outside is a stranger, no matter how good he looks."

"Okay, Momma."

"I'm only trying to protect you." Heat swelled up behind my eyes, clouding my vision. Giving me a fuzzy picture of the person I hadn't been able to protect.

"I'm sorry." Eve spoke in a quiet tone. "Oh, he's heading for the front door."

The doorbell chimed. I disconnected with Eve and pulled the door open. Water dripped from Dave's black hair to his wet face. He swatted a large drop off his ear. "I have what I need for now. I'm too wet to go in the attic today."

Sadly, I viewed a man soaked from his scalp to his probably ruined shoes. "I'll get you a towel."

The skin between his eyes creased. "No, thanks. I'll be back." Sliding into his truck, he drove off without hesitation. The rain was only trickling now, too late for him.

Before he turned the corner, Eve left her parking space and drove over.

I went inside, ready to meet her the second she parked in the garage and walked through the connecting door to her kitchen. "Don't ever ask me to be you again."

She lifted both hands. "I won't."

"You were so wrong to ask me to do that. Suppose he *had* been a killer?"

"I know. I'm sorry, Sunny." She grabbed mail from her table.

"I don't think you are. I think you were being selfish and inconsiderate."

Her phone rang. She looked relieved to have a reprieve from my gripes. Grabbing the phone, she carried it toward her bedroom. I fumed. Needing the reminder that she was in trouble, I stepped into her studio and glared at her former artwork and words on the wall.

"Detective Wilet wants to see us." Eve entered the room, lips tightening when she looked at her ruined paintings. She wrenched her gaze away from them toward me. "We need to go to the police station at three. There's new information in the Daria Snelling case. That's all he'd tell me."

In the den, we both checked the frameless clock. Twelve-forty.

"We need to eat. I have tuna in the fridge," she said. "I'll make sandwiches."

"While you're doing that, I'll go grab my estimate for Anna's window." I walked out, spied her nosy neighbor's son Royce driving away in his mother's five-year-old sedan, and scurried between the fences to the rear, wishing they were down so I could see into both yards. Could a burglar have hidden in either one?

On my street, Miss Hawthorne stepped out her front door and thrust on her floppy straw hat. Trowel in hand, she descended her porch steps, more light-footed than I would have imagined. Was she wearing her girdle? Even the thought made me aware of the moist heat now that the sun came blaring out.

A few steps from my house, I experienced excitement creeping through my chest. Surely the detective had more information about the break-in at Eve's.

A sudden rush of uneasiness replaced my content. Someone just broke into her house on the next street. We resembled each other. I scanned my surroundings and found cars normally home at this time of day were parked where they belonged. The front of my house appeared normal. I pulled the key out of the pocket of my jeans, opened the door, and peeked in. Quiet descended. Was it quieter than usual?

"Don't be stupid, Sunny," I told myself. Still, I wanted to get outside fast.

Ripping off my wet garments, I tossed them in the tub and slipped into similar dry clothes. I grabbed the estimates and hurried back out. Scurrying to Eve's house, I hoped my sudden fear diminished once we spoke to the detective. I rang the front doorbell to give her warning, let myself in with my key, and was struck with the urge to hug her. There couldn't be a connection between the break-in here and Daria's murder. I could never bear the thought of anyone trying to kill her, and I would do everything in my power to prevent that from happening.

I hadn't prevented one sister's death. That couldn't happen to my remaining one.

Chapter 7

"Why are you singing?" Concern tightened Eve's lips when I joined her in the kitchen. "What happened?"

I shook my head. "Nothing."

"I fixed us sandwiches. Come on, what's wrong?"

I threw the papers down to the table and wrapped my arms around her. A second later, her arms came up around me. We gripped each other, listening to each other's soft breathing. Feeling each other still able to do that.

"Missing her again?" she whispered near my ear.

I kept my head tight against hers. "I thought after time, pain is supposed to go away."

"That's what they say." She let me hold on a minute longer. When she let go, the expanding space between us felt safer. We ate without eye contact or words.

"Do you have time to check this?" I gave her the papers I'd completed.

She pulled a calculator from a drawer and worked with my figures. It didn't take her long, yet time kept still, not letting my thoughts wander from the solemn place they'd submerged. Without glancing away from the numbers, she reached for my hand. "These are correct." She tightened her fingers around mine. "Great job as always."

Gratitude for having her and for her normal attempt at making me feel intelligent made warmth heat the back of my eyes. But tears would never fall from them. "Thanks."

"Those notes about what we'll need to do to change that window look easy. It's pretty much what I'd figured." She went off to check her makeup, and I phoned Anna to give her the final estimate. She sounded pleased. She was such a pleasant person that I was sure she wouldn't complain unless our price sounded exorbitant. It was also okay with her that we couldn't start the job right away because we had other projects scheduled, and the lumberyard needed to order her glass blocks.

Hoping our larger ad in the parish paper brought us even more business soon, I called the lumberyard and ordered materials, charging them to Twin Sisters.

Eve was down the hall coming out of her bedroom. "I want to ask you about an item I saw in your room," I said. "Maybe it has something to do with the break-in."

"Really? What is it?"

She returned to her room with me and watched me pull open a drawer from a bedside table, and I took out a tiger-eye ring. "This looks like it belongs to a man."

"It did." She yanked the ring from my hand. "Why were you snooping around in here?"

Her attitude surprised me. "I was skimming through things while your soul mate that you're scared of went around outside checking the entrances to your house."

"And why did you do that?" She fisted her hands on both hips.

"What is your problem? I thought I might see something you overlooked when you tried to figure out what somebody broke into your house to find. What is it with you? Who is this for?"

"Me." She thrust the ring back where I'd found it and slammed the drawer shut.

"Eve?"

She stayed silent, facing down. She inhaled deeply and looked at me. "It was Dad's." My sister stomped out of her bedroom. When I followed, she spun back and closed her bedroom door.

I waited in the hall. "Why did you get such a personal item of his?" Our dad had died, and Mom lived in a retirement home. Men always gave Eve gifts. Dad did, too? An ache sat in my heart.

She didn't answer. I pulled on her arm, and she faced me. "I can't give you an answer. You'll need to ask Mom." She proceeded to the den. "We need to get to the sheriff's office."

Anger swirled with disappointment inside me. "I'll go in my truck. I have other errands." I scooted to my house, threw myself in my truck, and rolled onto the street. Huffing, I needed to remind myself my main concern was her safety. No matter how annoying she could sometimes be,

I needed her to stay alive. She might make me furious, but I loved her and our mother more than anything else in the world.

Detective Wilet was waiting. The smell of fired weapons caught on the back of my tongue. The odor of overheated coffee pots and worn-out leather assailed me before I spied new signs and yellowed diplomas on the walls. The detective sat us in two fairly comfortable blue foam chairs and took the swivel chair behind his desk cluttered with papers and pens.

I leaned toward him. "Please don't tell us you've found a connection between Daria's murder and the break-in at my sister's house."

He steepled his fingers. "I don't know of any."

Eve and I sighed with relief.

"What we have discovered is that you and Mrs. Snelling had an argument at her husband's funeral."

Surprise at his words slapped me back. "We didn't really argue."

His upper body shoved toward me. "Then what did y'all do?"

I glanced at Eve for help. She lifted both eyebrows. Great help she was. And I had hung out with the possible bad guy at her house? I faced Wilet and considered each word. "I'm sure you know Mrs. Snelling fell, and then her husband's ashes flew out of her urn. I just offered to help clean them up."

His bushy eyebrows squeezed closer together. "Why would offering to help make her yell at you?"

"Because…"

Eve placed her hand on mine. "Because Mrs. Snelling didn't want you to use a vacuum cleaner, remember?"

"Right." Pleased with the answer she offered before I could think straight, I smiled at the detective.

"I know she ordered you out of the church. That was only because you offered to use a vacuum?" His jaw tensed. A slight indention twitched along its right edge.

"Not exactly." I flipped thoughts back to that moment, recalling Eve's words. "My twin here kind of suggested I could have been involved with Mrs. Snelling's husband."

"I did not!" She straightened in her chair.

"Were you?" Wilet asked me. "Were you having sexual relations with Zane Snelling?"

I sang about Santa on his way and tried to quit, but considering sex with that man I'd only known from ashes in my pocket, couldn't stop myself or slow down. I shook my head, wishing he'd understand.

"Ma'am?" His black eyebrows became one thick line.

I caught my breath, swallowed, and swallowed again to stop the song. "I'm not really into sex," I explained.

"The thought of it often makes her sing or hum," Eve added. "She can't help it. Sunny has an emotional problem."

I stared at her. Hearing those words made me cringe and want to curl into a ball.

"Is there anything else?" The detective sounded annoyed, and I wasn't certain he believed either of us. "Did you remember anything else? Is there anything else you want to tell me about that incident?"

We shook our heads. My mind blanked. Maybe Eve's did, too.

The detective stretched his upper body forward until he was halfway across the desk, eyes aimed at mine. "I might want to question you again."

"Me? Am I a suspect? What did I do? You think I killed her?" I asked, getting no response. I pointed at Eve. "Daria kicked her out of church, too."

Eve's eyebrows shot up. "But that was because of you."

The detective stood, letting us know we should leave. Eve and I rose. The three of us were about the same height. My impulse was to argue with the man. Common sense said not to.

We left his office, nodding at people working at desks. Some of them knew us. Did all of them know why the detective had us come here? Would word scatter through town, maybe making the parish newspaper and even New Orleans TV stations, warning people we might be killers? How great would that be for helping our business flourish?

I gritted my teeth. Eve flicked me an angry look. It wasn't my fault that Daria also threw her out of the church. I drove off in my truck, while she spun away in her Lexus. Seeing my gas tank read almost empty, I pulled into the station I knew to have the lowest prices and waited in line. Did those drivers who glanced at me know I could be suspect in a murder?

I pumped gas, annoyed. Who did kill Daria? Had her husband accidentally drowned? And even if my sister and I often aggravated each other, I wanted her kept from harm. Not much I could do about us being murder suspects. The police needed to find out who killed Daria, which I hoped they'd do soon. I needed to visit my mother, a task I didn't do often enough for her, although I made a number of stops a week to see her at the retirement home. Right now, I had a special family purpose for speaking to her.

Besides, some of her friends were big gossips. They might help me learn what really happened to the deceased couple.

Chapter 8

Sugar Ledge Manor resembled an enticing vacation spot. Palm trees lent a warm greeting while crepe myrtles burst into clouds of pink near the pale blue stucco building sporting an archway with inviting benches and the sweet scent of roses growing nearby. I could imagine myself on a tropical island, the taste of Mai Tai in my mouth. A tall section in front led to suites and bedrooms on both sides. Cars belonging to residents, staff, and visitors rested in wide parking lots.

My mother's room was charming, as were the others I'd seen here. I wouldn't see her room today since she sat on a sofa in the main area. Next to my sister.

"Why are you here?" I nestled against our mother and held her twisted hand.

Eve thrust her nose in the air.

"It's nice to see you, too," Mom told me.

"Sorry, Mom." I kissed her cheek on the side opposite my twin. "I just didn't expect to find her here."

"She visits fairly often, you know."

I exchanged tight-lipped smiles with Eve, then nodded to the ladies, most with white hair, gathered round. "Hello," I said to include everyone on sofas and in wheelchairs in their regular snug semicircle for their afternoon Chat and Nap Group.

Mom's hair was snowy, even though she was one of the younger residents. She was soft and average size, not the parent Eve and I inherited our height from. She'd insisted on moving in here after a severe case of rheumatoid arthritis made her need help for everyday living. We'd each asked her to move in with us, but she deferred. She had made lots of friends here. A couple were snotty, but most were sweet.

"It's so nice to have both my daughters visit at the same time," Mom said to her friends. "They always did seem to know what the other one was doing, like ESP between twins."

Some ladies smiled and made pleasant comments.

"Mom, I'd like to talk to you. Could we go to your room?" I asked.

"Sweetheart, unless you're having severe physical or financial problems, you can speak in front of my friends. All of them care about us. Some of them can't hear too well anyway." She exchanged pleasant looks with the ladies.

"Here's the thing." I pointed to Eve. "Why does she have Dad's ring? I never saw it before, so I guess she hid it from me." Good grief, I was sounding like a spoiled kid.

Mom looked at Eve and then me. "It was the only jewelry he had, so I gave it to the oldest child."

"Just because she's six minutes older than I am?" My voice went shrill.

"Yes." Mom spoke with a nod as though that explanation should make perfect sense.

Eve gave me a smirk and cocky lift of her chin.

"It was only an old tiger-eye ring," Mom told me. "You'll get my wedding ring."

Yes! I awarded my sister a smug look. Jewelry had little meaning to me, but an item of such importance in my parents' lives gave that ring extra value.

Mom held up her left hand, drawing oohs from a few of her cronies. Her fingers on that hand weren't as twisted as the ones on her right, but most of her knuckles were large. A few tiny diamonds topped her ring.

Mom's friends compared their own rings or lack of them. I'd seen many of these ladies without their clothes while I'd worked at Fancy Ladies and wished I had not. They'd asked me to bring different size nightgowns, bras, and panties to their dressing rooms and were often naked when I returned. I tried to shove off images of sagging, wrinkled body parts. Probably because I feared mine might much too soon become that way.

The plumpest woman, Ida, with a snug polyester dress matching her hair, more blue than white, sat on the sofa adjacent to Mom's and pointed at a wheelchair-bound woman who was rubbing the thigh of a man asleep beside her in his wheelchair. "That is so sad."

Some other ladies nodded.

"If she wants to fool around, she should get married," Ida said. "Just like you, Eve. Why don't you just marry more of those men and then fool around afterward?"

Eve's mouth fell open. I felt she was struggling between giving a smart reply or feeling embarrassed in the midst of all these elders.

"What about you, Sunny? You still can't get a man interested in you?" Ida asked.

Heat flamed up my cheeks. "I don't want another one."

Ida nodded. "After my husband died, I never wanted another one. I already had a dog that expelled gas and snored."

I snickered, as did some others.

"But it's strange, isn't it," Eve asked the group, "that a young woman like my sister wouldn't want another man? You know what Sunny needs? An explosive romantic relationship."

"That would be nice," the lady who always wore three strings of pearls said.

"Yes, lovely," another agreed with a big nod.

I looked at our mom, who gazed at me wistfully. Maybe considering the grandchildren she'd wished I'd given her.

"Yes, one husband was enough for me," Ida said. "I loved my Oscar, bless his soul."

The tiniest woman spoke up. "But he kept running around with that hussy."

"Oh, I forgot. Then damn him."

Ida's buddies agreed.

"Ladies." I lifted my hand to interrupt them. "Eve and I have another concern. Have any of you heard about what happened to Zane Snelling and his wife?"

Puzzled expressions they gave each other answered my question.

"They weren't from down here," I said. "They moved here within the last three years and lived along Felicity Bayou."

"Oh, that's the woman who pushed her husband in their pond," Ida said.

My heartbeat raced. I was right. "How do you know that?"

"Because how could a man just slip in a pond that's been in his backyard?" Ida asked, dulling my enthusiasm.

"Wait. I might have a picture of their house." From her wheelchair, slender Grace, with thin orangey-dyed hair, shoved her hand down into the top of her floral print dress. Movement bouncing above her belt must have been her fingers digging in her bra. She drew out a cell phone that looked moist. "This slipped under my breast. It's damp down in there, but I imagine the thing still works."

While she tried to get to her photos, the newest woman to the group spoke up. "Well, people can drown in their yards. I almost drowned in a drainage ditch once."

"How can you drown?" asked another one who faced me and pointed toward the newcomer. "She's too fat to drown."

As entertaining as these women were, nagging thoughts of a killing remained. I didn't need to see a picture of the Snelling house since I'd seen it enough, but most of these ladies had lived in our community all their lives and heard rumors and truths. I raised my voice. "Did any of you actually know the Snellings?"

"He had affairs," Grace said.

I gulped. Eve and I gawked at each other. The shock registering in her face surely matched mine. Some residents nodded like they'd heard this gossip.

"Zane Snelling?" Eve asked. "The man who recently drowned in his yard?"

"Yes, he had two women besides his wife. Can you imagine?" Grace said, and I wondered if she had total control of her mental facilities. I hoped so.

"Do you know who they were?" I asked.

She peered to the side. Maybe she couldn't even hear well. Most of the ladies shook their heads no.

I spoke louder. "What about his wife?"

The ladies glanced at each other and shook their heads.

"That poor woman was killed not long after he died, wasn't she?" Mom asked.

"Yes. I hate to admit it, but I thought she could have pushed him in their pond," I said.

Ida's chins wobbled. "I think that, too. How could the man just slip in?"

The ladies came to life. They didn't wait for each other to finish telling stories of how they almost perished when they were little. It seemed almost every one of them had at one time or other fallen into a flooded ditch or bayou and almost lost their lives.

"I need to go." I kissed Mom's cheek.

"Me, too." Eve dropped a kiss on the other side of her face.

We bid the ladies goodbye, though some might not have heard. Eve and I waited until we were outside the building to speak.

"Should we tell Detective Wilet what we heard about Zane having affairs with two women?" I asked.

Her eyes, like mine, looked inside. Twin vibes connecting, searching ourselves.

"I don't think so. Mom's friends are interesting, but they don't always have their facts straight."

"I agree. I believe we need to investigate whatever we can on our own about what was said. If we bring the police false information about the Snellings, it would make us look like we're only trying to tarnish the other women's names."

"Then we'd look even more suspect."

I heaved a sigh. "We sure don't need that."

"I have to get home. Somebody's coming from the burglar alarm company to check wires in the attic. It won't be Dave." Eve's lips tightened, their edges aimed down.

"Talk to you later. Remember, the offer's still good for you to come and stay with me."

We separated toward our own vehicles. I sat in my truck, considering what to do with the information we'd received in the retirement home and wondering whether it was truth. I had seen a few people I knew slightly in church for Zane Snelling's funeral but didn't feel I could call any of them to ask if he had been cheating on his wife. The police knew how to find needed information. What I knew how to do was build things and make repairs, courtesy of our father creating interest and talent in me and my sister for so many years.

Starting my motor, I pulled out my phone and called Angela Stevens.

"Leave a message," is all her answering machine said. She might be still on vacation.

"Hi, Angela, it's Sunny. We have your ceramic tile. Give me a call, and we'll discuss when would be a good time to install it. Thanks." We had other jobs lined up but nothing major. A few teachers wanted to wait the handful of weeks left until their summer vacation for us to start projects at their homes. We would need to build up our clientele soon for us to have a chance at having the town council seriously consider bids from us. I needed more steady income to remain in this business.

I tried to work on ideas for increasing our production but found considerations about the Snellings shoving ahead in my mind. My one meeting with Daria had taken place in St. Gertrude's Church. I pointed my truck toward it. If I checked without any emotional turmoil in the building, maybe I could locate some clues about what really did happen that day. And possibly who caused his death or hers.

Chapter 9

Gravel and oyster shells crunched under my tires while I pulled in at St. Gertrude's. I parked out front, admiring the old wooden structure. The church stood near the highway a few miles south of town. Cars and trucks sounded extra loud, sweeping past. I'd only been inside once before the would-be funeral and that was some time ago for a wedding.

The structure was a comfortable size, nowhere near as large as the cathedrals in some cities. The biggest majority of churches in South Louisiana were Catholic. These long-standing country churches were the exception. I'd been raised in this religion but gradually let the practice of entering a church fall by the wayside.

Concrete made up most of the front yard, which would have remained more inviting if they had left trees and grass. To the left of the church stood the priests' small brick house. Rose bushes and half-bare short palms filled much of its front yard, where the two priests from Zane's funeral were planting a cypress tree.

I was glad they didn't look at me while I stepped away from my car. Out of their line of vision, I took my time checking around the sparse grass near the front parking lot. Somewhere out here was probably where a person from the funeral parlor had handed Daria the urn right before she walked inside.

The only item appearing out of place was a plastic cover from a water bottle. I picked it up, spotted a tall trashcan, and dropped it in. The *ping* when the cover hit made me consider that a possible clue to what happened to Zane may lie inside. With the receptacle almost empty, I could make out crumpled bulletins, a half-filled water bottle, and bits of paper. Unable to see quite everything, I tilted the can.

"Did you lose something?" a man asked.

Startled, I jumped. My hands jerked off the can, and it dropped on its side. Wet papers spilled out.

"No, I—uh, thought I did," I told the young priest. "I'll pick that up."

With dirt on the knees of his black slacks, he grabbed the trash and had it disposed of in the can he set upright before I could.

Relieved because he hadn't asked what I wanted, I considered what he and the other priest planted. "Oh, y'all do know that cypress trees will grow hard knees that are actually roots sprouting above the ground to breathe, right?" I asked. "The knees can grow two feet tall and cause problems with cutting grass." And might trip and drown someone, although right here that person wouldn't have a pond to drown in.

"Thanks for that information. I'll tell Father Prejean."

I stood an awkward moment in which he didn't go away. "While I'm here, I'll just go inside a minute. Say a few prayers." I didn't tell him I almost never went in a church. I certainly didn't say I'd look for anything tied to a murder.

He smiled as though I was doing something really good, forcing a twinge of guilt to crimp inside my chest. "I'll unlock the door for you." He trotted up the stairs to the narrow wooden porch and unlocked the church's front door.

"Y'all lock the church? People can't just stop by and pray?"

His lips tightened with his frown. "It's a shame things have gotten this way. Most churches are locked now when scheduled events aren't taking place. Too many people broke into them and stole or broke valuables."

"I'm sorry to hear that." And relief made me breathe deeper when he scooted down the steps and returned to the other priest. I would be alone inside.

I stepped into the church, the heavy cypress door creaking while it closed behind me. An old wood smell brought up images of Model T's and barefoot children walking miles to school and made my sinuses say *Wait a minute*. Faded statues of saints guarded walls right inside the doors, and wall-mounted glass cups held holy water for more protection. Stuffiness engulfed me. I dug for a sinus tablet from my purse and dropped it in my mouth where it melted.

A tiny table held fliers and stacks of folded bulletins. The comforting oak floor had developed a patina through the decades. The same type wood created a stairwell to the left. I couldn't imagine anything upstairs causing a person to trip down here. Standing at the rear of the church, I found nothing hinting of foul play in the area.

And what was I doing, believing I could discover something police didn't? I'd overheard a high school classmate say I wasn't the sharpest tack in the box. Just because I'd been kicked out of a club for top students and an honors class. Also she didn't know, but later I'd been thrown out of a nightclub when Kev and I were married and he started feeling me up soon after he'd made me disgusted with sex, and I belted out a chorus of "Frosty the Snowman" that drowned out the band.

Shaking my head, I dumped the cruel girl's words from my thoughts. Intelligence came in many forms. Just because I'd needed fewer multiple-choice items on a test than the rest of the class and other tests read to me didn't mean I was mentally deficient. A wonderful teacher explained that meant my brain didn't work the same as most others. She'd also let me know up to fifteen percent of the world's population was dyslexic, including Alexander Graham Bell, Churchill, da Vinci, Thomas Edison, and Einstein. Probably nobody read tests to them or called them names. With a smile, I bolstered my spirits with a remembrance of this esteemed group to which I belonged.

I ambled around the back of the church, snooping. A black umbrella, faded red one, and two wooden rosaries on a shelf probably made up their Lost and Found. Squeaking sounded from a section of the floor I walked on. A one-inch wide wooden threshold piece held down the end of the worn green carpet that ran down the central aisle.

Squatting, I eyed the carpet. As I'd suspected, back here it lay flat with no bumps. The slim piece gripping the carpet to the floor would not have made Daria fall. Besides, she'd already walked past that when she pitched forward. I was sure of it. Otherwise, Zane's ashes wouldn't have flown where they did, and none would have landed in my pocket.

Had she waited to get into this section of the church before dumping him?

Uneasy with a twinge of guilt nudging me for believing a murdered woman had killed her husband, I decided I'd better pray. Besides, I didn't want what I'd said to a priest to be a lie. Returning to the holy water, I dipped my fingers in and crossed myself. Sliding into a pew, I knelt on a padded kneeler.

The altar up front appeared small. The statues looked aged. Small rotating fans were mounted on square posts on both sides of the church. Sunlight danced through one of the exquisite stained glass windows.

I lowered my head, needing to concentrate on prayer instead of building design. My first prayers were general, a couple I used to recite by rote. And then I asked for guidance, knowing I shouldn't point the finger of blame at anyone. But I silently asked whether someone murdered Zane Snelling.

"Can I help you?"

I snapped my eyes open and jerked my head up. No, not a quick answer from God. The older priest, Father Prejean, stood next to my pew. He was tall with an angular face, extremely long eyelashes, and a shiny bald head.

"Sorry if I frightened you." He gave me a tight smile.

"No, I'm fine."

"I wondered if you wanted to go to confession or needed to talk to a priest."

"Oh, no, thank you, Father. I just…wanted to stop in a church to pray." Ugh, now I was surely going to hell.

His calloused fingers touched my hand. "I understand."

I sat back on the pew. "But I was surprised that a church might be locked."

"It's a sad comment on the day. You can still come any time, and we'll unlock it for you. We live right next door."

"Thank you."

He took a few steps away. Then he stopped and came back. "Oh, and I know about cypress knees. My family's from down here. There are different kinds of cypresses. The one we're planting doesn't grow knees. That type cypress grows mostly around water. That's why their roots need to come up for air."

Darn, why didn't the Snellings have the type without knees? And did one of those knees near the seating area we created trip Zane?

"I've seen a lot of those with knees in the swamps," I said.

"Yes. Anyway, thanks for telling us. You can stay as long as you like. I'll start hearing confession in a few minutes."

The second the outer door shut behind him, I hopped up. I didn't want to remain much longer and didn't want to confess anything. Retracing my steps toward where Daria tripped, I stooped to see beneath pews and kneelers. A candy wrapper lay under a nearby pew. A bulletin, light film of dust, and tissue lay under others. I walked around the rear and inspected pew seats.

The one across the aisle from where I determined we'd sat for what was supposed to be a funeral held what could be a few ashes in the seam where the seat met the back. Uneasiness shifted through me. Were those parts of him? Should I try to scoop them up? I had those ashes that were definitely his in my pocket back home and had no idea what to do with them. If I took more, what might that accomplish? Then suppose these weren't bits of a man but cookie crumbles? I could be inviting mice into my clothes.

Women's voices neared, growing louder. The front door opened, and three women walked inside. We told each other "hi" like people do when someone looks familiar, but no one remembers the others' names, and I headed out.

Sunlight from the open door struck a shiny item lying flush against the threshold piece that held down the end of the carpet. Past the women, I lifted that item. It was an ordinary silver metal nail file. What didn't appear ordinary was the thick, dry, tan substance on its pointed tip.

I slipped the file into my purse. Sound registered of cars stopping. More people were coming to confess sins. Were any of the women going to admit they had been with Zane Snelling?

I glanced back into the church. Grayish-white bits appeared ground into the nearby short section of carpet. Zane, lying in its fibers? A flash came of my oldest sister lying on our driveway.

With trembles running from fingertips of one hand to the other, I roared out a lyric and shared frowns with people entering the church while I ran outside beneath the darkening sky.

Chapter 10

I called Eve from my car and told her about what resembled ashes in the church. "And I found a fingernail file someone dropped at the edge of the carpet. I think there's dried glue on the point. Daria could have used this file to pry the urn open while she walked into the vestibule."

"Don't you think those priests and altar boys would have seen her do it?" Eve's skeptical tone deflected my idea, but only for a moment.

"She was walking ahead of them. She might have started working the file around the glue as soon as she got hold of the urn, which she probably did outside."

Eve mulled over my idea only a moment. "You probably won't bring those guesses to the police, right?"

"No, but it would help if they found Daria's fingerprints and urn glue on the nail file."

"Your prints might be covering hers. If that file really did belong to her."

I sighed. I was no good at police work. Remodeling jobs were coming in slowly. Maybe I should try to go back to selling double-D bras and thongs.

"Dave's company started putting a burglar alarm system in my house. I don't know if he'll come back." Disappointment tainted her tone.

I envisioned the muscular Dave Price—then pictured his hair dripping to his face once I sent him into the rain. "Sorry I ruined his visit to your house. I'm horrible at trying to be you. Remember that."

She exhaled a loud breath. "That's okay. If he doesn't come around for the work, I'll catch up with him someplace else." Leave it to my sister when it came to being with men.

"I want to learn more about burial urns," I said. "Maybe I can find out when Daria got Zane's in her hands."

"Good idea. Oh, you know Royce next door. He told me he noticed a strange man wearing a hat skulking around my house this week."

"Skulking?" Excitement swelled inside me. "That sounds like the burglar. Royce must have seen him."

"Maybe so."

My enthusiasm dulled. "Oh, it was probably just Dave taking measurements."

"No. I asked if it was raining. It wasn't."

The streetlight in front of me flipped to red. I stopped. "Let's take that information to the police tomorrow, and they can question your neighbor's son. While we're at the station, I'll give Detective Wilet this nail file."

"Do you think that's a good idea?"

"Sure. We might be solving his cases, so he should be pleased. And, Eve, you need to come and stay at my house."

"I want to be here when the alarm people come back in the morning."

"Call if you need me," I said, and she clicked off. Satisfaction swirled through my chest like when I'd scored an A on a reading test near the end of fourth grade. Suppose I was right, and Daria did pry that urn open and purposely dump Zane? What if her fingerprints and dried urn glue remained on that file? I would need to be careful to lift it from my purse without covering any more of them with my own prints.

Possibly Daria was in cahoots with the guy who snooped around Eve's place, and together they planned to kill Zane. Then that man broke into Eve's studio and smashed her paintings and wrote on her wall because he wanted... What?

My positive musings ended. The story building inside my head developed so well and slammed at a wall at this point. But the police could fill in any parts I missed.

In the morning, Eve called to say her alarm people wouldn't perform any more work at her house until afternoon, and she had phoned the station. Detective Wilet would see us, although briefly.

Parking at the police station, I waited for her in my truck. She drove up minutes later. Inside the office, two female officers hustling past turned to give us double takes, likely realizing, yes, the tall redheaded women heading to Detective Wilet's office were identical. A fresh coffee smell met us in the next hall, coffee spills staining the gray rug beside the pot, along with a small piece of chocolate someone's shoe squashed.

"You said you had new information." Wilet didn't waste time when we entered.

We took chairs anyway, and Eve told him about her neighbor's son visiting her and saying he'd seen a man wearing a head covering near her house. He hadn't described this man except for saying he wore a cap, so maybe Detective Wilet could get more information from him. Wilet looked serious while he took notes.

"And I have this." Using a tissue, I grabbed the nail file from the small inner compartment of my purse and held it out.

"Tissue?"

"No, what's important is the fingernail file."

His forehead creased while I told him my theory about how the file had been used, my throat tightening and words softening by the end of my ideas that didn't seem as convincing as when I'd said them to Eve.

"The woman who was just killed. You think she murdered her husband?" he asked.

I sucked in a breath and considered poor Daria. Someone just killed her. I peered down, feeling the detective's and my sister's stares. My face warmed like it did back in school after I was called on and gave some answer that made sense to me but nobody else.

I faced the detective. "It's possible. And what's on the tip of that file might be dry glue."

The detective took breaths while I felt his eyes searing my thoughts, judging them. He set the tissue and file on his desk. "Thank you for bringing me this information. And these items."

Eve and I stood.

"Will you let us know what you find?" I asked.

"I'll let you know when we have something definite. Thanks again." He tipped his head toward the tissue.

Grumbling started in my throat before we got outside.

In the sunshine, Eve spun toward me. "He thinks we did it. He really thinks we killed her."

What she suggested had begun to really sink in while I'd spoken to Wilet. "He believes I did it. Me. Maybe he's going to talk to your neighbor, but he certainly didn't believe my theory about Daria or the nail file," I said, more convinced of something else. "I'll bet he throws it in the trash before we're two blocks away."

"Well, he can't prove anything negative about us." Eve unlocked her car. She lifted her shoulders and rolled them backward. "I'm going to change and get to the gym. I need to get rid of some of this tension."

"Be careful, Sis. Your burglar alarm hasn't all been fully installed yet, and a man was snooping around your house this week." I considered my statement. "Maybe I'll come and help check things out when you're going inside."

"Don't be ridiculous. I have my busy-body neighbor and her son watching my place." She gave me a quick hug. "But thanks for worrying about me."

I drove off, still concerned about her and wondering what I should do. The police might think we were killers. They couldn't prove we were guilty of anything, I thought, while tension in my face relaxed. My breaths eased. Until I realized the harm that would come from them believing I or Eve had killed Zane.

They wouldn't be trying to discover whether Daria did it.

I needed to check into more myself.

What could I do? I drove aimlessly along the bayou, working to focus my thoughts. The urn Daria held high when she entered the church came to mind. I knew little about urns since at most funerals I'd attended, caskets held the deceased. I had attended only a handful of funerals with the departed in an urn and knew little about those vessels. It was time to increase my knowledge.

I turned at 6th Street and headed for the funeral parlor. Halfway down the block, I answered my phone on its first ring. Badeaux Lumberyard. The glass blocks were already in. Since the lumberyard was along my route, I made a quick stop. The job at Anna Tabor's house wouldn't pay my rent, but the income would provide quite a few groceries. Mainly, removing a plain existing window and doing an excellent job of installing this large unique one would get our company's name out there more. Anna was loud and spoke to everyone. Word of mouth from her would become another nice stepping stone in growing our business.

T-Joe in freight loaded boxes of glass blocks in my truck bed. I hefted a box, surprised to find it so heavy, and knew the next item I held, a funeral urn, would be much lighter.

Aiming my truck across the bayou at the next bridge, I reached the funeral home within minutes. I parked near the brick building and hoped the few cars parked at its side belonged to people who worked there, not mourners.

A cloying perfume of flowers clung to the air. The tan carpeted floor captured the sound of footsteps. The door to the viewing parlor was shut. Through an open doorway to an office I approached, I could see two men in pale gray suits speaking together.

The younger one stuck his head out. "If you'll please take a seat there, we'll be right with you," he said to me.

I sat on a tapestry-printed sofa and picked off a loose bright orange thread. Now that I was there, I realized my request would be different from what people normally came for and hoped they were receptive. I'd seen both the men in that office many times but didn't know them. They were involved in most funerals I attended.

"Sorry you had to wait. Please come in," the hefty one with thick white hair said once he walked out. He gave me what I imagined was a compassionate hand squeeze to match his sad-eyed expression.

"It's no problem." Surely he believed I wanted to plan a loved one's funeral. Would he be turned off by my request to learn about glue?

"Have a seat please." He pointed to padded chairs near the front of his desk. The other man was gone, probably behind the closed door beyond this room. "I'm Toby Hensley. How may I help you?"

I sat and glanced around, considering how I might ask so that he'd tell what I wanted to know. I couldn't say why I wanted the information.

Trailing ivy sat atop tall file cabinets. Pictures of crepe-myrtles in full bloom hung on the wall. A framed picture on his desk showed a dog with unusual colors: brown splotches beside a white belly and the rest of him gray with black spots. One of his eyes was blue, the other one brown.

"Is that Fritz?" I asked.

"You knew Fritz?" Smiling, he lifted the picture, admired it a moment, and handed it to me.

"He was the first Catahoula hound I ever saw. Such unusual great colors. And I love their eyes." I considered how attractive Fritz was and unwillingly recalled how much he'd barked in the yard close to mine. I stared at the man sitting across from me. "Oh, you're Miss Hawthorne's grandson."

"Step-grandson." His eyes went hard. He thrust his hand out to retrieve Fritz's picture, looked at the dog, and replaced the photo on his desk.

"Then you're also a hunter," I said, knowing most of this breed's owners here used them to hunt.

"Not anymore." His clipped response made me aware that the sport went away with his dog.

I'd been saddened to learn Fritz managed to get loose from Miss Hawthorne's backyard fence when she'd kept him. She had told me Toby lived in a townhouse that didn't allow animals. He was in the process of buying a house with a yard to keep Fritz in when he got loose. No need to ask whether he'd ever found his beloved animal.

"I'm so sorry." I was also sorry to recall rumors that Toby hadn't been especially kind to that animal.

"Yes." He lowered his head with the same reverence he wore beside caskets at funerals.

"Sometimes Miss Hawthorne is working in her flowerbeds when I pass, but I probably don't have as much contact with her as when I worked in sales. Do you get to see her often?"

He grimaced. "I saw that green brassiere you sold her."

"Ah, sorry for that. She wanted it." The garment was the shade of stagnant swamp water that I couldn't imagine anyone wanting to put on her body. Miss Hawthorne selected it from a clearance tray. And why had she shown it to her grandson? *Step-grandson.* He hadn't said that like he felt especially attached to her. My guess was he'd seen the bra hanging to dry. Maybe he held it against her that his dog managed to get out of the fence.

"Yes, well, what can I do for you?" His demeanor once more went all businesslike.

"I'd like some information about burial urns. How are they sealed?"

"Sealed?"

"Toby, I'm especially interested in Zane Snelling's burial urn. Did his wife get it here?"

His eyes focused downward like he was concerned about a large paperclip on his desk. Was he wondering about the purchase of the urn or whether he should tell me? He lifted his gaze toward my face. "She did. And you liked it?"

"It was pretty." I remembered some nice etching on the container before she dropped it. "His wife fell when she entered the church, and the urn popped open."

His chin reddened and tightened nearly to a point.

"Can that normally happen with those vessels?"

"It's very unusual. Urns are normally sealed."

I scooted forward in my chair, ready to prove Zane's murder. "Do you know what happened with the one holding Mr. Snelling?"

He studied the dog's picture. Reached out and touched it. "I don't."

"Do you know what Mrs. Snelling did with the urn? Was it placed in a tomb or mausoleum, or did she keep it at home?"

"I have no idea. I wasn't personally involved with that service."

Voices in the hall drew his attention toward the doorway. I glanced back there. A woman dabbed her eye with tissue. A younger male used comforting tones to speak to her.

"Did you have a newly deceased," the man in front of me asked, "that you'd like to check into for burial vessels or services?"

"Thank goodness I don't." Seeing him start to rise, I stood. "Thanks for your information. Oh, and one more thing. What about the ashes? Are they just poured in the urns?"

A grimace tightened on his face. "A person's ashes are sealed in a plastic bag before they are placed in a vessel." He barely glanced at me with a brief nod and strode past me to the people in mourning. I checked the dog's photo, wondering again how Fritz had gotten out of the hurricane fence that day and hoping someone nice now owned him.

I drove from the funeral parlor pumped up with my knowledge. I had no idea what I could do with it. Besides learning a slight bit about urns, I discovered Toby seemed to have cared about his Catahoula hound much more than he cared about my cheerful neighbor. If he'd had more time without customers coming in, I might have gotten him to show me the different styles of urns. I recalled seeing a wooden carrier holding an urn at one funeral I attended and learned family members had rented it. Why hadn't Daria done that? Was the carrier too costly? Or had she been making certain the urn top would pop open and nothing was in the way of her dumping him?

How had Zane's ashes so easily escaped if they were sealed in a plastic bag? Unless a sharp fingernail file ripped the bag open.

Nearing a house with a bay window out front reminded me of the window Eve and I would soon change. The thought of installing an unusual one for this area excited me. With that window facing the highly traveled street, people would notice and ask about it, just like I was certain some must have inquired about the Snellings having a mansard roof. Word of mouth about any good jobs we did was great for business. I paused at a stop sign. No cars were near, so I dug my phone out of my purse, scrolled, and found Anna Tabor's name. I pressed her number and drove on, smiling when she answered.

"Hi, Anna. It's Sunny. The glass blocks came in. We'll be able to change your window this week."

"Oh, hey, Sunny. Listen, something's come up. I don't think I'll want any work done on my house right now."

"Oh." Disappointment crushed my spirit. "Well, maybe a little later."

"Sure. I'll let you know."

"Great. Thanks for giving Twin Sisters a chance."

"Right, definitely," she said, but something sounded wrong in her tone. She didn't seem to mean what she said.

I sensed the added weight of the hefty boxes of glass blocks in my truck bed. I'd charged them to our company, which so far kept a very limited bank account. Getting Eve on my phone, I found her interested in what I'd learned at the funeral parlor, but not so pleased about our cancelled job.

"That's okay," I said. "If we'd need to, the lumberyard should let us return the glass blocks. I have them with me."

"What about the ceramic tiles?"

"In my truck bed? What about them? Now we'll be able to do that job sooner for the woman you work out with."

"Sunny, I just saw her when I was leaving the gym. She was going inside. I told her hello, and she wanted to tell me something. She changed her mind, too. We won't be installing any tile at her house."

I tapped the brakes. "You're kidding me."

"I wish I was, especially since this sounds like the same thing with Anna."

Stopped in the middle of a street in my neighborhood, I considered the consequences of what was happening. Our business could crash before it really got started.

"Word must've spread fast that we're being considered as murderers," I said.

She stayed quiet. "That could be happening."

"I think I need Momma." Struck with the urge to seek our mother's comfort, I mainly hoped to receive input about what was happening to our business from the Chat and Nappers. Those women learned about more things that occurred in town than I did from their visits from family and friends and news from staff members. Maybe they could direct me toward a murderer before the business my sister and I hoped would provide years of comfort instead swooped down to a rousing crash.

Chapter 11

The Chat and Nap Group hunched in its semicircle of sofas and wheelchairs, the strong perfume of one of them tainting the air. A triangular walker with a central wheel leaned folded against the end of a paisley loveseat. Most of the women's faces lit when I approached.

"Hi, Sunny," one woman said.

"Nice to see you again so soon, Sunny," another of my mother's friends said.

"I'm glad to see all of you, too," I said and meant. These ladies were gentle souls, hoping for more in their declining days than the aches striking their joints. So did my mom. She sat on the floral printed sofa, blending with it in her favorite pink polyester blouse and white polyester slacks.

"Hey, Mom. So glad to see you again." I settled beside her once someone moved over to give me space.

Mom took my face in her hands and kissed my lips. "Hello, Sunny."

"We're all the same as last time you saw us," Ida told me, her voice loud enough to be heard in the next room, "except Grace is more constipated than usual." She nudged her chin toward the slim wheelchair-bound woman.

"Sorry," I told Grace, who nodded what I assumed was her appreciation of my sympathy.

"You're back here again so soon. What's up?" Ida asked me.

Her buddies leaned forward, awaiting my answer, apparently not shocked at her rude questioning. Of course she was right. I did have an ulterior motive for coming to visit my mother and her friends.

"I miss my momma." I hugged her.

"How sweet," one lady said.

Mom smiled her pleasant small smile. She knew I was here for something else.

"I wanted to see you," I told her and sat back, pressing against the sofa, "and I'm not busy with work."

"Twin Sisters," Grace said with a nod. "I've heard of y'all. You and your twin do good repair work."

"Thank you. The trouble is we don't have any work to do right now. We were getting quite a few calls for jobs and had some things lined up, but our customers started backing out."

Some ladies nodded. I wasn't telling them anything they didn't already know.

Mom patted my hand. "Just give it time. You'll do fine."

Two ladies eyed each other. Their guarded looks said they didn't think our business would do fine.

"Okay, y'all, give," I said to them. "What do you know? Why don't people in town want us to work for them now? Because we're suspects in Daria Snelling's death?"

The newest member of the group spoke up. "And your poor workmanship might have made her husband trip and fall in the water and drown."

"What?"

Mom squeezed my hand. She didn't appear shocked at any of our statements. "I'm sure you didn't kill anyone, dear. And the work you and Eve did was fine."

I spread my hands toward the gathering. "Our work *was* fine. We did everything we were supposed to do. Eve and I dug the foundation for a seating area, and we put down sand and crushed stone. Then I developed high fever and achy legs and needed to leave."

"But you're all better now, right?" Mom touched her lips to my forehead to check.

"Yes, I'm fine."

"Good," one lady murmured.

I needed to tell them all the rest of what happened. Townspeople they'd speak to needed to hear the whole truth. "Eve finished putting the pavers down by herself, and they looked great." I noticed my voice had risen, my tone pleading with them to believe me. "Our workmanship was excellent," I said, keeping my voice level.

"We believe that," Grace said, nodding.

"Nothing we did made Zane Snelling trip." My reinforcement made a couple more ladies give me small nods and smiles. "And of course you all know Eve or I wouldn't kill anyone."

The majority of them gave me nods. One raised an eyebrow, appearing skeptical. We sat quietly, most of us gazing down. Clicks sounded on the vinyl tile while two residents moved past with walking canes. A kitchen worker greeted us, the rubber soles of her shoes sucking at the floor.

I was the person police suspected most in Daria's murder since she'd yelled at me. Now I'd learned townspeople believed my sister and I did shoddy work that caused a man to trip and drown. Our business was sliding faster than Zane would have slid into his water. "I'm sure all of you know about his ashes falling at the beginning of what would have been his funeral. Do you know what happened after that? After they picked up the ashes?"

"They had a small memorial service," Mom said.

"Was his urn buried?"

Most of the women looked at each other. Some shrugged. None of them seemed to know the answer to my question.

Mom squeezed my hand. I smiled at her, not having noted she'd gripped it. She knew about most of these problems facing her twin girls. Her thin-lipped smile with compassionate eyes reminded me that she believed we could handle anything.

I touched her soft cheek, appreciating her love and trust. "We'll be fine."

"I know you will."

"Oh, I know something, too." Sparkly-eyed Edith Truxillo waved her hand. "I know the name of a woman that dead man was seeing."

My heart raced. "You do?"

"Her name is Lillian. My brother Andrew lives close to her house. Every Saturday at noon, she wears a bikini to cut her grass. My brother sits out on his lawn to watch her."

I hopped up and kissed Edith. "I love you."

She gave me a wide smile. And her brother's address. I knew exactly where I would spend my lunchtime Saturday.

* * * *

Noon Saturday swept in with a soft westerly breeze and the roar of a starting lawn mower. The temperature was warm for late spring but definitely not hot enough for bikinis. Except for Lillian. My mother's retirement home friend had given me the phone number for her brother Andrew who lived across the street from Lillian.

"Yes," he'd told me on the phone, "I knew Zane Snelling. Well, I didn't really know him, but I knew who he was. He used to come to her house all the time. Uh-huh, her name is Lillian, but I don't know her last name.

I can tell you she looks good, and things sure swing around on her when she wears a bathing suit."

I sat in my truck across the street and a couple of houses down from Lillian's. The stoop-shouldered gent setting up a folding chair in the front yard next door must be Andrew. I knew for certain when he plopped himself in the chair and stared at her with a wide grin. She didn't work up a sweat, strolling behind a self-propelled mower in her tropical-print bikini that barely covered her jiggling breasts and swaying butt.

I sat with a hand on my door handle, trying to decide what I would say when I approached. *Hello. You were having an affair with Zane Snelling, weren't you?* No, that wouldn't work. *You knew Zane Snelling, and I attended his funeral, so would you tell me all you know about him?* Not hardly. *Did you happen to kill a Mr. Snelling?*

Harboring frustrating thoughts, I noticed motion in the car parked a few feet ahead of me. A woman with big hair sat in the driver's seat peering out her door's window. Part of her face that I could see reminded me of Daria Snelling's. I had seen this person at Zane's funeral, sweeping up ashes, and guessed she was Daria's older sister.

She must have also heard about her sister's husband having an affair. Was she here to confront this woman about causing anguish to Daria, who was now also deceased? Or maybe she would only watch Lillian and leave without saying a word.

I needed to speak to her before she took off.

Shoving my door open, I stepped out of my truck. Daria's sister was doing the same. Face stern, she steamed across the street toward Lillian.

I remained in place to watch.

Long-legged Lillian spotted her coming and waited, her mower idling. The lawnmower's whirring kept me from hearing what Daria's sister told her that made Lillian's face twist with anger. She swung her arms out like she'd gotten into a serious argument. The older version of Daria bent toward her, pointing an index finger at her face.

I stepped closer to hear and spied some neighbors appearing to get earfuls from the pair. Moving to the edge of the next yard, I heard bits of what they were yelling about, their words shaking me to the core.

"Yes, I had sex with him," Lillian screamed, "but you did much worse! You're his wife's sister."

On the driveway beside Lillian's house, a young boy wobbled on his tricycle. A woman, probably his grandmother, rose from a chair near him and stomped toward the women yelling at each other. "You two watch your mouths," she hollered. "There are children around here."

"Right," I said although no one heard my words while I strolled up to the pair of angry women. "Sex is nothing to raise your voices about."

Lillian grabbed Daria's sister's arm and pointed toward the yard on the opposite side of her house. The two stormed there, away from me and the child and his elder.

Zane supposedly had two lovers. One was Lillian. Daria's sister was really the second one?

I was tempted to turn off the lawnmower to hear them better, but the grandmother eyed me with a sneer. She wouldn't want her grandson to hear more of their words, but I wanted to. I shifted closer to the side yard and focused on listening. The women spoke quieter. At times their voices rose, letting me snag bits of their argument.

I couldn't distinguish the voices, but heard one of them expected to get something Zane owned. If I heard right, he possessed a fortune.

Daria's sister's voice became evident as it rose. She recently learned about Lillian, who said she had known she wasn't the only woman he'd been seeing.

"He wasn't having relations with Daria anymore," Daria's sister said in a raised tone.

Lillian laughed. "You're a fool if you believe that."

A horn tooted. A twentyish male driver wearing a broad smile gave both women thumbs up, pausing their discussion.

"This isn't finished!" Daria's sister snorted. Storming away, she glanced at me before crossing the street to her car.

I strutted up to Lillian. "Hi." I pointed. "That was Daria's sister, wasn't it?"

Lillian's jaw fell open. She raced into her house and slammed the door.

Not knowing whether I should turn her mower off, I left it alone. Maybe she'd come out soon and cut more grass, although that didn't seem likely. I crossed the street to my truck and waved at the older man who sat glued in his lawn chair. He'd probably enjoyed Lillian in her swimsuit on many Saturdays but most likely had never been as entertained as moments ago with the women arguing.

I strode up to him. "Hi, I'm Sunny, the woman who called you about Lillian," I said while he nodded. "Do you know the person she was arguing with?"

"Can't say I do." He shook his head, his pale blue eyes bright. "But I sure as heck am not gonna miss this next week. That was a nifty show, wasn't it?"

"Pretty nifty." I grabbed a piece of paper from a pad in my purse and wrote my phone number. "Would you call me if you hear anything else that's as interesting as that was?"

He agreed, and I drove away, calling Eve. "Obviously I wasn't the only person who'd heard about Lillian. So did Daria's sister." I relayed all of the events that took place.

"Fascinating," she said. "So here's my news. Dave Price is here! We're not getting romantic—but hopefully one day soon."

I gave a small laugh in response, noting I didn't especially want her to get romantically entangled with him, but not certain why.

"He's with a helper," she said. "They're almost finished putting in the alarm. Why don't you stop by to see how it works?"

"No thanks. I can figure out how an alarm works. If somebody goes in your house after it's set, the alarm goes off. That's a no-brainer."

"Okay, but actually, I know being deceitful with him that day you pretended to be me has been bothering your little conscience."

"Yes, big time. And I don't think my conscience is so small." I shoved my foot at the four-way stop, slamming my brakes extra hard.

"If you come over, Dave will see that we're twins. We won't tell him you pretended to be me, but at least he'll see there's double me." She chuckled. "Maybe your conscience will get some relief if he sees you for yourself."

Did I want to? Did I want to see him around my sister and see her being flirty with him? Of course another worker was there with them. I envisioned Dave. Taller than me. Broad shouldered. Eyes that made me want steaming chocolate. My body enjoying a sizzle while being around him.

Wow, did I think that? Why wasn't I singing about snow or maybe Rudolph?

"I guess I might stop by."

"Good. Give Dave a chance. You'll like him."

I couldn't tell her how much I feared I liked him already.

Chapter 12

Seeing the glass replaced on the sliding door of Eve's studio made peace settle inside me. But not for long. Her art room instantly stifled when she brought in her guest.

"Sunny, this is Dave Price. Dave, my sister Sunny Taylor."

"Also known as E," he said with a grin and then I remembered what brought this on. "And you're identical twins." He sandwiched my hand between his.

My body heated from his touch and my remembrance of my hip and leg jammed against his. I forced my voice to work. "Nice to meet you."

"And you, Sunny." He gave my hand a little squeeze.

Flirting? Being nice? His usual handshake?

I hummed a bar.

Eve raised an eyebrow at me. She knew the Christmas tunes came when I was frightened or considering myself in sexual situations. She probably thought I feared him. I shook my head, mouthing *no* at her. Turning my back to Dave, I pointed my thumb toward him and nodded to let her know I believed he was okay.

Immediately, I regretted that decision. She stepped around me to get closer and started hitting on him. "Dave and his men did an excellent job of installing a burglar alarm."

"Actually, they did most of the installation," he told me. "We placed motion detector sensors on all the entrances to your sister's house. The man who completed the work just left."

"Great. I'm glad she finally decided to get an alarm system." I sighed, content to realize I could stop worrying about Eve.

"Yes, Dave is such a convincer." She stood so close to him, she needed to lean her head back to peer at his face. Then she actually grabbed the man's shoulder—at first rubbing as though brushing a leaf off his shirt—and then holding on to him.

I hated her actions. I hated when she made me take her place for that science exam, and I hated when we were six years old in dance class and Lana what's-her-name said, "I like your short set," and I proudly replied, "Thank you," and she said, "Not yours, your sister's." I also hated this moment, when she was almost pressing up against Dave. Any other animosity I'd had toward her before was regular sibling stuff. Worse right now, Dave didn't seem to mind. He stood without taking a step back from her or even swaying his torso a pinch away from hers. Actually, he smiled at her.

What was she doing? "Remember what Ida said?" I mentioned, breaking the moment between the pair.

Dave cocked an eyebrow at me.

"She's talking about one of our mother's friends at the retirement home, one who shares lots of opinions, some of them unsavory," Eve told him. She faced me, a new crease in her forehead. "And which of Ida's many statements were you talking about?"

"Specifically, she said something about you and—" I faked a little cough, figuring she'd fill in that I meant *men.*

And then I recalled Ida's entire statement. She had told Eve she ought to *marry* more men instead of just sleeping with some of them.

I didn't want her to marry Dave. We weren't even one hundred percent positive he wasn't the person who broke into her house, although I had to admit to being ninety-nine percent certain. A twinkle of interest sparked his eye. He glanced from one to the other of us, seeming to enjoy watching us annoyed with each other.

The angry expression left Eve's face, replaced by a smile. "Oh, Ida thinks I should get married again," she said to him.

"That part of her statement was not what I was referring to," I said. "It was the part about other men." *Lots of them.*

My bait didn't work. She kept her goo-goo eyes trained on Dave, making certain he heard the suggestion about marriage.

"Is there a problem between you two?" One of his eyebrows lifted.

"No," I said too quickly.

"Absolutely not. We *love* each other." Eve drew out the love part, maybe trying to imprint the word in his mind. She shoved up closer to him.

My head felt like a pressure cooker ready to explode from building annoyance.

"Eve, we inserted a simple code in the burglar alarm," Dave told her, stepping back and soothing the charged air a bit by a change of topic. "But I suggest that you insert your own."

"If you think I should, then let's do it," she said.

"It's not difficult to get numbers or words into the system. I'll tell you how."

A sudden twinge of uneasiness made me hum. Eve glanced at me. I shook my head, trying to warn her not to let others know a code that could let them gain entry into her house.

She smiled at him. "I would love for you to insert them. And how about a little wine now that you're finished?"

"Thanks. I'll have water."

He did quick work changing the code while I once again checked the studio, which felt much safer than before. Eve had used three coats of paint to cover the words *WHERE IS WHAT'S HIS?* She'd thrown out her paintings with *X*'s slashed across them and started over, giving a fresh, empty feel to the room. Her current painting on an easel in the center of the space made me shiver. Bright red, yellow, and orange circles filled almost every inch of the canvas. I glanced at Dave. Had she told him this painting was supposed to represent her anticipated encounters with him?

She still wore a happy smile. Maybe she'd already begun to fulfill those fantasies.

"Sunny, come sit down," she said, stepping ahead of us to the kitchen. "And you can write down the numbers for the code."

"How many numbers did you use?" I asked Dave.

"Only four."

I crossed my arms and didn't budge behind my sister. "Just tell me what the numbers are. I can certainly remember four of them."

"You don't have to be snappy." She grabbed a water from the fridge and gave it to Dave, along with a pleasant grin.

"I'm not snappy! What're the numbers? I need to go."

"Six, one, nine, two," she said.

Dave lifted his water bottle toward me. "It's always good to write them somewhere."

"Then do it." I stormed out of Eve's house. She'd probably told him I was dyslexic, so he figured I couldn't get my letters or numbers straight. A common misconception. Most of us had problems with sound recognition, and some had more problems than others. And then there was the mistaken belief that people with dyslexia lacked intelligence.

Or maybe that was true. Maybe I was dumb for leaving my sister alone with a man who might harm her and who tempted me. Okay, there, I allowed myself to think it. No man had done that in such a long time. Maybe never. Or maybe I thought I wanted him because she wanted him first, I considered, slamming myself inside my truck. Yes, she'd wanted and gotten other men, but none of them had attracted me. I tore away from her house, not certain how I felt about myself or my sister or the person with her.

At home minutes later, I mulled over the break-in at Eve's. Other concerns came. Was what happened at Eve's connected to Daria or Zane? And was Dave somehow also connected?

Maybe right now I just wanted him to be.

What could I do about all these things happening around me? The police believed I could have murdered Daria. Her killer must be found for them to know otherwise. Nobody in town wanted to hire Twin Sisters Remodeling & Repairs since Zane's death. With no income at all from that source, I would be financially strapped. I especially hoped no hurricanes decided to slam into town this summer since my roof wouldn't withstand that type winds. I was grateful that I'd been diligent about putting money aside, but what I'd saved was nowhere near unlimited.

Something concerning me, too, was being so bothered by my sister. Most of my life I'd loved having a twin. She was like another half of myself. We accepted each other's problems and goofs. When my dyslexia was discovered, I anxiously waited to learn Eve was dyslexic, too.

Testing confirmed she wasn't. Teachers commented about her advanced performance in classes. Soon afterward, a kind reading teacher who knew much about my condition made me feel I was like every other child in school. I just happened to have been born with this situation in my brain that made me work harder. Other people need to work hard at different things, she'd said, making me feel good about myself. Until I overheard a teacher saying if those of us with special needs couldn't do what the rest of the students did, then we should fail.

I'd slunk away. I wanted to be like everyone else. Starting to blurt Christmas carols as a result of being a terrified child that awful day didn't help my self-esteem. Lack of confidence probably made me stay with Kevin after I discovered what a jerk he was.

Hearing a crinkle, I looked down and realized I'd been popping chocolate chip cookies into my mouth and chewing one after another.

Growing wider or with mid-life zits from too much chocolate wouldn't help. I stowed the cookies away but still wanted something to chew on. Grabbing a handful of peanuts in the shell, I took them outside and ate. I gazed a couple of yards down, but didn't see Miss Hawthorne outside. How had Fritz gotten out of the fence behind her house? I peered in the direction of Eve's place as though I could see through houses in-between ours and focused on listening. A car sped by. Someone's door slammed. No sound of my sister crying out in fear. Or pleasure.

Envisioning her pushing closer to Dave, I wished her back to the last town she'd lived in. Nobody broke into her house there. Nobody gave me confusing thoughts about romance.

Right now, I needed to work on discovering why two people died, and my main concern was keeping Eve safe. I hopped in my truck and aimed it toward the police station, hoping that since Detective Wilet was off a couple of days during the week, he might be there now.

* * * *

"So Zane Snelling was having an affair with this woman named Lillian? And his sister-in-law, too? Both at the same time?" The detective sat behind his desk, taking notes of my statements.

"Yes," I answered. "I think so."

He stopped writing. "You think?"

"I'm pretty sure."

"Of what? That he was seeing both women or that he was seeing them at the same time?"

"Ummm." I gazed off to his right, replaying the words I'd heard in Lillian's yard. I looked him in the eye. "It was hard to make out the exact things they said since Lillian's lawnmower was still running, but I really believe he was seeing them both at the same time."

Wilet let out what seemed an exasperated exhale. "I'll note that." With his lovely full lips squeezed tight, he jotted words. Of course he wouldn't tell me what information they already had about this case. "Ms. Taylor, you've also told me about Mrs. Snelling being in a store with some man soon after her husband's funeral."

"She looked happy with him," I added, pleased with my info's importance.

"He might have been someone who expressed condolences and asked about the funeral. She could have just smiled and said it was nice."

"But it wasn't. It was awful. She dumped him. I know it was on purpose."

His cop face said he didn't look convinced. "We checked with clerks in the grocery store. Nobody remembers her with a man that day. It is a small store."

"But she left without any groceries."

He spread his hands. "The woman had just lost her husband. She was distracted and could have forgotten why she'd gone in there."

"A woman doesn't often grocery shop the day after she buries a person she loves."

"Maybe not." He focused his stare on me. "Now. Can you tell me anything you know for certain?"

"Like?"

He waited to respond. Appeared to want to nod. "Like exactly who murdered Daria Snelling?" The detective rolled big shoulders forward, his lips pursed. "It would give that person a lot of relief to admit what happened."

I straightened. Stared at him, indignation racing with fear through my body, making my back shake. He was waiting for me to confess.

"I didn't kill her. I only saw that woman twice, first in the church and then at her house. And she was already dead."

"So you went to her house why?"

"I went there to have her take her husband's ashes out of my pocket, but she didn't because she was dead." I was wearing that jacket and pressed gently against the pocket. "They flew inside here when Daria tripped in the church."

"I'll need that jacket."

"What?" Damn. I hadn't meant to let him know about the ashes. "It's my favorite one."

"You can probably have it later." He held out his hand.

I shrugged out of my best cover-up. "It's silk. It'll need to be dry cleaned if it's messed up."

"We'll try to be careful with it." With a smirk, he took the item I gave him and looked in the pocket. "Have you been working with cement?"

"Not since y'all have everybody in town believing my sister and I messed up with a job. And I surely wouldn't wear silk for that kind of work."

He laid my jacket across the rear of a chair beside him. "When we found you and your sister at the Snelling house, you told us a different reason for being there. You didn't mention ashes or a coat."

"I probably forgot."

He pressed his thick upper body toward me. "Maybe you forgot to tell us something else. Remember what I said about confession making a person feel better?"

"I need to go." I barely got the words out before I stamped out of his office.

"Think about it," he called.

I flipped around and poked my head back in the room. "What did you learn about the man with a hat snooping around my sister's house?"

He spoke without looking up at me. "Have you ever seen a meter reader without a cap?"

I drove away, fuming. I was also humming, which made me realize how concerned I was. Was his entire investigation aimed toward me? I took deep breaths. Maybe Wilet only seemed to be unconcerned about the information I brought him. He was a trained detective. He probably already knew everything I said. Except for Zane's ashes in my jacket. So now he also thought I'd withheld information, which was true. He probably didn't even check on the man with a hat at Eve's house, only figuring it was someone checking a meter. And he could be right.

Calming down, I recalled past rumors that Detective Wilet had also had affairs. Wait, it was women from my mom's Chat and Nap Group who'd once told me that. They lived such limited lives. Few of them ever left Sugar Ledge Manor. Possibly they invented some of those stories to tell each other to add interest to their days.

What if they'd done that with what they'd said about Lillian and Daria's sister?

I tapped my brakes. If those ladies fabricated events only to have fresh things to say to each other, had I just fueled those stories by bringing their imaginings to police?

I dug my phone out of my purse. I'd call Wilet and apologize. Tell him I wasn't certain about anything I'd expressed about the women.

Wait, I *did* know about Lillian and Daria's sister. I'd seen them arguing. Had I heard them mention Zane Snelling's name? I didn't think so, but he must have been the man they were arguing about. One of those two said she'd expected to get something from him. Could that item be what a burglar broke into my twin's house to find? How was that possible? She didn't have anyone's fortune.

I reached the corner of Second and Canal. I'd call Eve and tell her what happened.

My cell rang before I could press her number. "What're you doing?" she asked when I answered.

"Getting ready to call you. What's new over there?" Maybe hers would be better than mine. I could use some cheering up.

"Guess what? Dave's coming for supper tomorrow."

My spirits lowered. "That's nice."

"I can't wait. I'm using your recipes for shrimp gumbo and potato salad. You don't mind, I'm sure."

"Of course not." I struggled to gain enthusiasm in my tone. "It's good that he's going over. I guess. I mean, you really think he's safe, right?"

"Definitely. You assured me of that. Okay, gotta go. I'll let you know how things turn out."

"Thanks," I said dully and clicked off. I imagined her painting filled with vibrant colors that represented her anticipation of a relationship about to start with that man.

What was wrong with me?

Driving down my street, I passed Miss Hawthorne working in her front flowerbed and didn't feel like waving back when she lifted her trowel to acknowledge me. The brim of her hat shielded her eyes, but I could make out her wide smile. I gave my horn a light tap to return her greeting.

Inside my house, I moved around, unable to sit still with jumbled feelings. I wanted my sister happy. I wanted her to find one man she could stay with forever.

I just didn't want him to be Dave Price.

What is wrong with you? I asked myself, circling the kitchen table. I didn't want a man. I didn't want him.

I probably still feared he could harm my sister. I stopped and stood in place, anticipating my song.

Nothing came.

My experience with Detective Wilet must have caused my confusion. He hadn't believed me. He caught me off-guard so that I told him about the ashes, then he took the ashes and jacket. Nothing I could do about that. But maybe I'd learn something from Daria's obituary. I strode outside and grabbed the local newspaper from its white tube attached to my mailbox.

A couple of yards over, Miss Hawthorne's movement grabbed my attention. She knelt, head down, digging. The flat of pink petunias near her knees waited for her to set those flowers in the ground. Her shirt was open at the top, and darn if that didn't look like the avocado green of the bra I'd sold her.

Probably the sun and its angle inside her shirt made it appear to be her old bra. Maybe since her step-grandson mentioned it at the funeral home, I imagined I saw that thing.

At least the remembrance of that dreadful bra made me smile. A real smile, I realized, pleased to find my mood lifted. On my front stoop, I flipped through the paper, looking for mention of Daria's death since I hadn't seen it yet. The obituary showed four people's faces with long write-ups. And then came the name *Daria Snelling*. No picture or other information displayed except the date she died. No relatives or funeral arrangements were mentioned.

What should I do now?

Eve, in one of her rare appearances in her fine stainless-steel kitchen, came to mind. She would be grocery shopping today and cooking tomorrow. And after a while, in would walk that charming man. They would eat two of my best recipes and then—

I needed to go somewhere. Since Detective Wilet seemed focused on me being a killer, I had to find out who really did it. St. Gertrude's Church might be helpful. There I'd found the nail file that could have pried the urn open. Maybe I could locate other clues if people weren't around.

I grabbed a phonebook and flipped to listings of churches in the yellow pages. St. Gertrude's little square listed its mass schedule. They held one on Saturday afternoons. Tomorrow was Sunday. They held three masses in the morning but none in the evening.

Sunday afternoon arrived, and I found it the perfect time to be driving up to a church. Getting into a different place would make my mind leave my sister and her guest. At the moment, I preferred to think of murder. I hummed and parked. Trotted to the porch and pulled on a door. To my surprise, it opened. My peripheral vision let me see both priests strolling over from their house. Maybe they wanted to talk to me, perhaps with new information. I watched them and waited.

The younger one trotted up the steps. "Hi. Nice to see you again. Are you coming for confession?"

"Yes." The word popped out of my mouth before my mind could work.

He held the door open for me to walk inside first.

Oh no, what nasty sins was I going to admit to this man?

Chapter 13

"It's hot in here," I said, entering steamy St. Gertrude's and dipping my hand in holy water. I made the sign of the cross. A priest was following right behind. The old floor croaked when I took another step. Possibly the church felt extra hot this time because I was about to enter a confessional, something I hadn't done in decades.

"We've had some trouble with the air conditioner. I'll go check on it," the young priest told me.

"Thanks, Father."

"Oh, I'm not a priest. I'm a seminarian, Jessie Landers."

Since I didn't want him to know my name, I gave him a brief nod and withheld introducing myself. He went off toward a thermostat, and relief relaxed my breaths. If he wasn't a priest, I wouldn't need to confess anything. The pastor hadn't heard me say I was here for confession.

The door behind me creaked open. I rushed to a side aisle to get away from the entrance before Father Prejean came inside. Three older women walked in. Two of them glanced at me, gave me small smiles, and moved to a pew near the confessional in the rear. I suspected they were regulars—those Catholics brought up to believe they needed to go to confession once a month, or more if needed, like once a week if they'd entertained a really bad thought.

I scurried farther away from that small box, wanting to search for items like the nail file that might become evidence to prove Daria killed her husband. We didn't do it, and I still figured she did, although hearing her sister and Lillian argue, I wasn't so sure any longer. What I needed to find to prove our innocence was beyond me. Searching here might let me discover something, anything. At least I was contributing toward the investigation. I wasn't sitting at home wondering what my twin might be doing with Dave.

Father Prejean shoved in through the front door and headed toward the confessional.

I scanned pews in the center of church. A crumpled pink tissue lay on a seat. An open songbook on another. Two small pencils without erasers. A brown umbrella near a kneeler. But no sign of any of Zane's ashes.

"Oh, Father, that woman was first."

My body froze. I could not believe someone said that.

The seminarian walked across the center aisle toward the priest, pointing at me. "She came in before those other ladies."

Heat flooded my face. "No, that's okay. She can go in now. I'm not in a hurry." I thrust my finger toward the tall woman standing at the end of her pew. Beyond her, Father Prejean waited in front of the confessional, eyeing both of us.

"Oh, no, honey, I know what it's like to wait. You came first. You just go on in," the woman said.

I recognized her as my mother's friend, Ruth Ellen Molaison.

"How nice," Father told her. He nodded at me. "You can come right in, little lady."

Surely he hadn't noticed my height when he called me little. I considered protesting, but Father opened his slim door and swept inside, the door clicking shut.

I swallowed. Could I knock on it and tell him I changed my mind? Say I'd never done anything wrong?

Others in church stared at me, making me feel as toasty as if I'd been placed in a broiler in my wool scarf and coat. Taking a breath, I shoved my short sleeves up over my shoulders to let more air reach my skin and slid between the navy curtains.

On the kneeler inside, I sucked more air into my lungs. Inhaled the strong odor of antique oak and burnt incense that sank down my throat. Dark-paneled walls swallowed me. They didn't match the painted white walls of the church. There were dark corners above. Bits of light angled in from under the curtain, reminding me my mother's friend out there might be able to hear. I'd need to speak quietly—if I could get my voice to project past my mouth. My heart slammed against my chest wall.

"Why are you singing?" Father Prejean's face drew close to the square screen between us.

"Sorry. Habit. I hadn't realized I was doing it."

"That's fine." His eyes widened. Pupils expanding, he stared at me. Then leaned back and with an exhale, faced his entrance door, waiting.

"Father, I haven't done this in such a long time. I might forget some things I'm supposed to say."

"Take your time. We're not in a hurry. Just say whatever comes to you."

Bits of recalled childhood actions and words returned. I crossed myself. "It's been so long since I went to confession that I actually can't remember the last time." Now he might kick me out, saying I didn't belong.

"That's fine. Good." His voice soothed, putting me more at ease.

I needed to come up with something. "I probably fibbed a few times. Especially to my mom. About why I didn't visit her often enough."

Father nodded without looking at me. This was going well.

"And I fibbed to this man." I didn't plan to tell him about Dave. But maybe telling him was a good thing. I couldn't tell anyone else, not even Eve. "My identical twin thinks she's in love with him, but she was kind of scared of him and wanted me to take her place when he came over, so I did. I made him think I was her."

A small grin played on the priest's lips. "Go on."

"Everything came out okay."

He gripped his chin while staying quiet.

I sucked a deep inhale through my nose. The slightest relief relaxed my chest. "And I've been jealous of my sister."

Father nodded. "Sibling rivalry. Very common."

"Exactly. And do you know what kind of person she is?" Whoa, what was I going to tell him? I checked my intentions and realized I'd been ready to blurt that she'd had various lovers over the years. But who was I to judge? And this was my confession, not hers.

"Sometimes I'm resentful because Eve doesn't have as many flaws as I do. She always seems happy."

Was I jealous because she took such pleasure in romantic relationships? Had I complained about sex with Kevin because I had no idea how to enjoy having relations with a man? What would that feel like?

I probably shouldn't be thinking of such things in a confessional.

A small knocking sounded. Inside Father's tiny room, he was tapping his foot. Oh, sure, he didn't want to hear about all of our bickering.

Footsteps sounded past the confessional. A floorboard creaked. People out there waited for me to finish so they could come in. I should wrap things up now and leave.

"Father, I also lied to a priest." That got his attention. His face snapped toward me. "Actually, your seminarian. Just now he asked if I was coming to confession, and I told him yes. That had not been my intention."

"Oh? Well, Mr. Landers is a forgiving man."

"What I really wanted to do was look for clues to what happened to a man you buried here a few days ago. Or tried to. His ashes fell all over."

He nodded. "Mr. Snelling."

"Correct. And I believe he was murdered."

The priest's head pulled back.

"Yes," I said. "You know his wife was killed soon after he died. My sister and I found her, so the police think we did it. We didn't, Father, I promise."

He stared at me, face closer to the screen, eyes narrowing. Did he believe he was eye to eye with a murderer?

"Father, have you seen anything or do you know of anything unusual about either of the Snellings' deaths?"

He pushed himself away from me and seemed to think a minute before he replied. "I can't say that I do. But this is your confession."

The tiny room squeezed into an even smaller space. "I *really* didn't do it." I watched him, hoping he wouldn't say if I told him the truth about the death, God would forgive me.

Sweat broke out across my brow. "So, Father, if you think of anything concerning the newly-deceased couple, please let the police know." I sucked in a breath, released it. "That's about it. People are waiting to see you, and I'm not ready to think back to everything I've done wrong."

"Someone mightier than I am knows and forgives. He forgives you." Father used a soothing tone.

I felt suddenly secure—warm behind the eyes. "Thank you."

He gave me a penance of five Our Fathers and five Hail Marys, made the sign of the cross toward me, and said a prayer that God would guide me. "Good luck," he said as I ducked out past the curtain.

I kept my eyes diverted from people waiting near the confessional. Had I stayed longer than most people so now they believed I did terrible things? If my mother's friend overheard that I'd fibbed to Mom, I did not want to see shame in her gaze. Instead, I would try to make up time spent with my mother.

Walking toward rear pews, I glanced at seats, searching for ashes but not knowing what I would do if I found some. The police confiscated my jacket with what I'd captured of Zane Snelling. If I found more of him, would I return to the confessional and ask Father for a small brush and container? Probably I'd need to knock on his door but first wait for a person telling him her sins to come out.

A massive wave of guilt concerning the Snellings' deaths washed over me, taking me by surprise, making my footsteps falter. No, Eve and I didn't kill either one of them. But maybe we could have done something to stop their demise. Had Father's hint of my guilt caused this feeling? Adding it to Detective Wilet's suggestion that confession was good for the soul made me consider that both of these discerning men might know much more about me than I knew about myself. Or that I was willing to admit.

I didn't see the seminarian inside the church and glanced around the back of the building again, but didn't find anything that might help with the investigation. I did feel a strange sense of comfort from having the familiar penance and then reciting those prayers.

Maybe I'd done a good thing. What next? My thoughts ran to my sister's house, but I jerked them away. I needed to focus on clearing our names and discovering who killed Daria and maybe also her husband. In my truck, I aimed for Lillian's place. If she was home, would she let me in? It was nearing suppertime for most people. She'd surely be angry if I bothered her while she was eating.

Was she really having an affair with Zane? And if so, why would she admit it to me?

A lyric from "Silver Bells" assured me I was alarmed. I wasn't sure why until I scrambled through mental pictures and determined I was afraid of reaching the door of another woman I barely knew, ready to confront her, and instead finding her dead.

Chapter 14

"You? Forget it! Go away." Lillian slammed the door in my face.

I was never so happy to have that happen. It meant Lillian wasn't dead. I rang her doorbell again. When she didn't answer, I used the brass knocker to clack against her merlot-colored door.

She yanked that door open. "Stop bothering me, or I'll call the police. Get away from here."

Just what I needed. The police wanting me for something else. I shoved my foot in the doorway, cringing when she slammed the door against it. Pain shot back to the spurs in my heels. "Lillian, you saw me here when you argued with another woman, but you don't know who I am or why I was here."

"I don't want to know. Leave me alone." She pushed against the door. The pressure sent aches up to my shoulder from my elbow I also used to block it.

"I knew Daria and Zane Snelling."

She released pressure on the door. "And?" Her tight lips and chin softened a bit.

"I know about your connection to them." My next words came faster. "I'm not any kind of investigator. I'm just a regular person who cares. I care about what happened to the people who died. I don't care about your relationship with either of them. That's your business."

Her chest rose with her sigh. She wore a snug knit shirt, shorts, sandals, and her hair in a bun.

"I'm not here to hurt you."

I touched her hand. She jerked it back.

"I need to talk to you, Lillian. Please let me in."

Her stare appeared vacant, like she was seeing inside herself, trying to make a decision. I gave the door a gentle push. Taking a step back, she allowed me entry. "But just for a minute," she warned.

"Fine. That's enough." I slid past her into the den and sat on the edge of her tan leather sofa. Wooden blinds hung on windows. A local newscaster spoke from a television.

"All right." She didn't sit.

"I know you and Zane were having an affair."

Her firm stance faltered. She sank to the upholstered chair beside me. "I'm not saying that's true." But she looked curious, waiting.

"And the woman who showed up and argued with you Saturday was having an affair with him, too. She was his sister-in-law."

Lillian stood, her narrow jaw set. "It's time for you to leave."

"I'm not here to judge you. I didn't know Zane or his wife, but I captured some of his ashes. They dropped in my jacket pocket at his funeral. I want to preserve them."

My hostess took a moment to consider my words. Lines of tension in her face relaxed. She sank back to the chair. "You have part of Zane? Where?"

I sucked in a deep inhale. "I'm sorry to say a detective just took my jacket. I've been trying to take care of the ashes and didn't want them stuck in a police station. I plan to get them back."

She lowered her head, then looked up to face me. "I was at the funeral. I ran toward him when she fell, but realized I couldn't just scoop him up and take him with me, so I rushed out the side door before I burst out crying. I drove here and sobbed all day."

"You really cared about him. That woman who came here, she's Daria's sister, isn't she?" I needed to keep her talking before she decided to quit.

"That's her older sister Kellie. Isn't that horrible?"

I nodded. Who was I, or Lillian for that matter, to decide? "And you knew he was seeing Kellie?"

She hung her head. "Yes. I've been around. I know men often sleep with different women." Lillian's lips twisted. "Of course Daria was having an affair, too."

"What?" I straightened, shoulders high. "Is that true?"

Her face scrunched up. "Sure. That's why Zane was planning to leave her."

My head jerked. "Zane Snelling was going to leave his wife?" Was all of this information the truth, or just something he'd told this woman?

"That's why I think she killed him."

"You do?" Gratitude swelled in my chest. "So do I."

"Zane and I were talking on the phone. A lot of time they kept the speaker on 'cause he was a little hard of hearing, and he'd forget to change the setting or didn't bother since he only called me from their house when she wasn't there."

Smart choice.

"So we were talking that day, and Daria walked in. She had told him she was going to the mall but probably changed her mind since she showed up home so early."

"And then what?" My breath went scant with this new information.

"He told me he needed to go. She was back. Then he probably thought he hung up, but I heard them start arguing."

I leaned close, hands clasped. "About what?"

"She'd heard us. She had gone in through the front of the house and heard him talking to me on the phone. That's when she knew he was planning to leave her." She shifted forward like she was ready to shove herself up. "I've told you enough."

I pushed my arm out, hand lifted as though telling her to stop. "And Daria went into a rage because he was seeing you?" My tone suggested I sided with her. I needed her to tell me more.

"She yelled at him that she'd been involved with a lover long before he had other women—and she still had her man—and he was so much better than Zane ever was." Lillian stopped. Her gaze dropped to the Aztec rug on her floor.

"Lillian." My calling her name got her to face me. The vacant look in her eyes suggested her thoughts remained elsewhere. "When you and Kellie argued, you said he had a fortune."

She drew her head back, and I sensed she was ready to snap shut like an oyster inside its hard shell. I rushed toward my point. "If he did, I'm not trying to find it. I don't care about his money. I'm only trying to discover why he died. It's really important to me."

She rubbed an index finger over the edge of her chair, looking down at first and then lifting her gaze toward me. "Zane told Daria he was going to leave her sorry ass stone dry without anything. He yelled that he was going to go cancel everything that was in both their names. First, that big insurance policy."

"Okay, good. And then what did Daria say?"

Lillian sank back. "Nothing."

"Nothing? He told his wife all those things, and she didn't say anything back to him?"

Gazing at that rug, she kept shaking her head. "I think that's when he went outside, and she went after him. But I can't prove it." Lillian's eyes were misty when she faced me. "That afternoon, I found out he was dead."

We eyed each other. I was letting her feel her words, that the man she apparently cared very much about was forever gone.

"I think she killed him," I said quietly. "I believe she ran after him and shoved him, and he tripped and hit his head on a cypress tree or its roots. Then he either fell in the pond, or she pushed him."

She kept nodding. "That's what I believe, too."

"You do?" My breath eased.

Water rimmed the lower edge of her eyes. "She probably stood there and watched him drown."

Reaching out, I gripped her hand. "I am so sorry."

Eyes sad, she gazed into nothingness. Moments passed before she blinked and stood. "Daria knew Zane had gotten a fortune from his grandpa. But she didn't know where he kept it."

I stood with her, hope welling inside. Maybe her information could somehow clear up some things surrounding the break-in at Eve's and Daria's death. "Do *you* know where he kept it?"

"No." She kept eye contact, and I believed her. "I was just interested in him."

"Oh, Lillian, I am so sorry. But your information should really help clear things up." My body relaxed, my nostrils releasing a long, silent exhale.

"I won't tell any of this to police."

Disappointment dropped through me like a boulder off a cliff. How could I prove my innocence without her statements? Lillian's eyes tightened to a squint. Her lips pressed into a line as her expression grew darker and mean. A touch of fear chased up my neck. Someone murdered Daria. Could that person be facing me now?

I took a step back before noticing I'd done it and struggled to withhold the tune as she stepped toward me.

"It's time for you to go." Her shoulder knocked against my arm when she swept past and yanked the front door open.

"Thank you." I dashed outside. Darkness swallowed the front yard. "If you think of anything else, call me, okay?"

She slammed her door.

I jumped into my truck and drove off. Then determined I hadn't given her my phone number. Or even my name. I smiled, a real smile of satisfaction. She wouldn't know where I lived or how to find me.

Driving north, I yanked my cell phone out of my purse and punched in number two. I needed to tell Eve about everything I discovered.

Wait. I snapped my phone shut. Dave was at her house. They had probably already eaten the food she'd prepared. She might have brought him into her studio, pointed to the canvas filled with massive splashes of bright colors, and announced, "That's you—and me. It's what I've been anticipating."

"That's fine," I said to convince myself and drove to Swamp Rat's Diner. I would treat myself to a large meal surrounded by other people, not stuck inside my house alone eating leftovers or a ham and cracker sandwich.

Swamp Rat's resembled a gray tin shack squatting between thick cypress trees as though it needed to pee. Leaning a pinch to the right, the building gave diners the fear that if too many of them stepped inside, it might tip over. When Eve and I started our business, we offered to make repairs in exchange for a couple of gift certificates, but the owner said the shack wouldn't fall or sink into the swamp. The leaning added to the charm and enticed some people to come in just to find out whether the building would stay upright.

A picture of nutrias, the large swamp rats with two long yellow teeth that came over from Texas, took wall space outside the door. Reaching the screen door, everyone seemed to forget to worry and took pleasure in the aromas of fried and boiled seafood. I enjoyed those enticing scents while I walked inside and exchanged greetings with people. Immediately afterward, my phone rang.

"Hey, you called?" Eve's voice made my smile vanish.

"I did, but I didn't mean to." And I didn't want to hear about what she and Dave had planned.

She giggled. "No, it's okay," she told someone.

"I need to go," I said, following a waitress to a table.

"Please stay," Eve said.

I quit walking. "Why?"

"Not you, Sunny."

I clicked off and sat at a table and accepted a menu then asked for a beer. I lifted my menu and stared at it so people wouldn't try to talk to me and imagined what my sister meant. Had she been talking to Dave? Did he already want to leave her house?

I wished I hadn't hung up so soon. She would have kept talking to whoever was with her, and I would have gotten most of the story. I would eavesdrop, exactly like Lillian did with Zane and his wife.

For now, I didn't want to think of them. I wanted to think of Dave being at my sister's house and her trying to keep him there to do something more than eat and him saying he wanted to go.

With a smile, I ordered a seafood steak covered with a creamed crayfish sauce and sides of grilled asparagus and fried sweet potatoes. During the brief wait, I sipped my brew and mulled over what Lillian told me. My enthusiasm built since someone else confirmed what I believed. But if Lillian wouldn't tell any of her story to police, what could I do with her information?

I took immense pleasure in my cup of seafood gumbo appetizer and the well-seasoned entrée and veggies. I ordered a chocolate explosion dessert. My great meal satisfied, but I felt ready to explode myself from the rare treat.

Heading toward Eve's house to share information I'd discovered, I hoped I would not find a truck still parked out front.

One of Eve's neighbors was having a party. Cars filled the driveway two doors to the left of her house, and a number of other vehicles sat along the street. A couple of pricy models parked in front of Eve's place. No truck sat in her driveway.

"Yes," I said.

Dave might have gone over for supper, but he hadn't stayed for dessert. I was ready to visit my sister but realized I harbored mixed purposes. Would I really be digging it in? I'd drive home and talk to her tomorrow.

After I dressed for bed, I plopped in front of TV and mindlessly watched. Then slept better than I had in some time.

In the morning, I still savored the thought that my sister hadn't been able to get a man to stay for a romantic interlude. He wasn't just any man. He made me smile and grow warm when I thought about him.

Conflicting with my pleasant thoughts about what occurred at Eve's house was the mental image of Daria running out her backdoor after her husband once he'd told her he was leaving. He was going to cancel everything in both their names. Daria probably confronted him again when he was near the pond in the area where Eve and I had worked. Maybe he reached our pavers first. Or she could have shoved him right before he reached them. His wife watched him die.

Lillian had agreed with me about that but also frightened me. Possibly, she was the person who actually killed Zane after she learned he was also having an affair with Daria's sister. Sure, she told me she'd known, and it hadn't mattered, but should I believe her?

Could Lillian have envisioned that scene near the pond because it really happened? Or instead of Daria going after Zane and shoving him, was it her?

Daria supposedly went shopping at a mall. The nearest one would take an hour and a half for a round trip. A woman could spend many hours shopping there. I had no idea what Daria's shopping habits had been. Suppose what she'd told the police was true? That she had shopped for a while, arrived home, and found him dead in their pond.

My pulse sped. I needed to talk to my sister. She'd help me sort through the truth. I hopped in my truck, drove to her house, and rang the front doorbell. A minute passed with no sound inside. I rang the bell again. Still no answer. Possibly she wasn't home. I could dig out my key and go in but preferred not to because I didn't want to spook her since her break-in.

Ready to go home, I tried the doorknob. Her door opened.

"Eve," I called and tensed, waiting for her new alarm to blast.

Since I didn't hear her, I dashed inside to the alarm's keypad near the door, ready to punch in the four-number code she'd told me to make the noise stop.

But the alarm wasn't going to go off. I inspected the keypad. It hadn't been set.

"Eve," I called. "Girl, I need to talk to you." Stomping through her den, I prepared to chew her out for not setting the system. What good did it do for her to have one if she didn't set it? Even if she was inside, there was a setting for that purpose. Being in the house was the best time to keep the darn thing set.

I tromped toward bedrooms. Her bed was made, and her bathroom door stood open. "Eve," I called, but nobody answered.

Fear pricked the skin on my legs, my vocal cords starting to vibrate. Where was she?

I ran down the hall and crossed the den toward her kitchen, calling her name. The studio room door stood open. I tiptoed in, fearing what I would find.

Beyond the sliding glass door, my sister was walking across her patio from the left. She had probably turned off her alarm to go to her friendly neighbor's house to borrow an egg or slice of bread.

I smirked, happy to see her okay, unhappy I'd been so frightened. I would fuss at her about starting to set her new alarm. Eve was grinning. I wore a frown, ready to complain.

Movement out on the right grabbed my attention.

An arm swung up. A man's hand held a pistol. Aimed at her.

I trembled, fearing I was about to lose my last sister. "No!" I roared and flew across to the studio. I grabbed a can holding paintbrushes and threw it all against the glass door. Running to that sliding door, I slammed my fists against the glass, punched code numbers into the keypad beside it, and shoved the door open. I might not scare a killer, but a screaming alarm that would alert others would.

A shot rang out.

"Eve!" I shrieked.

My twin fell to the ground.

Chapter 15

My body shook like a hurricane was slamming against me. I shoved the door open wide and dashed outside. The shooter was running off.

"Eve. Eve, be okay," I cried through fitful lyrics, hating that I couldn't stop, hating that my sister lay on her side, dying.

When I stooped near on the patio, her back expanded. Eve reached toward me. "I wasn't hit. Just give me a minute."

"You're alive!" Joy shot through my trembling body. I looked up to see the man who shot at her was no longer around. I stayed with my sister, rubbing her shoulder, massaging her back, and whispering, "You're all right."

She remained down. "Sunny, I'll be fine. Just go call the cops, okay?"

I'd dropped my purse in her house. "I'll be right back." Afraid to move her, I ran inside and punched 9-1-1 in her phone. I gave the information and rushed back toward the open door.

That's when I realized the burglar alarm I'd set hadn't gone off.

Eve was sitting up, moving cautiously. She sat with elbows on knees and was feeling the side of her head when I walked outside. "I have a little hickey and some achy joints. I'll most likely have a few bruises," she said. "But I'll be fine."

I sat close, still gripping the phone, and wrapped my arms around her.

Her tears wet my shoulder. "I'm sorry," she said with a whimper. "That was so scary."

"Why should you be sorry?"

She drew back her head and wiped her eyelashes. "You know."

I sucked air through my nostrils. "That wasn't your fault."

A siren's wail rang out, approaching. It would frighten away an intruder that might still be lurking.

"Are you sure the bullet didn't hit you?"

She shook her head and winced, touching the knot growing on the side of her head. I inspected her face and lifted her hair in spaces to check her scalp, making certain I didn't find blood beneath the red hair.

The siren stopped near. A car door slammed, and a cop with freckles ran into the backyard.

"I'm okay," Eve told him. "My sister yelled, and then I saw a man across my patio pointing a pistol at me, so I threw myself down. I'm sure that's why the bullet missed me. He ran back there." She pointed to the slim pathway between the fences behind her house.

Backups were on the way, the cop said, and more sirens approached. He and other police who ran up checked behind Eve's house. Some scrambled around the neighborhood.

Eve told me and the police she'd gone next door to borrow a couple of slices of bread, was heading back to her house, and noticed a man approaching on the opposite side of her yard.

"Who was it?" I asked.

"I couldn't see his face. He wore one of those roll-down camouflage knit caps like hunters wear when it's really cold, so I couldn't see anything about his face or even tell you about his eyes. What I can say is I saw his arm raising a gun pointed at me, so I wasn't checking his clothes."

"How large a man was he?" the cop asked, writing on a pad.

"Medium. I don't think he was anyone I knew. He was stepping on the other side of the patio when Sunny yelled." She shivered and squeezed her arms around me. "Thank you."

I could only nod, my throat so tight it couldn't release a sound. The backs of my eyes sizzled.

Eve's slight quiver intensified, building to violent shakes. She squinted, her face tightening as though she was experiencing extreme pain.

"You need to go get checked," I said, and the officer concurred.

"No, I'm fine." Shrugging out of our hug, she attempted to stand. Immediately she jerked her leg up with a grimace and sank back down.

"You probably hit the concrete hard. Your ankle might be broken," I said. "And you might have a concussion."

She swallowed. "All right."

"An ambulance is on its way. Are you sure you don't know the man who was here, or can you tell me anything else about him?" the cop asked.

She shook her head and touched the side of her scalp.

"You saw him and warned your sister," the questioner said to me. "What was he wearing?"

"I just saw a pistol in his hand. Oh, he didn't have long sleeves, I don't think."

He jotted information, and I squatted next to my sister, touching her arm. "You need to stay away from this house."

To my surprise, she didn't look ready to argue.

"You should stay somewhere else for now," the young man said. "And it's probably best if you don't remain anywhere close." Approaching sirens shut off. Medics rushed near with a gurney.

"Go stay with Nicole," I suggested. Medical technicians tended to my sister, and I told the deputy, "Nicole is her daughter who lives in Houston."

"That's probably a good idea," he said.

"Don't call her yet." Eve's pinched expression pleaded with me. "Don't tell her what happened until we know for certain how I am."

Against my better judgment, I agreed. I grabbed her purse so she'd have medical and insurance information and tailed the ambulance to the hospital, praying my sister would be all right. I sang out, then realized I was imagining life without her.

"No!" I shouted and shoved aside the image of her dying.

I needed to do something constructive. Mentally replaying the scene with the man's hand and the gun, I worked to shove my picture farther to the right, to remember his clothes or his face. I imagined a pause button keeping him inside my view.

Nothing else would come.

Eve's burglar alarm was faulty. That was a major problem. I grabbed my cell phone, called information, and connected with Dave Price's office.

"I'm sorry. Mr. Price isn't here at the moment. Can I help you?" a pleasant woman's voice said.

"Yes. I'm Sunny Taylor. Mr. Price recently installed a burglar alarm at my sister's house. Her name is Eve Vaughn. And the alarm doesn't work."

"Oh. I'll be sure to tell Mr. Price."

"Please do. And have him contact me." I gave my cell number.

For long moments after we disconnected, I gripped the phone. My mind returned to the scene that angered me so much last night. The scene of *Mr. Price* and my sister fulfilling her fantasy of him that she'd painted so vividly. I mentally apologized to her for those wayward thoughts right before an Emergency sign ahead at the hospital made my gut clench.

The only thing I cared about concerning the man now was his product that was supposed to protect my sister but did not. I threw my truck into park and sprinted up the ramp behind her on the gurney.

"Is she all right?" I asked the medics. "She didn't get worse?"

"I'm fine." Eve lifted her head off her pillow.

"Good. Lie back." I trotted inside the hospital beside her, through a large number of people sitting in the emergency room, along with a strong odor of chips and sound of a crinkling bag. I moved beyond this into one of a number of smaller rooms, immediately assaulted by the sounds of fast-talking voices and suctioning on the floor from staff members' soft-soled shoes.

The phone I'd tossed into my purse warbled.

"Sunny, this is Dave Price," he said when I answered.

I stopped. My sister's gurney rolled past. A flood of emotions surprised me with their wallop. Fear for Eve. Contentment from hearing from this man? No way. I cleared my throat. "You sold my sister an inferior product. The alarm system she bought from you was supposed to keep her safe."

"She isn't?"

His tone made me recall that Eve and I had feared him. Should that concern still hold true? I didn't think so.

"No. Well, she's not hurt badly, but your alarm doesn't work."

"That would be highly unusual. I'd like to check it out. Would that be okay with her?"

I glanced ahead at her being rolled through a curtain. "Let me call you right back." Disconnecting, I stepped to the curtain.

A male nurse intercepted me. "They're taking her for x-rays and other examinations. She'll be fine. You can sit in the waiting room over there. We'll let you know when you can see her."

Fighting the urge to knock him down and rush after her, I turned around and walked outside. I wasn't ready to sit in a room and wait. Sunshine and coolness of the air felt strangely discomforting. So did mounds of lavender and white petunias slanting down from the sloping land the hospital was built on. Dark clouds should overhang this day. Cars pulled into a large apartment's parking lot next door. A line of vehicles headed for the high school. How many of the locals who taught there and the people living next door knew my sister? Our town was normally safe. Would people who knew Eve believe what just happened at her house?

I struggled with my singing instinct. No, *this* sister would not be taken. I refused to believe she would.

Looking at Dave Price's number, I called him back. "There's a little complication with asking my sister about things being okay at her house. Let me get in touch with you later to tell you when you can come out there."

Without questioning he agreed, and I paced. I strode down one slope toward the huge parking lot and paced up the opposite end. On my third trip down, a woman I didn't know well walked from the parking lot calling my name.

"You look like an expectant father waiting for a baby to be delivered," Sue Ellen Granger said. She gave me time to explain. I chose not to. She'd bought lacy black bras and body huggers from me. Now she wore her too-black dyed hair upswept, and her make-up too showy. Her dress and heels were the latest style, as always.

"No. No baby today."

Apparently giving up on my telling who I had in the hospital and why, she said, "I hated to hear you left Fancy Ladies. You helped me the most over there."

"Thanks. It's just that I learned your tastes so well, I could tell what you'd like in undergarments." I'd also known she wanted the most expensive of everything.

Sue Ellen leaned close. "Not like those ugly things your neighbor Faye Hawthorne wears, right?" She grinned, then glanced around like she was checking to make sure no one walked up behind and heard.

"I prefer not to talk about what other people buy or wear." I wouldn't mention I'd heard that the woman in front of me way overspent on all her jewelry and garments. I was, however, glad to have her distraction. Chatting kept me from the constant worry. I glanced at the doors to the emergency room. The male nurse wasn't coming out. Still, soon I would go in and check on Eve.

Sue Ellen kept her head close to mine. "Jeanne Pearson saw her buying a horrible green bra from you."

She needn't say anymore. Jeanne probably told half the town what my sweet neighbor bought. "If she did, she might not wear it anymore."

"Or maybe she never did. Just like that step-grandson of hers."

"Toby?"

She leaned her head closer. "That man never did wear any underwear. Not when he was a boy and not even now that he's a man."

I hadn't known him when he was a child because they'd lived elsewhere. Some of my customers used to tell me their spouses went around commando. But him? "Surely he sometimes wears briefs or boxers," I said. "He works at the funeral parlor. He does funerals."

"I know. He gives new meaning to hanging loose."

"I need to go. Nice seeing you." I darted to the door before she could say anything more or ask who I had inside. And why did she bring up gossip about my neighbor and her grandson?

"She isn't in a room yet." The male nurse sat at a desk with two others.

"Do you know anything about her?" I asked, but he shook his head. "I'll be in the waiting room. Please let me know as soon as I can see her."

I joined a dozen other people in the cramped seating area. My mind raced through events and people. My reaching Eve's house. She didn't answer. She was out back. I wanted to gripe at her. A man wanted to shoot her.

And then there was Dave. Why hadn't his alarm worked?

"Your sister's done. You can see her now," the nurse told me.

I scrambled to reach Eve. Instead of writhing in pain, she was sitting on the side of the bed. A bump had risen on the corner of her forehead. "Undo me," she said the second I darted in, "and you can help me get dressed." She pointed toward ties in the back of a hospital gown they'd put on her.

Relief swept through me. "Is she okay?" I asked the nurse entering information on a laptop on a rolling stand near the bed.

"I'm fine." Eve untied the top strings on her gown and tried to reach the others without waiting for me. I grabbed the next two and pulled, getting her loose. A large plastic bag holding her clothes sat beside her. She put on her bra, which I hooked, then she carefully shrugged into her pullover shirt.

"We didn't find broken bones or anything else obvious," the nurse said, focusing on me. "But she'll need to be watched for a while, especially with that knot on her head. The doctor sent a prescription for pain pills to the drugstore she uses."

"You're leaving town," I told Eve without offering room for discussion.

"Yes. I'm going to Nicole's."

"Great."

A nurse wheeled Eve out, and I drove her to her residence, where she insisted on going after picking up the medicine at the drugstore's drive-up window. Contentment and anxiety jumped through me, making my stomach relax but my arms and scalp tense.

"I'm so glad you're well." I parked out front of her house. "But I'm concerned about bringing you anywhere near this place."

"If I'm going to leave town, I need to pack some things."

"I'll drive you to Houston," I said, and her eyes went from oval to round. She knew how horrible I was at driving in big cities. "But before we go inside here, let me walk outside your house and check."

Moments passed in which I imagined she feared what might be found around or inside her place. "Okay," she said.

Not extra brave myself, I grabbed my phone from my purse in case I needed to make an emergency call and dug a crowbar out of the long toolbox in my truck bed. I could swing the heavy tool or throw it at any threatening person I might come across.

Creeping around the right side of her place, I didn't find a person hiding or any windows broken. I turned to check the neighbor's house. From what I could see, nobody watched. My body went into fight-or-flight mode as I crept toward the rear, ready to round the corner to the patio.

Before moving there, I shot my gaze at the narrow space between the two fences in back where I'd seen the shooter run.

No person came into view. A tune tried to come. More fully aware and needing silence, I stopped it. My shoulders and chest tucked themselves as I stood still. Didn't breathe. Didn't sing.

No sound carried of footsteps or voices. The only thing I could hear was the water Eve's angel poured into the fountain. Forcing courage to give me strength, I tightened my grip on the tool in my raised hand and rushed forward, ready to aim it or strike.

Nobody stood back there. I swerved my head from one side to the other, searching for the slightest detail that might suggest someone was around who shouldn't be. Finding everything as it was before, I checked Eve's backdoors. The sliding door was locked, as was the entry to her kitchen. Satisfied, I rushed to the opposite side of her house and discovered no person or broken windows.

"You can go in," I told her out front at my truck.

"Sunny, I can drive myself to Houston. I know the way to my daughter's house."

"I know you do, and you're a good driver. But you have bruised areas that will probably start to ache more, and with that swelling on your head, you might have a concussion. What if you're driving out there and black out? Besides, if you need to take pain pills, they could make you sleepy. I don't want you driving."

Opening the truck door for her, I shoved my shoulders back, attempting to bolster my bravery.

She stepped out, looking at me. My twin wanted to show courage, I could tell by the lift of her chin. "It's really not encouraging to go inside with you standing there holding the crowbar like a guard with a sword."

"Sorry." I still held the tool aloft. I shoved the crowbar back into the toolbox while she emerged.

"If it'll make you feel better," she said, "when we go in, you can grab that gun from the drawer and keep it out while I pack."

I unlocked her front door and shoved it open. She and I stood in the doorway, peering inside, shoving our heads forward and turning them one way and the other to check for intruders in the area we could see.

"It looks okay." Rushing inside ahead of her, I yanked open the drawer holding the pistol near her sofa. "It's still here."

"Does that surprise you?" Her face paled in a mask of fear.

I shook my head and waved her on toward her room. I inched through the den, her kitchen, garage, and studio, my breathing much more relaxed once I found no one hiding and no signs of a break-in. Her voice lifted from the area of the bedrooms. She was probably talking on her phone, but I needed to be sure. I rushed down the hall to her room, praying I wouldn't find an intruder there with her.

"What's with that?" Standing beside her bed that held a partially filled suitcase, cell phone in her hand, she pointed to the raised gun I gripped.

"Sorry." I'd rushed in with the weapon pointed, which made it automatically aimed at her. Lowering my hand, I shuddered at the possibility that I could have bumped my arm darting in that way and accidentally shot her. Good grief, I was no good with weapons.

"Oh, I was just talking to Sunny, not you," she said into the phone.

I spun around and slouched away from her, keeping the pistol aimed down. Glancing into the other bedrooms and bathrooms, I made my way back to the den. There I yanked open the drawer for the end table, ready to drop the gun inside. But if I did, could it go off? Taking a breath, I used a gentle touch to return the weapon to its holding place, not shutting the drawer tight in case we needed it out.

This situation was awful. I considered going to fill up my truck with gas while she prepared for her trip to Texas but then stopped myself. I wasn't going to leave her alone now. I could fill up my tank along the way with her safely inside my vehicle. Same for getting something to eat.

But would she be safe during that trip? She was right. I didn't know how to drive in large cities, and the one where her daughter lived wasn't tiny. I could mount my GPS on my dash, but that thing often distracted me and had me driving a distance away from where I'd been headed. Possibly, I could have Eve drive my truck once we reached Houston. Surely Nicole or her husband Randy would later direct me back toward south Louisiana.

I stepped to Eve's room, ready to make the suggestion. At her door, we almost bumped into each other.

She grinned at me. "Want to help me finish getting my things together?"

"Of course. Would you mind driving my truck once we're about to reach Houston?"

She shook her head. "We don't need that. You're not driving me there."

"Who is?" For some reason, I almost dreaded the answer.

"Jacques. He's leaving soon."

"Your ex-husband Jacques?"

"Yes, and his new wife."

Chapter 16

I assisted my sister with placing bright colorful panties and bras in her suitcase for a ride I didn't believe she should take. She squeezed in a couple more pairs of shoes. We placed garment bags over the dresses and tops she chose to bring.

"Don't worry so much," she said.

I felt the frown lines that remained between my eyes ever since she told me her plans to ride with them. "I need to worry. You need to stay safe."

She patted my arm. "Okay, we'll both do what we have to do."

"So Jacques was the only one you could think of to call for your son-in-law's new cell number?" I threw an emerald green nightgown atop the other things in her luggage.

"Yes." She pulled the silk piece out, folded, and replaced it. "I didn't want to just show up out there, and Nicole's phone was off. I'm sure she's teaching. I left a voice message and a text that she hasn't responded to. The number I have for Randy isn't working anymore, and if you want me to go there today, I am not making you drive me."

"So you figured since Jacques and his wife were in town a few days for Zack Snelling's funeral, they would be heading back to Texas soon and you might catch a ride?"

"No. I forgot if you even told me how long they'd be around. His name just came up first in my mind when I wanted Randy's number. Jacques sounded pleased to have me call, and he offered a ride there."

I wore a grim smile. "I wonder if they were planning to leave right when you wanted to go, or if he changed their plans."

Eve shrugged, followed by the doorbell's ring, making both our heads swerve toward the front entry. She and I looked at each other. My sister lifted her suitcase, and I took her overnighter and dresses. She unlocked and opened the door before I could issue another warning.

Jacques Thibodaux stood right outside, his broad smile widening while he devoured her with his eyes. "Hello, Eve," he said, leaning in to her for a hug.

"Thanks for offering to bring me," she said, drawing back from him.

His gaze swept down her body. It rounded her face. "You hurt yourself."

"Not bad."

I withheld the impulse to shove him back and remind him of his marriage, which was no longer to my sister.

"Hello again, Jacques," I said.

"Sunny." He nodded as though he'd just noticed me. Seeing what I held, he seemed to get the message and grabbed Eve's things. "I'll take this."

His wife sat in the front passenger seat, facing ahead in their fine Audi. Jacques popped the trunk open and moved items around to squeeze in my sister's gear, while she stood still. Melanie turned her head and made eye contact with Eve. She swayed her gaze across my sister's body, inspecting her down to her heels.

My discomfort swelled, urging me to shield Eve with my arm. I'd start with blocking her breasts, where the younger woman sizing her up seemed to want to make the most comparison. Eve stared back at her. Neither woman changed expression or spoke.

Jacques slammed the trunk and returned to Eve's side. "This is Melanie." He tilted his head toward the car. "And, honey, this is Nicole's mother, Eve." He knew, of course, that his wife and I had met at the supermarket.

The tongues of all us females seemed frozen since not one of us said a thing. Eve and Melanie didn't reward each other with any sort of acknowledgement. Jacques opened the door for my twin to sit behind him.

"Did you take your pain meds?" I asked.

"Yes, and I'll be fine." She gave me a swift hug.

"Give my niece a hug for me."

She nodded, and Jacques shut her door. His newest wife glanced back over the seat, fixing Eve with her stare.

Have a good trip, I almost said, but there was no way Eve would unless somebody knocked out the woman in front. The chill would have Eve freezing. When Jacques invited her on the trip, had he known he was also inviting major trouble? Or had he believed Melanie was as content with his gifts to my sister as she'd pretended to be with me when we'd met at the store?

I released a breath. The best I could wish for was that the pain pills might knock Eve out, and she would remain that way for the trip. At least she would stay physically unharmed.

Or possibly, I realized, Eve might even find it amusing to make the other woman so uncomfortable.

Once they drove out of sight, I connected with Dave and used a snap in my tone. "You can come to my sister's house now to fix your defective system."

"I'm in the middle of a meeting. I can be there in forty-five minutes."

"Fine." Getting weak from hunger, I knew there would be little left here except a few diet items in the pantry or fridge. I scuttled across the street and between fences to my house. Inside, I threw ham between crackers and ate a couple of these sandwiches.

Taking only enough time to drop my used dishes in the sink, I rushed back toward Eve's place. Right before I reached her house, I slowed, pulling back, wondering if someone could have already broken in. It made no sense that a burglar might smash a window or door here moments after I dashed off, but all of the dreadful things that occurred these last days defied logic. Someone had smashed the door to Eve's art room right after she left for the gym. And waited to kill her once she walked next door.

This is ridiculous. No way to live, I told myself as I took measured steps around her house, phone in hand. I swung my head one way and another, searching for thugs hidden on one side, the patio, and the opposite side of Eve's home. I was reaching the driveway out front when Dave pulled in.

Before he'd taken two steps from his truck, I said, "My sister was almost killed because of your malfunctioning product."

His forehead creased, lips went tight. "Did it shock her? Possibly there was an unusual short in a wire." Real concern gripped his face.

"Not that I'm aware of. What I do know is that your system didn't work when an intruder came."

"Another one? Somebody else broke into her house?"

"He didn't actually break in." What did I want to tell him about what happened? Not about a man out back with a gun pointed at her. Suppose it was him? That thought flashed into my mind, but I didn't really believe it. I searched inside myself for my feelings and believed the chance was extra-slim to none.

He looked at me with his thick eyebrows raised. He was still waiting for me to give him more facts about the intruder.

I chose not to. "Come in and see for yourself." Digging the key out of my purse, I unlocked Eve's front door.

Dave didn't step forward. Instead, he stood with his head cocked, his focus appearing to reach into distant spaces. He drew his head back straight over his neck. "The alarm's not set now," he said, and I knew he'd been listening for it to go off.

"It's not. But even when it is, the thing doesn't work."

"That really is strange," he said, stepping inside with me. He glanced toward the studio. "Did something happen in there again?"

Yes, I walked into it and saw my sister outside walking to her patio from a neighbor's house. Opposite her, I watched a man's hand come up with a gun.

A flutter came from my chest worming its way up my throat. Aware of it, I clamped my lips shut.

"Chestnuts roasting on an open fire?" He eyed me with a curious expression, confirming I'd just hummed aloud.

I shook my head. "Eve's studio is good. Just find out what's wrong with her system and fix it, or else pull the thing out so she can get one that works." My bluntness may have surprised him, but I was concerned about my sister.

He shut the front door and stepped to the nearby alarm box. "I remember the numbers she wanted in here," he said, still not asking why the owner of this house wasn't around. As his finger stabbed numerals in the box, my righteousness remained surfaced. That emotion gave way to warmth when he turned back and reached. His hand grazed my thigh. Our gazes gripped each other.

"Sorry," he said, moving his arm to his side. "I need to try the door."

I stepped out of his way, and he grabbed the handle on the front door he'd just shut. Dave yanked the door open.

"See?" I said. *WAAA-WAAA-WAA-WAA WAA* the alarm wailed before I could chew into him and add, *It's broken.*

He shut the door, glanced back to the den as though looking for something, and unclipped his phone from his belt.

"What did you do that's different?" My words competed with the noise blast.

He lifted a hand as though asking me to wait and punched a number in his phone. "It's Dave," he said into it seconds later. "I'm just testing a system."

My chest rose as I sucked in more air, ready to lift my voice to a scream above the screeching through my sister's home. Before I could speak, a deafening silence descended. I waited long moments. Would it come on again?

"Your sister doesn't have a landline?" Dave asked. I shook my head, and he started tapping numbers into his phone.

Mine rang. I grabbed it from my purse that hung on my arm.

"The alarm went off at my house!" Eve shouted.

"Yes, but it's okay."

"No. The company just called me. Somebody set it off!"

"Eve, everything's fine. It was just Dave."

"Wait. He's calling me." Her click put me on hold.

I heard him speaking in his cell phone. "Eve, this is Dave Price. I set off your system. I'm inside your house with your sister because she wanted it tested to find out if it worked." His eyes lifted toward me. "My company always calls the homeowner right away when an alarm goes off to make certain it wasn't them. It's automatic, so I wanted to let you know what happened."

He listened to her, nodded, and spoke a little quieter, taking steps away from me.

"Hey, Sunny." My twin's now calm voice followed a slight click on my phone that signaled she'd hung up with her caller. "Dave said the alarm's working fine. He'll make sure you know how to use it."

Annoyance slammed to the surface. Words of protest came to mind. Then I relented, concern for her winning out. "Y'all both showed me and told me about it right after they installed the system. I know how to make the thing work. For some reason it just didn't when that guy was out back, ready to shoot you."

She stayed quiet. So did I. The moment I'd seen a pistol pointed at my sister returned. I squeezed my eyes shut, blinking the image away.

"It's okay, Sis. I appreciate that you're having things checked."

"I know how to do it." I wanted to protest as much as I'd yearned to do when an elementary student down the hall filled with students yelled and said I was dumb.

"I'm sure you do. Just remember this. You were really snappy when Dave was showing you."

I recalled the situation. I'd felt as though I'd intruded into an intimate moment between them. Then he had suggested I write the alarm code, even though it was so short a seven-year-old would recall it. My eyes flitted toward him now. He turned his face from mine and stepped farther away as though not wanting to pry into my conversation any longer.

Eve released a yawn. "I've been so sleepy."

"How's the trip going? Has Melanie talked to you?"

"Not at all." She spoke quieter. "It got really tense in here, but that pain med put me to sleep. What woke me up was that automatic call telling me my house alarm went off, and then she and Jacques both asked what happened while I was frightened and speaking loud, so I did get to hear her voice."

How uncomfortable she must be with that tension from her ex who still cared about her and his wife. Sympathetic thoughts went out to Melanie, too, with her husband doing all he did for my sister.

"How's your head?" I asked. "And the rest of your body?"

"I'm okay. None of it really hurts right now. That medicine works great."

"Good. I need to go see what Dave wants to show me. Take care of yourself. Call me."

"I will," she said, and we clicked off.

Replacing the phone in my purse, I gave my attention to the man now facing me.

"Ready?" he asked, and I nodded. We moved to the alarm box near the front door, and I waited to learn what part of the setting process I'd missed the first time.

"I see that it's not set." I stared at the obvious green glowing message: *System disabled.*

"That's right. So now you'd just put in the code."

I pressed nine, one, six, two. "And because we're in the house, I would press *Home* and *Enter* so it won't start blaring whenever one of us moves." After I did that, I pressed more buttons to tell the system no one was here.

I glanced at Dave, watching me without speaking.

A minute later, I yanked the front door open and held it that way more than ninety seconds. "See? It doesn't work." Righteous anger rose inside me.

He kept his gaze level at my face. "You put in the wrong code."

"What? There are only four numbers. I know what they are, and I know how the rest of this thing works, too, but this one isn't working right."

His face showed no emotion.

He didn't follow me when I stepped outside and shut the front door. I called Eve. "What's your code?" I asked without a greeting.

"Six, one, nine, two. Is that what you put in?"

"Are you sure it isn't nine, one, six, two?"

"Sunny, you were really upset when we told you the numbers and wanted you to write them, remember?"

"Never mind." I clicked off. When I marched inside, Dave stood near the sofa. He said nothing while I proceeded to the alarm box and started the setting process over. I stabbed in numbers my sister told me. *Alarm Set* glowed in green, and I grabbed the front door handle and yanked the door open. Seconds later *WAA WAA WAA WAA* sounded.

I slammed the door, rushed to the alarm box, and shut it off. Eve might get an automatic call that her system had gone off, but she'd know what caused it. My humiliation grew as I faced the man in the room who phoned his office and said it was just him trying a system again. My face had grown warm.

"Do you want to check out the box near the backdoor and the one to the room where your sister paints?" he asked me.

I shook my head. "I made a mistake. I'm sure they all work fine." It was me who didn't.

"All right. But don't hesitate to call anytime if you have a problem with the system, or if you have any questions."

"I'm good." I thrust the door open wide so he had no question about why I did so. "Thank you for coming."

He paused in front of me as though wanting to say something. I turned my face away, and he stepped outside. I reentered Eve's house and slammed the door before hearing him drive off. I threw myself onto the sofa and sat with elbows on knees, gripping my head. *Dumb, dumb, dumb* kept swirling inside my mind, along with pressure building in my chest, and an anvil slamming through my scalp. I couldn't even remember a short alarm code, and I'd thought I could solve whatever happened at my twin's house and a murder or two?

Dragging myself off the sofa, I locked the front door and plodded back to my own place. Drained of spirit, I went to bed and put my dull brain to sleep.

Morning didn't break any better. I shuffled around, considering my fate. My sister was gone. So was our business. And I couldn't recall four numbers, so maybe my brain was gone, too.

I needed to check on Eve. She answered on the third ring. "How are you doing?" I asked.

"I'm good, Sunny. How're you?"

She meant because I'd messed up. "Fine. And Nicole?"

"It's strange to see my daughter with a stomach so large. The pictures she sent didn't do her justice. It's wonderful being with her again. I can't wait for that baby to arrive."

"I'm sure they were glad to see you."

"Yes, but after she and Randy saw the knot on my head and my scratches, you would swear I was an invalid. I want to help with Nicole, not the other way around."

"That's okay. Stay safe," I said and disconnected before she could mention yesterday's incident with Dave and the alarm.

Fear for my sister made my arms tremble, pulling me back to a day I never wanted to revisit, a moment that changed my life, that slung it to hell. The low hum in my chest wanted to blast into a full-blown holiday tune.

I was eight....

Chapter 17

I was outside with my big sister. She stretched on her side on the driveway. Her hand holding our mom's cell phone was open. So were her eyes.

"Crystal, get up." I pushed her arm with my toe.

She didn't move.

"Come on, quit playing around. You better get up, or I'm going inside." I started walking to the house.

That teenager didn't say anything.

I turned around. A red circle was spreading on the back of her favorite turquoise striped shirt.

"Crystal!" I screamed. "What happened?"

"Sunny, Sunny, pick up Crystal's phone!" Her best friend—I couldn't think of her name—was yelling at me from the phone by my sister's hand.

"I got it," I said but my arm was shaking so much I could hardly hold anything.

"Did something happen? Is Crystal hurt?"

My teeth hit against each other like popcorn popping like crazy. "Uh-huh."

"That sounded like a gun. Sunny, was that a gunshot?"

I was a kid. How did I know anything? I stared at the big tree in our yard. The moss on it moved slower than my arms. "I don't know. Maybe."

"Oh, Sunny." She made a small sound like a cat, or maybe a cry. "I'll call an ambulance. They'll come right over there and take care of Crystal, okay?"

I couldn't make any more words come out. Getting my legs to hold me up was hard enough.

"Is anybody around there?" the girl on the phone said. "Anybody who might've hurt her and could hurt you right now?"

Why would anybody hurt Crystal? Or me? I looked at our house and oak tree and Momma's azalea bush with pink flowers. No cars or trucks were on the highway. Nobody was on the next-door lot we rode bikes on. "I don't see anybody."

"What about a car? Did any cars pass by awhile ago?"

"Yeah…maybe."

"Did you see it?"

"Uh-uh. I was shooting hoops." I hiccupped. My eyes stung.

"You need to be strong. Stay right there, or you can go inside and hide if you want. I'm calling an ambulance. They'll be right there to see about her, okay?"

I nodded and put down the phone. Then I trembled and knelt by my sister. "Your friend's getting the ambulance. They'll make you better."

Stuff started twisting around in my stomach. I ran to the grass by the driveway and threw up the beignets Momma made for breakfast. My mouth tasted gross. I could go hide in our house or behind that bush—but I wouldn't leave my sister. I stooped beside her.

"Crystal," I whispered.

One blond curl covered her left eye. I pushed it back. Her blue eyes stayed open. But she wouldn't look at me. Her mouth was open a little bit.

"Did you say something?" I leaned my ear close to her lips. "Crystal. I need you. Please wake up."

She didn't move. I shook her arm. She rolled, and her face went down on our driveway. "I'm sorry." I turned her so her face was up again. I was shaking like crazy and looking at the road by the bayou. Where were Momma and Eve? They went shopping a couple of hours ago.

The wind moved her azalea bush. I stared at that bush, hating it. Moss in the big oak moved a little. I hated that, too. I wanted my sister moving, not them.

I needed my momma. What I needed more than that was my big sister to stay alive. Crystal couldn't die. She was *sixteen.* A teenager needs to take care of her little sister, not the other way around.

Nobody took care of me like Crystal. That's why I stayed with her while Momma and Eve went shopping. I kept staring at moss in that tree and breathing, trying to think of things except my sister on the driveway. I had stayed home 'cause they went to get my twin Eve something nice since she finished third grade with all A's. My report card was pretty good, but Momma always told people dyslexics can't expect to do as well, so people understood why Eve did better. They'd buy me something. I told Mom to pick it out. I wanted to shoot hoops in the driveway, and my new friend might come over. Nobody lived by our house around this bayou, but my friend might bug her momma enough to bring her here.

Crystal was shooting hoops with me like always, but then her phone rang and she walked around the driveway with it, laughing and saying, "Oh, sweet."

I got mad 'cause she stayed on her phone too long. She told me quit bugging her and she'd get off sooner.

And then that sound—*POW.* I threw the basketball and missed the goal and turned to tell Crystal that almost sounded like a gun. I'd heard some on TV, and hunters around here shot rifles and things.

I needed to quit thinking about that. My eyes felt on fire. My nose was running. I wiped the back of my hand under my nose and kept sniffling. I wanted to cry like crazy. Tears stung my eyes, trying to come out, and I shivered so much I really needed to pee, but I wasn't going to wet my pants. And I sure wasn't gonna leave my sister.

Crystal kept so still. My chest hurt like a bunch of hiccups stuck inside. But if I let them pour out of me, I'd cry. And if I started crying now, I would never ever stop.

No, I would never cry. I needed to be strong for my sister.

Probably I wouldn't cry if I was singing. The first song I thought about was "Happy Birthday." But I couldn't sing that to her now.

Humming started in my throat. "Jingle bells," I sang real soft. I kept singing more of the words and started to feel a little bit better. My eyes quit burning. I sang parts of the song louder and watched Crystal keeping still.

Other noises started. I hummed low so I could hear the sound better.

Sirens. That ambulance was coming. And Momma and Eve might get home soon, and I wouldn't be alone with my sister I loved more than anything else in the world. Crystal kept her eyes open. She wouldn't talk to me or look at me.

I sang my guts out.

Chapter 18

I was an adult now. Still, every nerve ending in my body trembled. Tremors that started in the skin of my legs inched to my torso till they found my neck. My fingers and head shook like cement pouring from a mixer. Lyrics of one Christmas carol after another rushed from my mouth.

Just as suddenly, I stopped. My body and thoughts calmed.

One sister died at my side. A drive-by shooting, her killer never found. I had one sister still alive. I would do everything I could to make certain she remained that way.

I'd purposely left out telling Detective Wilet some information that might be important to this whole case. In my mind, I wrapped together the killings of Zane and Daria Snelling and almost my twin. That couldn't happen. Needing to make certain the detective was in, I called and discovered he was. I made an appointment and an hour later sat across from him in his office that bore the smell of newly-brewed coffee. No cup sat on his desk.

"I'm glad your sister's okay and went to stay at her daughter's house in Houston," he said. "I have your sister's cell phone number. Would you also have that information for her daughter? A phone number and address?"

I provided what he wanted. "And you know that when I arrived at her house when the gunman was there, I set off her alarm to get his attention, but the system didn't work."

He nodded, and I gulped and forced out my guilt. "It wasn't really broken. I had just put in the wrong code."

The detective watched me a second. "But you do know it?"

"Yes, and how to make the system function. I hope she never needs it again."

He made notes, probably correcting what I'd originally said—that Dave's system had malfunctioned. While he jotted words, I mentally retraced my actions yesterday evening with Eve's alarm. When I left her house, I had forgotten to set it. I didn't need to tell him that but would correct it as soon as I left here.

"There's one other thing I should mention," I said.

He waited, face stern, maybe thinking I was ready to confess to Daria's murder. "I'm listening."

"I had left a message on Daria Snelling's answering machine."

Elbows on desk, he gripped his chin. "Yes."

"Did you know that?"

"Why don't you just tell me about that message?"

"Well, you know how I told you some of her husband's ashes landed in my pocket when she tripped—fell—when his funeral was starting? And then you took my jacket away. I don't suppose you're done with it yet?" I hoped but didn't suppose he'd readily give it back.

"Why did you say she tripped, but then corrected yourself and said she fell?" he asked, eyes harsh, totally ignoring my questions.

"There wasn't anything on that floor for her to trip on. I know construction. I checked." I was leaning forward.

So was he. "What do you mean, you checked? When?"

I spread my hands, not understanding why he didn't already know this. "When I brought you that fingernail file I'd found in the church?" I made my final statement a question to make certain he understood what I was talking about and then explained more of the possible connection. "That nail file with what may have been dried glue on the tip."

The diversion of his eyes, that quick shift so they held on the air to my left instead of on me broadcasted that something wasn't right. "You threw it away, didn't you? As soon as my sister and I left this place, you tossed it in the trash." My voice rose with accusation, along with my body I'd pushed forward, coming halfway out of my wobbly chair.

His broad chest shoved forward. The detective stabbed me in place with his eyes. "What we do with evidence and information in a case isn't something our department shares."

The most I could hope for was that they were having the file examined. At least considering the item.

"What message did you leave on the Snellings' answering machine?" he asked, and I repeated the words I'd used and suggested how I thought that might have caused Daria to break in at Eve's and write *WHERE IS WHAT'S HIS?*

"But then Eve and I found her dead. So I went to the church to look for clues for whether she really tripped, and I discovered that nail file she could have used to pry open his urn and rip open the plastic bag that held him."

The detective's shaking head made me quit talking. "Ms. Taylor, it's time for you to know that what's going on is extremely dangerous."

"Yes, deadly," I said.

"You saw that with the break-in and destruction at your sister's house and now that someone returned there and wanted to harm her. You need to back away. Let our office take care of all this." He pressed back in his seat. "Did you have any other information to share with me?"

I released a breath. He didn't want me to gather information. Now he does? "No, nothing."

He reached a hand forward. With fingers spread wide, he set it on his desk. "Maybe the best thing you can do right now is consider getting out of your house, too. Go out of town and stay in Texas with your sister."

"I'm good. Did y'all find the bullet in Eve's yard?"

His chin tightened. "Yes. So now all we have to do is locate the gun that fired it, or even better, the person who owns that pistol." His eyes went hard. "Leave it alone. Let us do our work."

I shouldered my purse and left his office. Once outside I fumed. He wanted me away from his case, but his case involved *my* sister. There was no way I would leave it until her would-be killer was found.

The only thing positive about what I just heard from the detective was the suggestion that he no longer considered me or Eve suspects in Daria's murder. Or maybe he still did, and this was just a postponement of checking into our guilt while he dealt with concern about the things that happened at Eve's house.

I drove there. Letting myself in the front door, I listened a moment and gained reassurance that yes, I had forgotten to set the alarm. The house felt eerily quiet. I rushed through it, checking her art room and then all the others, making certain no windows were broken or new damage done. I found no evidence of intruders.

Back in the foyer, I took my time to clear my body and mind of stress, and set Eve's alarm. This time I made certain I didn't press *Home*. With only a few seconds to let myself out before the wail sounded, I stepped out and locked the door.

I didn't plan to check so intently on Eve's place while she was gone, but found the need to do so now pushing me around to make sure no criminal element was ready to try to get in. I'd do so quickly since the sun was shining on this clear spring morning, and I didn't really believe any threatening person hid nearby.

This time starting around the left side of her house, I looked first for a person. No one was there. I stepped near Eve's window, searching for scratches or scrapes without seeing them. My shoulders squeezed tight right before I reached the backyard. Not allowing myself to step back or hum as my instinct urged, I walked forward. My eyes nailed the space beyond the fountain on the opposite side of the patio where a man had stood pointing a weapon at my twin.

No, I wouldn't allow the person who'd done that to pull a song out of my throat.

I rushed across the concrete, taking a glance toward the rear to make certain the small pathway between fences was empty and moved to the opposite side of her house. The enticing scent of boiled crayfish teased my nostrils. Next door, Mrs. Wilburn sat in her backyard peeling some.

"You're having crayfish early today," I said, walking toward her.

"I boiled a few." Right beyond her sat a burner with a butane bottle and a steaming short boiling pot. Her plastic tray held a pile of red peelings. With the nimble skill of a native of the area, she peeled another crustacean, dropped the peelings in her tray, and tossed the meat of the crayfish into a bowl that held a dozen others.

"You can peel crayfish like that, and not eat any?" I asked, admiring anyone with such willpower.

"I eat them boiled often enough. My son likes them best with onions and bell peppers in an omelet. I'll fix him a late breakfast after while."

"What a nice mother you are to peel these for him before you cook his meal." And why didn't the lazy guy do this himself, I wanted to add.

"He's not here often." She didn't slow down or glance at me while she finished another and moved on to the next one. It was a reddish-black crayfish that told me its shell was hard and the season might end early this year.

"Mrs. Wilburn, did you see anyone that didn't belong around Eve's house lately? Or anything suspicious?"

She tilted her head up to look at me. "I told the police everything I know. I didn't see anything."

I held her gaze, finding it strange to believe this was true. She always knew what was going on. She bent her head down and continued her peeling process.

"Did the police question Royce?"

"No."

I figured that. Discouraged, I stepped away from her.

"She's gone, isn't she?" the woman who didn't look up at me said.

"What makes you say that?"

"I just know it." She tucked her chin even more toward her neck. The woman was done with conversation.

Not sure I was glad she guessed or knew Eve left town, I made a quick check of the other windows of Eve's house. It was probably good that this neighbor knew, I decided. She might keep a closer watch on my sister's property and report anything out of line to police.

The uninhabited house for sale across the street was set back from the road. The wide parking area out front was where Eve had waited in her car while I impersonated her. I gritted my teeth, a low groan in my throat, unable to believe I had done that childish enactment. One day I should apologize to Dave for being such an impostor.

Large lawns with perfectly-kept flowerbeds fronted other homes down my sister's street. Nobody was out on those lawns. I had the feeling that with such a distance between their places and hers, people in them hadn't seen what occurred in the back of her house. Surely police questioned the residents, also asking for a call in case they saw someone who didn't seem to belong. Most of them had surely seen me. Even if they hadn't known my identity, they'd probably thought I was my twin. I skittered to the skinny grass trail behind her place to my street.

"Hello, Sunny," Miss Hawthorne called, head down as she plucked a weed from her flowerbed. Her straw hat's wide brim hid her face.

I hurried my step closer. "Good morning. How did you know it was me? I didn't see you look up."

She used the hand holding her trowel to shove back the brim of her hat. Dirt flecked from it to her nose. "Oh, silly me," she said, brushing her nose off. She aimed her small garden tool toward my feet. "I could see those shoes."

My bronze flats glittered in the sunlight. "So you only saw the shoes coming and knew it was me?"

"I've told you I admire them."

"And I should get a new pair, but these are so comfortable."

"I understand. We women do like our shoes."

She'd worn the same pair of wedge heels each time she had shopped with me at Fancy Ladies, only in different colors. I'd told her I liked them the first time I saw her in a pair, and she must have wanted to keep me happy for each of her visits after that.

"Miss Hawthorne, have the police come to talk to you about an incident at my sister's house?"

Again digging out weeds, she was nodding before I finished asking my question. "I'm sorry that happened. And I'll sure keep an eye out for anything that doesn't seem right."

"Thanks. I really appreciate your help." I took a few steps toward my house.

"I saw the man's shoes."

With a quick spin, I was back to her, satisfaction pushing hope higher up my chest. "When? What did they look like? Did you see his face?" I wanted to pump questions into her until she gave all the answers we needed to get my sister home and safe from harm.

My neighbor pulled off her hat. She wiped sweaty brown hair with one-inch gray roots from her forehead. "I just realized it," she said and stood. "That I saw the man's shoes."

"Tell me what you saw."

"It was yesterday morning. I was working out here." Her vision seemed to go inward while her words stopped.

I squeezed her hand. "And what did you see?"

"I thought I might've heard a little *pop*. But you know how that is? It happens all the time, it seems. You think it's gunfire, but it's a car or somebody's lawnmower."

Yes, I knew the sound of a gun's pop.

When I kept nodding, she continued. "I looked up anyway, just in case." Anticipation made my heartbeat race. "But I didn't see anything different. So I pulled out more weeds and then heard somebody running on the street. The unusual thing was the sound of the soles hitting the road. You know sometimes people run on the street nowadays, but they always wear those tennis shoes with rubber soles. These sounded like hard soles."

I tightened my grip around her fingers when my stomach fluttered. She was about to solve the mystery.

She pulled her hand away. "I didn't get to see anything about the man that I recall. He'd already run past me. I only saw the bottom of his pants and his shoes. The shoes were black. And black pants, I think." Her gaze met mine as she appeared to come out of a trance. "Anyway, his pants were a dark color."

"Think about it more. Maybe he was wearing a hat. Dark glasses."

She shook her head. "I really didn't look that far up."

"Which way was he going?"

She pointed in the opposite direction from my house.

"Can you think of anything else?"

She shook her head. "No."

"Would you tell the police what you just told me about this man running on our street yesterday with dress shoes right after you heard a gunshot? He might have come between those fences from Eve's backyard."

She brushed off her knees. "I'll go call them right now." Carrying her trowel, she made her way to her door.

"Thank you so much. And speak to Detective Wilet."

She waved without looking back at me while she walked inside.

The fellow who'd shot at Eve wore a camouflage hat to hide his face. Maybe while he ran to escape, he'd pulled it off so he wouldn't call attention to himself. Officers might ask some people along our street about this. They might also search yards to discover whether he could have thrown the hat away. Or maybe I was clutching for any hope.

Rushing into my house, I called Eve. Her voice, an echo of mine but with the smoothness of newly melted butter, tugged a smile to my face. "Hey, Sis," I said, savoring the connection with her while she was secure. "We might have someone who can identify the man who shot at you."

"Great! Tell me about it."

I relayed the details Miss Hawthorne gave me.

"That's encouraging," Eve said, her voice not as enthusiastic as before.

"Yes, so how are you? And your beautiful daughter?"

"Nicole's terrific of course." Her tone lifted. "About the same as yesterday."

"And you?" I felt she was putting off answering this question.

"The hickey's gone down. It's just that there's a little discoloration forming on my face."

Was she telling me all? "Send me a picture." When she didn't respond, I repeated the request. "I want to see what you look like. The lowered bump on your head. That little bit of discoloration."

She hesitated before answering. "All right."

We'd talk again soon, we agreed, and hung up. I gripped my phone, watching it, waiting for a text that would show a picture of her face to come through. Long minutes passed. Still nothing changed on the surface of my phone. I texted her.

Come on, send that picture.

In short order, she shot back a message.

I'm waiting for somebody to get home to take a good picture of me.

I didn't wait to send a response.

You're stalling and making me worried. Come on, send a selfie.

The time it would take her to open her camera, snap a photo, and forward it to me counted down like a slow second hand on a clock through my mind. Finally the *bleep bleep bleep* of an incoming text came.

My breath caught in my throat. My gut jerked like someone punched it when I saw her. The woman starting at me didn't look like my twin except for her red hair and blue eyes, but one of those eyes was partly shut. The deep purple-black of the sky with an imminent storm surrounded that eye, the lower edge of discoloration lodging below the apple of her cheek.

I dragged my focus higher up, toward her hairline, where the bruising clustered around what resembled the budding growth of a buck's horn. Except it was on my sister's head.

I pressed her number on my phone, words of concern about her wellbeing swirling through my mind.

She wasn't answering. I left a message: "You look awful. See a doctor out there. Take care of yourself."

After time enough to listen to what I said, she sent a long text instead of speaking to me. She wanted me to be the better-looking twin for a while. She'd seen a doctor at the hospital here before she left for Houston and didn't need another one so soon. She would take care of herself. I should do the same.

I was out of crackers, so I wolfed down a ham and bread-and-butter pickle sandwich on bread while deciding what to do next. First, I'd follow up with my neighbor to learn whether the detective told her anything of value or if he got her to recall something else.

Walking out front, I stepped along the edge of the street to her house. She was again digging out front.

She held her brim back. "Hello, Sunny. I made that call for you."

"That's terrific. What did Detective Wilet say?"

She wiped her damp forehead, smearing dirt from her fingers across it. "Oh, I didn't talk to him. I just gave the information about the man running out here on the street to the officer who answered."

Disappointment certainly showed in my eyes. Instead of complaining, I said, "Thank you for calling their department." Should I contact the detective myself to make sure he learned exactly what she saw? I headed home.

"Sunny." The aged voice came from Miss Hawthorne. For the first time ever, I saw her out of her yard. She was striding to me, face pink while she fought with the breeze to keep her straw hat on. "There's one other thing I remember about that man running on the street," she said, and I felt my hopes lift. "His pants had cuffs."

Cuffs deflected my expectations. But if I pushed her for more, she might recall other things about this person who could have shot at my sister. I asked the question with the best possible answer first. "Did you see his face?"

"Oh no. My head was down, and this hat was in the way." She shoved it farther back, accentuating her statement.

"Think, Miss Hawthorne. Did you see his hand? If it held a gun?" I asked, and she shook her head. "Maybe you saw the bottom of his shirt. The color of it." My statements made her keep up her head shake. "Well, what about his pants? Were they slim fit, or maybe you noticed the fabric. Were his shoes tied or slip-on?"

She'd stopped shaking her head, so maybe I'd hit on a remembrance.

"I don't recall any of those things. Just that his pants had cuffs. I noticed because they had this little green thing hanging from one cuff, and my Graham always used to insist on cuffs on his pants, whether they were dress trousers or everyday ones he wore around the house." Her shoulders lowered, and the excitement in her eyes dulled. "But I believe cuffs on men's pants may have gone out of style."

"Thank you so much for that information. Would you like to come inside? Cool off. Have a glass of iced tea or cold water?"

"No, thank you, hon. If I had time, I might ask for a sip of wine, but I need to get back to my work."

Wine? And leaving her yard? I realized sometimes you thought you knew a person, but they hit you a homerun instead of a bunt.

She sauntered toward her house, and I stepped inside mine, considering what I might do with what she told me. The ring of my doorbell startled me until I figured my neighbor had come back with a more important recollection. Anticipation bubbling in my chest, I didn't check the peephole and yanked my front door open.

"You look happy today," Dave Price said.

My eyes automatically checked out his slacks. Not black, but navy. No cuffs. Tied black dress shoes.

"I thought only your sister did that."

"What?"

He gave his head a little tilt. "Checked me out."

The impact of what he said struck me. "Oh, no, I didn't … " Knowing this man had just seen me inspecting his lower half sent a blush burning from my cheeks down my neck. Was he a bad guy? No way, not with the draw his body had on mine. This was all ridiculous—the suspicion, the attraction. "Come in." I stepped back.

"I went to your sister's house to check on how her alarm was working, but she didn't answer. Eve's all right, isn't she?"

"Yes. And her system is working just fine." The fewer people who knew she'd left town, the better.

His gaze swept my den, making old embarrassments try to surface because my home wasn't nearly as impressive as my twin's. But I was who I was, and that was good enough I reminded myself. I didn't offer him a seat. I liked standing beside him. Eve loved standing closer to him. I wasn't going to keep him here in case he'd ask more about where she was. "Thanks for coming by. I'll tell my sister you checked on her and her alarm."

He turned to go then nodded toward the bare wall near my front door. "Maybe you'll consider our company if you ever decide to have your own alarm system installed."

"I will."

He went out, and I locked the door. Leaning back against it, I considered how he made me feel, especially since my eyes had roamed over him and then he stood beside me. Attracted, yes. But he was Eve's, possibly the man she'd been looking for all her life. Fighting an inner struggle, I shoved myself off my door, knowing I needed to go somewhere and do something that would keep her alive.

This new information from Miss Hawthorne might not be much, but at the moment it was all I had. Even though I'd kept up with some women's styles, especially in undergarments and lingerie during the time I'd worked at Fancy Ladies, I hadn't paid attention to cuffs or lack of them in menswear, which the store never carried. My aged neighbor thought cuffs in men's slacks were out. If she was right, it might not be too difficult to discover who'd bought them. I hopped in my truck and drove downtown to Sydney's Menswear.

A sign on the door announced they were closed for a funeral. I checked styles in the display windows. None of the pants were black, although some were dark navy. A fourth of the slacks bore cuffs, but this place wasn't known for being most up to date. I headed for the mall where Daria had supposedly returned from to find her husband drowned. And if townspeople's ideas were correct, he supposedly fell in that pond after tripping on the seating area we created for him.

All About Men was the store holding the most menswear that didn't cater to garments for teens. The moment I walked in, the strong tang of dye and a saleswoman met me. The thirtyish woman wore a striped suit and her long brown hair down over her shoulders. "Can I help you find something?"

My eyes located pairs of black pants, although most tended toward navy and gray. Instead of checking all the hundreds of items, I asked, "Do you carry pants with cuffs?"

"Sure. What kind of pants were you looking for? Dress slacks? Work pants? Slender cut or wide leg?" She led me to a circular stand holding many pairs squeezed together and a sign saying Up To 75% Off.

"I'm not sure yet," I said and touched a few items.

"What size did you need?"

I noticed I was thumbing through size forty-eights. Surely a man running on the street wasn't that large. I moved to the opposite side of the rack. "These." Looking down each pair, I noticed one thing. They were made of a coarse material or else some fabric more like double knit. No wonder they were all about a fourth of their regular prices.

"Listen," I said when my salesclerk started thumbing through cuffed garments in the size I stood near, "I want to know if cuffs are in style. Do a lot of men wear cuffed pants anymore?"

"Of course," she said, making my shoulders droop, not giving the answer I'd hoped for.

"Okay, who? Any men in particular?" I urged.

"You've got to be kidding." She glanced at the entrance, probably hoping someone would come in and draw her away from my questions and buy something.

I gripped her arm, regaining her attention. "I'm deadly serious. It's really important that I find out."

She slipped her arm away. "Cuffed pants are always in style. The majority of them look great." She shifted her shoulders forward. "Actually, I find that lots of men who wear them are tall."

"Why's that?"

"Because anything that's not a straight line cuts down a person's height."

I knew that, although it had never been my problem. My mind swirled to men I knew who were extra tall. Not many came to mind, except for the one I'd stood next to less than an hour before. I was taller than most when I wore heels.

"You seem to have many pairs with cuffs." I skimmed their items.

"Yes. It just depends on what a person likes."

Ready to give up on the whole idea, I recalled noticing at least two people who wore black pants. With cuffs? I hadn't looked that far down.

But now I was plucking at straws. "What about priests? They wear black pants. Do they buy them with cuffs?"

"I've been working at this store four years, and I've never seen a priest come in. They probably order their pants from those places where they get those other garments they wear for masses."

"Thanks for your help," I said. "I won't be needing anything today."

Her forehead creased, and I wished I had a man I could purchase slacks for—although I didn't really want a man again, and with our business seeming to crash before it ever got on firm footing, I'd barely have enough money to buy pants for myself.

What a silly idea this had been, I told myself driving away. The only lead I had that might be worthwhile was that someone running on the street wore cuffed pants. His pants—dress or casual, I didn't know—were probably black. So were his dress shoes. That knowledge had made me even pull toward priests breaking into my twin's house and smashing her paintings and writing on her wall and returning and shooting at her?

Sheez, I was getting carried away with attempting to become a detective. Surely I wasn't created to do their work or even that of an officer who wrote parking tickets. But I couldn't let myself wallow in self-defeating thoughts. Where was someplace else I might check into, and what did the person who broke into Eve's house want? I still didn't know what *WHERE IS WHAT'S HIS?* on her wall meant.

Mental images came of items I'd like to learn more about. Zane's ashes in my jacket, but they now resided at police headquarters. A metal fingernail file with what resembled dried glue on its tip that I'd given to Detective Wilet, but who knew whether he checked on that? Then there was the burial urn Daria dumped. What was it made of? What type sealant did funeral homes use for them? I could learn much of this information on the web.

I turned into the parking lot of a burger joint and used my cell phone to pull up photos of urns, instantly recognizing the one Daria had carried and spilled. As I'd thought, it was made of pewter, one of the least expensive. Maybe she couldn't afford the finer ones, but I believed her husband seemed worthless in her eyes. Some funeral urns could be unscrewed, I read, but I didn't think that was the case for the one used for Zane. Sealants came in all varieties, although some were fastened with ordinary glues.

I headed for the funeral parlor to discover their typical adhesive and hoped that might help lead toward information I could give to police. With the saucy info Sue Ellen Granger had told me about him outside the hospital, I certainly knew where I would not look when he stood.

So the moment Toby Hensley got to his feet, where did my eyes aim?

I checked his shoes and above them first, skimming for cuffs, which he did have, but they were on the slacks of his charcoal gray suit. And then my gaze slid upward, although I didn't want it to, but those words about his lack of undergarments made me do it without thinking. The flush I felt from my neck to my ears made me jerk my eyes to meet his.

Toby's face filled with annoyance, probably because I tapped only once on the open door of his office and walked inside. I'd stepped past a few people milling in the carpeted foyer.

"What type of glue do y'all use on urns?" I asked without a greeting.

"Why?" The skin between his eyes folded into a deep crease. He glanced beyond me toward other individuals.

"It's important for something I'm working on. And was a sealant used on the urn that held Zane Snelling?"

His head pulled back, his eyes narrowing. Was I insulting the funeral home's integrity since Zane fell out of the receptacle they'd sold to his wife?

"People out there," he said with a lift of his hand toward them, "are waiting for me to open the viewing room for a wake. They have lost someone they love. They're in mourning. Is a sealant more important than that?"

Behind me past his open doorway, two women were consoling each other. I had lost someone dear to me. "No, it isn't."

"Then I'll walk you out." He stepped toward me.

"I recently learned something interesting from your grandmother," I said, again skimming his shoes and slacks.

"*Step*-grandmother." His word sounded harsh. "What was it? That I never wear boxers or briefs?"

Actually, she'd told me about someone's shoes and cuffs, and a woman outside the hospital had gossiped to me about this man's lack of underwear. But those words coming from his mouth and the fury in his raised voice stunned me.

"She tells people that and other ridiculous things she creates that get stuck in her mind. That made-up story gets her a lot of attention and shocked faces. All the woman does is dig in her flowers, wearing a hat so large it doesn't let her see any of the world around her."

Soft voices with a woman's crying assured me I needed to go. I wouldn't disrespect these mourners' loss with my questions. I nodded to the people with sad eyes on my way out.

If Miss Hawthorne made up the tale of this man always going commando, even under his suits, had she also created a story about a running man wearing black shoes and black cuffed pants? Or had she developed this picture in her mind to entertain herself while she piddled in her yard? Maybe she heard some noise outside and decided it could have been the sound of a man dashing down the street with dress shoes? Her mind could embellish the story even more. Was there any way I could find out?

My cell rang, the regular picture from that number looking like me. "Hi, Sis," I said. "How are you? Is the face improving?"

"I don't know, but I'm coming home."

Muscles tightened in my neck. "You can't do that. Not yet."

"Yes, I'm coming back. They treat me like I can't take care of myself. I can't stand it."

"No, Eve." I gripped the phone tighter to my face. "There's still a man on the loose out here who wants you dead."

Her long exhale sounded. "I guess that is worse than being treated like a baby who can't fend for herself." Her voice had softened.

"It definitely is worse. Your face looks terrible."

"Thanks. Nicole just started her pregnancy leave, so she's around me all the time. She worries about every little new touch of purple or yellow that comes out. But I'm healing. I really am."

"So you have some yellow near your eye, too, huh? Send me a picture."

"No. You'd just do the same thing." She coughed, the kind of cough that sounded forced. "Now changing the subject, how're things there? Have you seen Dave?"

"He came to check on you and find out if your alarm was still working. I told him it was. And I thought I was finding out some important information, but it seems it's not. Do you know much about Miss Hawthorne?"

"You sold her a girdle quite some time back that she still wears and a horrid green bra that wouldn't match anything except algae. And her grandson works at the funeral home, doesn't he?"

"Do you know anything else about either of them?"

"Uh-uh. Did Dave ask where I was?"

"He didn't, and I didn't offer that information." What else could I tell her? I made myself cough. Like my sister, I knew how to flip a conversation. "Did you know that your busybody neighbor's son likes crayfish omelets for breakfast?"

"I don't blame him. I've had that for other meals during the day but never in the morning."

"She boiled some and was peeling them for him."

"Mm, I might come home before crayfish season ends and maybe she'll fix some for me."

Nothing should entice her back here until the man who was after her was caught. "The season's not ready to end. Stay there and stay safe."

She quieted a moment. "Is our business getting any calls?"

"Ha ha."

"Sweet dreams. See you soon." She clicked off.

I hoped her last statement to me wouldn't come true. The police needed to hurry and catch the man trying to kill her. I got ready for bed, hoping things would look better in the morning. A nagging fear told me they wouldn't.

Chapter 19

In the morning, I phoned the detective covering Eve's case and asked to come in. He didn't have time, but wanted to know what I needed.

"Did you get the message that my neighbor Miss Hawthorne called in yesterday about hearing a man running down the street soon after she'd heard a noise that sounded like a gunshot?"

"I did. So do you have anything new? I need to leave."

"She might not have told your office this, but the man who was running wore black dress shoes and black pants with cuffs." When a snort left his nostrils, I rushed on. "Come on, Detective, give me something. My sister wants to come back home."

"Don't let her."

"I'm trying not to. Please help me."

"I can tell you this much about what we've learned. Zane Snelling had been taking line dance lessons in town."

"I know. That's where Eve met him."

"Well, Lillian took those lessons, too. Maybe he went to her house for help to learn some of the steps better." When I released a chuckle, he quieted. He didn't believe what he suggested any more than I did.

"You have to leave this case to us," he said. "These are dangerous people. We'll get the perpetrators."

But will it be in time? Will you solve everything before Eve insists on returning to her house?

I called Eve and relayed the new bit of info.

"I don't know which one Lillian is, but I do know a few people from that class." How nice to hear a small amount of enthusiasm in her tone.

"Give me names, and I can call them," I said.

"Oh, no, I'll make some contacts, see what I can find out."

"Great." The slight tug of the lifted corners of my lips felt alien but welcome. My twin and I might be making a little headway in finding perpetrators ourselves. At least she could make calls from Houston, which would keep her away from our city.

It was no use contacting people about possible jobs for us. By now everyone in town knew Daria had been murdered. They still weren't assured that inferior workmanship by our company didn't cause Zane's death, and I couldn't look at bills that were creating a pile that frightened the shadowy corner of my kitchen counter.

Instead, I returned to Eve's house. Pulling into her driveway, I peered back at a truck I heard slowing while it passed. The driver was Dave. I doubted he could see me when he glanced toward my truck and then slid his gaze over the house, possibly like me checking to make certain things looked okay. An unusual tug built inside. I shoved my hand up to the truck's horn, wanting him to stop so I could bring him inside. Be alone with him.

I yanked my hand down. What was wrong with me?

Waiting long minutes until he passed, I slid out and went inside. Dave's presence on the street made me think to check on the newly installed alarm. I pressed the correct numbers on the control pad and entered *Home*. I wished I'd paid attention when I first heard the code instead of acting so self-assured. I might have stopped a man from firing a gun at my sister. When I imagined that scene again, a thought of a song came, but I shoved the urge off and walked through rooms. Everything looked the same as before, including her studio holding that single large bright painting. I set the alarm for nobody inside and went out and locked the door.

A crayfish omelet for breakfast was really what drew me to return here. I checked Mrs. Wilburn's backyard, didn't see anyone, and strode to her backdoor.

Before I could knock, she yanked the wooden door open, the screen door between her and me surely still locked. "Can I help you?" She had watched me outside Eve's house and, I felt certain, could tell my twin and me apart since she'd snooped on Eve's activities so often.

"Mrs. Wilburn, your son told police he'd seen a man with a hat snooping around my sister's place. Had you seen him, too? Do you know if it was someone from the gas or electric company reading a meter?"

Her face pinched up, tight lips pushed forward. "I didn't look. I don't have time to sit around and stare out of my windows all day."

I forced back a snort. "I guess you have to cook a lot. And peel crayfish and things for your son."

Her head jerked back as though I'd slapped her. "Royce normally peels his own."

"You're talking about me?" Dark-eyed Royce swooped beside her, annoyance written in his tone to his mother and his frown at her.

"She said you usually peel your own crayfish," I told him. "That's good."

"Why? Did somebody think I was stupid and needed to have my momma still peel them for me?"

"No." I fought the temptation to reach out and try to yank the screen door open. I'd be most satisfied if one of them would invite me in so I could learn more. That wasn't going to happen. This young man or his mother might have been the person carrying the strong smell of boiled crayfish at Zane's funeral.

I needed to get answers while I could. "Did either of you know Zane or Daria Snelling?"

She shook her head.

"I didn't," he said.

She turned on him. "Isn't that the woman you cut grass for that time?"

His cheeks tightened. "I don't remember."

"We have things to do," his mother told me. "I hope your sister's doing well."

"She is. I'll tell her you're concerned." I got most of those words out before she shut the wooden door in my face. The lock clicked.

She knew Eve was out of town although we hadn't broadcast that news. I trotted to my twin's backyard, sat on the ledge of the fountain that she'd left on to appear as though she remained inside, and sent her a text asking what kind of work Royce did.

Three dings came from my phone with her message.

Cut grass a couple of times. Tried being a professional gambler in Vegas awhile. Probably piled up tons of debt. Why?

Just an idea. Maybe nothing. Later.

I cast my gaze toward their house. With no windows in my view, they couldn't see me. What if Royce needed to repay a lot of money and decided to break into Eve's house? It would have been easy for him to smash her sliding backdoor that day after he'd seen her leaving to workout at the gym. My heart rate increased as I considered that possibility, which would bring us closer to getting life normal for her. After police arrested whoever was causing the threat, she'd be okay.

Royce might have also been at Zane's funeral. But so what if he was? The only problem was if he lied to me about knowing either of the Snellings. Then suppose Royce wanted to steal from Eve's house. He could have smashed the paintings for meanness. But why write that question on her wall?

My main concern was why he would have come back here with a knit hat pulled low and tried to shoot her?

Unless two people were involved.

I pushed up from the fountain's ledge, satisfied that the odor of bleach from the water and sound of it pouring out of the angel's pail onto plastic goldfish planted me into reality. Surely only one person had wanted to harm my twin. I hoped I or the police would discover that person soon.

Reaching my truck out front, I found a patrol car passing. The driver stared at me, and I waved with a smile, content to find officers checking on Eve's house. I drove to mine, needing to figure out what I might do next. One thing that came to mind was taking the picture of Daria to salesclerks at the supermarket. I could ask if they remembered seeing her and the man with her the day after Zane's funeral. That man might hold the real clue to the people who died and the threat to my sister. But neither of the Snellings' obituaries had provided a picture. Their deaths were mentioned. Zane's had told of the funeral arrangements but nothing else.

At home, I unlocked my backdoor and walked in.

My body went stiff when I found someone inside.

Chapter 20

"Go back!" I insisted to my intruder.

"I love seeing you, too." Seated at the table, Eve lifted her Sprite in salutation. "Now give me a hug." She stood, and I struggled with the desire to both hold her and chase her away.

I gave in to my first instinct and wrapped my arms around my sister. How wonderful she felt, how comforting to have her near. Until I recalled why I didn't want her around. I loosened my grip to inspect her face. "The knot on your head is almost gone, and your color's nearly normal. Just a little yellow and purple around the eye."

"To match our business's shirts," she said with a wide smile.

"I think we can shove them in the back of our closets."

"Still nobody's trusting us, huh?"

I shook my head. "But at least you're okay. Now go away." Instead of leaving, she sat. I joined her. "How'd you get here? You've been texting me. And your car's still in your garage."

"Jacques drove me here."

"Eve, he and his new wife brought you to Houston when they were going home. But your ex-husband certainly didn't drive five or more hours just to bring you back here. And I sure hope Melanie was with him."

She shook her head. "Melanie left for a trip with some girlfriends right after we got there, and he hasn't heard from her since."

"How did you know that?

"Darn it, he's been calling me every day, saying he wanted to check and see if I was all right."

I reached out and grabbed her hand. "You need to discourage him."

"I do. That's one of the reasons I wanted to get away from there. I said I was coming to your place and knew Jacques wouldn't keep calling when I'm here. He knows you'd tell him off if he did." She stood and tossed her empty drink can in the trash.

"But you can't stay around here. Whoever was after you is still out there. If he sees you..." A hum buzzed in my throat.

"I hadn't heard 'Silver Bells' in a while."

Up on my feet, I faced her. "I love you, and you can't go to your house. That's where you've been threatened twice. You have to leave town. This time I'll bring you."

"I love you, too. And I love my daughter and her husband who're driving me crazy." She shifted away. "They check me out every minute. Both of them know if the purple under my eye blends into the yellow. They're using mental markers on my cheek to determine how far the bruising extends in a day. I can't stand it, Sunny. I want to wait on my very pregnant child, but she keeps shoving me to the sofa, insisting I lie down, take it easy." Shoulders lowered, Eve quit talking.

I gave her a minute. "So what did you plan to do to keep a killer away if you stay here?"

"No one will know. We won't be seen together. We won't even go out of the house at the same time." She tilted her head toward my hall. "My clothes are in the mauve bedroom."

Her idea just might work. But only if police caught the man who was after her really soon and we weren't both out at the same time. Let whoever wanted to get her attack her house again while it's unoccupied.

"I want to borrow your truck and go see Mom," she said.

"Uh-uh. She'll know who you are, and then all her friends will know, and word will get out that you're back and that guy will come after you again."

"That won't happen. I'll take care of it." She scooted past me, and I followed to the mauve bedroom, where she retrieved her purse from a shelf in the closet. Hanging inside that space were other items we'd packed for her to take to Texas.

"I can't believe Jacques just drove you back here." I shook my head, amazed that we could be so alike, yet so different. "Girl, you've got the first man you divorced still wanting you even after he finally remarried. And your second one. Stan, who slept at your house while he was in town."

"But I told you we didn't sleep together. And did I tell you he's engaged?" She slipped off the heels she wore and retrieved shoes with heels that weren't as high.

"I'm glad he'll get married again. I like Stan."

She sat on the edge of the bed to slide her feet into the shoes. "And I love knowing who he's engaged to—Dave Price's sister! Now Dave and I will have an even closer connection."

"Oh."

She stood and rubbed a finger over my lips. "Get that frown off. Be happy for me. After all the threats I'd been getting, something good might be coming my way."

Forcing my lips into an upward curve, I leaned my forehead against hers. "I'm happy about anything positive that comes to you."

"Good." She slipped on wide-rimmed dark glasses and pulled a section of hair down to cover the bump on her forehead. "Now give me your keys. I won't be long."

I gave her orders about staying secure and trying to look like me as much as possible. I also warned her to check my rearview mirrors to make certain no one was following her. While I tried to think of more caution she might take, she slipped out the door and took off with my truck.

I was concerned about her, but sitting with fear wouldn't help anything. I needed a new plan. And I couldn't step out of my house while she was in town.

She'd given me new information to consider. Her first husband brought her back to south Louisiana. Jacques probably didn't drop her off here and turn right around and start driving back to Texas. Would he try to contact her when she wasn't near me? And where was Melanie, his new wife?

What about Dave's sister and Stan? Was that connection a good one?

I called Dave's office.

"I'll see if he's in," the secretary said.

While waiting, I experienced conflicting emotions. The man tempted me. This situation between his sister and Stan concerned me. I wasn't sure why but needed to know more about it.

"Hello, this is Dave." His deep tone drew me to him.

"Hi. This is Sunny Taylor. Could you meet with me?"

"Yes. Is there a problem? Did your sister's alarm quit working?"

"It's something I'd like to talk to you about in person." We couldn't meet here in case Eve came here, too. "Maybe the Midtown Coffee Shop? Tomorrow morning at ten?"

"I'll be there."

"Good." I hung up. No, my sister was not going to learn about this meeting. It might only entice her to be with him, or she'd try to stop me from what I had planned. I couldn't believe how much I looked forward to meeting with this man.

Chapter 21

Eve had been gone much too long. I called her. Apprehension slammed to the surface when she didn't answer by the third ring. She picked up on the fourth.

"You're still with Mom?" I asked.

"I left there twenty minutes ago. I'm shopping at The Craft Store. Do you need anything?"

"Not from there. What are you getting?"

"Sketch pads, drawing pens, other art supplies. Just looking around. I don't have anything I'd need to paint with at your house, and I miss my hobby. With these, I'll have some kind of release."

The type of release she preferred wasn't going to happen. No men would come around her until all threats were dissolved. "Don't talk to anyone. And don't be long."

"Yes, Mother." She clicked off.

When she finally arrived at my house, I'd prepared a quick meal of her favorite, shrimp creole.

"Yum." She entered the house sniffing toward the stove, hands holding different-sized bags. "I might move in forever so you can feed me."

"But with no guys." I nodded toward her purchases. "It looks like you bought enough to sketch for months."

"Since I've never done any art work without paints and canvases, I had no idea what I might like best." She showed me inside one bag, which held pads and colored and charcoal pencils.

"Good. What happened with Mom? I'm sure she knew it was you."

Eve plucked the cover off one pot. Inhaling, she closed her eyes and wore a smile of appreciation. "I was hoping I'd catch her in her room for a change, but she was sitting in the foyer with her ladies."

As my eyebrows lifted and my mouth opened into an O with concern, she raised a hand.

"Don't worry. She smiled when she saw me coming, but before she could say my name, I gripped her face with both hands and leaned in for a kiss on the cheek and whispered in her ear that she shouldn't mention who I was. She didn't."

"So none of the ladies knew it was you?" I asked, relieved.

"Miss Grace asked which one of the twins I was, so I said, 'You know I look prettier than Eve.'"

I grinned. "Then she never figured that you are Eve."

"Nope. I got to hold Mom's hand and let her know I was doing well. Of course she'd heard gossip about things that happened, so my visit reassured her."

"I know that pleased Mom."

"She'd like to see you soon, too."

"I'll get there."

Eve fixed a salad while I cooked rice I'd bought. We both sipped Chablis. Supper gave us a chance to visit with another glass of wine along with a nice meal and great conversation, which mainly consisted of her telling me how wonderful Nicole looked with her big belly and sharing lots of pictures of the same. She showed me Nicole and Randy, the soon to be Mom and Dad, and the baby's room done up in yellow and white stripes, not frilly yet not masculine either. They didn't want to know whether they'd have a boy or a girl but were sure to welcome one or the other fairly soon.

"I can't wait," Eve said.

I lifted a glass and clicked it with hers. "To the soon-to-be grandma."

"Isn't that hard to imagine?" she asked, and I had to agree.

After cleaning dishes together and putting them away, we watched a relaxing comedy on TV and then chose to get to bed early, neither of us mentioning what remained foremost on my mind and surely on hers.

I hugged her and held on an extra moment. "Let me know if you need anything, Sis."

She nodded. Her concerned eyes and half smile assured me what she needed was peace from all threats.

Concern kept me turning in bed. Morning came without me feeling refreshed. The cheer in her voice didn't dispel my notice of her new lines of weariness. Her lip corners and outer edges of her eyes turned down until she noticed me entering the kitchen. She seemed to force both up.

"Good morning. I was looking for a place to set up my drawing material." She held up a bulging bag.

"How about the dining room table? That's a large space I never use."

"Great. Thanks." She took her things there. I fixed grits in one pot and in a skillet, smothered onions, bell peppers, and mushrooms and poured seasoned scrambled eggs over them. As I added cheddar cheese while this cooked, she dumped the bag on the table, sorting materials she'd use. She sat in front of it all and did nothing.

After the toast popped up, I walked in to tell her breakfast was ready. Eve was still staring at a large blank sheet of a sketchpad. She joined me in the kitchen to eat. Unlike the previous night, we spoke little except her telling me she enjoyed this meal.

"Did you call some people from your line dance class," I asked while we cleared the table, "to see if you could learn anything about Zane and Lillian having a thing together?"

Her head shake and deep intake of breath let me know that working on solving crimes also remained utmost in her thoughts. "I realized I don't know that many people from our class, but I jotted the names of a few."

"Grab your list and get busy." I handed her a phone book and pointed down the hall toward the bedroom where she'd have the list and more privacy. Hoping the people she knew had landlines and were home, I figured she'd feel more useful trying to discover a way to protect herself than looking at a blank sheet of paper without inspiration to put anything on it.

A little before nine-thirty, I peeked through the open doorway into her room. She sat on a brocade chair she'd pulled next to the bed. Her phone and notepad sat on the bedspread. "Any luck?"

She shook her head. "Some of them aren't home. A couple of women I talked to knew Zane, but only that he wasn't very good at learning even the easiest dances like The Freeze. One woman said she met a person in class named Lillian, but doesn't know anything about her except she can do the Macarena real well. I'm going to call a couple of others and the instructor, but she works during the day, so I'll try her later."

"Great. We might get somewhere with at least one person from the class."

Eve's eyes shifted to the purse on my arm. "Where are you going?"

Before I could mumble a lie, the phone inside my purse rang. I grabbed it, hoping it wasn't the man Eve thought of as her soul mate cancelling our meeting. "Hello," I said, not mentioning our company's name as before.

"Is this Twin Sisters' Remodeling and Repair?"

"Yes! It is." My cheerful voice gained interest of my sister who kept watching me. I couldn't wait to tell her about the new job we were about to get.

"This is Marsha Ellis. I talked to Eve about y'all possibly remodeling my kitchen," she said, making my smile stretch wider. "Tell her I changed my mind. I won't need any of that work done."

I swallowed, my smile leaving. "Thanks for letting me know."

Eve's continued stare made me feel she could intercept my thoughts, as sometimes we'd seemed to do in the past. I slid my gaze toward my purse where I deposited my phone. She didn't need any new concerns or disappointments.

"Somebody saying you won a trip or thousands of dollars?"

"Something like that. I need to run some errands. In case I'm not back at lunchtime, help yourself to something from the fridge."

"I know where you keep food. Thanks."

A short drive took me to Midtown Coffee Shop. I swept my glance across the three round metal tables topped by blue and white striped umbrellas out front. The rich aroma of mocha and cinnamon pastries greeted me the second I opened the door. I looked beyond the few customers seated inside, keying in on the man who made my breath catch. He looked at me, his closed lips pulling into a partial smile, drawing my body toward his. Who was this person with such appeal?

His smile widened while I approached.

"Thanks for meeting me," I said, unable to stop my own lips from smiling.

"No problem." He stood and pulled out a chair beside his.

Seated, I thought a little small talk might be best to ease into the questions I planned to ask him. "I'm surprised you had this time of day free."

"I just needed to change a couple of things around, but that's fine. What can I get you? Breakfast? This espresso is excellent." He tilted his head toward the cup in front of him.

"I had breakfast, thanks," I said, biting off *with my sister*—that almost spilled out my mouth. "A large cappuccino, please. Nothing else in it."

While he went for my coffee, I struggled with questions I planned to ask and my feelings about him. Yes, darn it, the man I watched standing at the counter with wide shoulders and nice buns looked good, although his appeal seemed to come more from somewhere inside. When the barista made a machine churn, Dave glanced over his shoulder. Renewed eye contact with him made my cheeks burn. The rest of my body also heated.

"Maybe it's cooler outside," I said when he returned and set a cup in front of me.

He looked toward the door. "It was almost ninety degrees this morning, and the air conditioner is on in here. But if you want to, we can move out there."

"No, that's fine. I just had a little warm spell."

"Is it something you get often?" He lowered himself beside me.

I shook my head. *Only when you're close.* "Thanks. So I hear that you have a sister."

"Yes, the same as you." His satisfied smile expressed his pleasure. "We're the only two."

My lips squeezed together with the grim thought of the one we'd lost. "We had another sister. She died when we were young." Anger flared inside. "Some stupid person drove past our house when we were outside and for entertainment, I guess, shot her." My shoulders felt the trembles first. Tremors worked themselves down to my chest where they vibrated and regurgitated in "Silent Night." I squelched the song and the tremor of my body with Dave's arms warm around me, holding me close, keeping my head tight against his.

"I am so sorry," he said near my ear. "Sunny, I'm truly, truly sorry." He gave me a squeeze.

I sucked in a deep breath and drew back. "Thank you."

He shook his head, a sorrowful look tugging down the outer corners of his eyes. "I can't imagine what you've been through."

I sighed. "It's been so hard to lose her." I peered at the table, then up at him. "That's when the idiotic singing began. I was alone with Crystal when it happened, and I was so scared and I wouldn't let myself cry because I'd never stop, and instead, I sang. The only songs I knew— Christmas carols." My voice came stronger and louder. "So I don't have an older sister any longer, and any time I get scared, I still sing them."

He watched my face, his eyebrows lowered. Dave placed a hand over mine.

"I tried to get help, some counseling," I continued, unable to stop this sad story of my life, "but not much helped." Spent. My body and mind and word bank had exhausted themselves. How could I have told all those things to him? The only one I'd said this to was the professional who said little and didn't help. Pressing back in my chair, I felt my hand slip away from Dave's.

He sat straighter, giving me the courage to do the same. "You are a strong woman, Sunny. I admire your courage in all you've had to face."

I nodded, silent at first. "Thank you."

Just then, I noticed the older couple at the next table. Their eyes turned down the minute I looked at them. So they heard. No matter.

"Now we need happier talk. Tell me about your sister." I stirred and sipped my cooling drink, trying to divert attention away from myself and allowing him time to speak and me to move my thoughts in a different direction.

"Ah, she's a sweetheart." He took a swallow of his coffee. "In fact, Penny has never been married, and now she's engaged to a man your twin divorced."

When he stopped talking, I didn't respond, again stirring in my cup, not giving away whether I already knew what he told.

"I think Eve's divorced more than one man," he said. "This one, I believe, might be her first? Stan Legendre."

"He was her second husband."

"Anyway, he seems like a really great guy, and my little sister's nuts about him. That's all that matters to me."

Peering out the corner of my eye, I wouldn't look directly at Dave. What would he or his sister think if they knew Stan slept at Eve's house the night before Dave showed up there to talk about installing an alarm? Yes, she'd said they didn't sleep together, but was that a fib?

"You seem to like your sister a lot." I dabbed at my lips with a napkin he'd brought.

"What's not to love? She's kind and considerate and always calling her big brother from her place in Shreveport to check on him." His gave his head a brief shake. "And I'm the one who really should be checking on her."

Did his adorable sister know her fiancée had given my sister expensive jewelry and other fine gifts since their marriage ended? "She sounds really sweet."

"She certainly is, even while being confined to a wheelchair."

My hand jerk made coffee splash on the table. I'd been bringing my cup to my lips when he told me this surprising information. "A wheelchair?"

His lips went into a tight line. "A car accident two years ago. Some drunk guy ran into her while she was driving. Since then she lost her job and doesn't have much of anything left. Except hope."

I shook my head, sympathy oozing out to this unseen young woman.

"Being in love with Stan has given her the main joy in her life since the accident."

Dave's words sent my mind and emotions swirling as though in a tornado. She owns little, but does have this big brother. She may know about Stan's previous wife, my sister, who has much, and he's given much more. Suppose she wanted her big brother, seated beside me, to crash into my sister's house and grab all those things of value that Stan gave her. *WHERE IS WHAT'S HIS?* Could that be what was meant?

"What's wrong?" Dave stared at me, forehead crinkled. He set his cup down.

I shook my head. "Nothing." With a napkin, I wiped off the coffee I'd spilled. Lowering my uptight shoulders, I tried to relax the tension in my forehead and chin. My attempt mustn't have been too convincing because he leaned his upper body toward me, concern gripping his face.

"Why exactly did you want me to meet you here today?"

My mind skipped through thoughts, trying to pick one. *I wanted to learn more about your sister and Eve's ex. I wanted to be around you. And I certainly didn't want anyone connected to you to be a potential threat to my sister.*

He looked at my hands, which I'd tucked together near my chest without thinking. His gaze made me realize I'd also drawn back from his nearness.

"Hello, Eve." A man's words made me twist around. She came in here? We'd be seen together, a potential major problem.

I didn't see Eve, but a young man wearing a suit, tie, and pleased expression, stepped up to me.

"I'm not Eve. She's my twin."

"Oh, I didn't know she had a twin. You two are identical." The grin he gave me had seduction written around the edges, making me shiver and wonder if he was considering that I might have moles in the same hidden places she did.

"Yes. Well, we're not quite identical." I turned my back on him.

Dave kept hard eyes trained on the man standing behind me. After a beat, the man's footsteps moved on. Dave's gaze lowered toward mine. "Is Eve around? I haven't seen any sign of her."

"She's fine. And her alarm system is working fine, too," I said, evading his question.

"Good."

I wet my throat with a small sip of the cooled cappuccino. "I wanted to apologize for all the commotion I caused by saying your alarm didn't function properly when actually I was the one who didn't work it right."

"That's fine. No harm was done."

"So thank you for the coffee. I can repay you for both of these." I pointed to my cup and his.

"No way. But that's all you wanted? To apologize again?"

And sort my feelings, which were now even more scrambled. "Yes. Thank you for the drink." I lifted my purse.

He leaned and touched a kiss to my cheek.

With a small tremble, I stood. No smile came to my lips before or after I strode away. This man my twin thought of as her potential forever mate might actually have been the person who broke into her house, ruined her paintings, and wrote on her wall once he couldn't get into the rest of the house to steal valuables. He'd have done it for his younger handicapped sister he seemed to adore. Disappointment roared through my system with the thought that the only man who appealed to me since early in my marriage might be proving what I had known—that no man was ever meant for me.

Chapter 22

The other threat to my sister came to mind while I slid into my truck. Someone shot at her. I couldn't imagine Dave in any circumstances firing a gun at Eve or anyone else. And why didn't I want him to be involved? Again I wondered if there could possibly have been two people, one who smashed the glass door and got inside, and another one for some different reason later trying to kill her?

My humming about winter wonderlands let me know I didn't want to stay with that thought. I turned my radio full blast to a country music station, ripping away my hums and pictures of a dead sister.

What about Daria and Zane? I still believed she killed him, but who killed her? And why? I wondered when the first song stopped.

I needed to brush all this detecting off my shoulders. I wanted to rush to solve Eve's problems but couldn't connect all of these recent tragic events. Surely the police had much more information than I did. Maybe, even at this moment, they were closing in on a killer.

I punched my volume button up even more until a refrain vibrated against my truck's windows, and I belted out lyrics about love in the wrong places. Twisting my upper body helped suck away more of my body's tension.

Considering what I'd just learned, I decided where I might discover more. Besides, it was too soon to return home, and I didn't want Eve to see me until my emotions calmed. I aimed my truck in a new direction and soon trotted inside the retirement home. Mom's lady friends sat in a clump. One was napping. Three of them leaned toward each other while Grace drew her cell phone out from deep in her bra and then showed pictures on it. Mom was nowhere in sight.

"You're back already? Miriam will be glad to see you again," one of them said.

"Or are you the other one?" another asked.

"Where's Mom?" I asked instead of replying. No telling what some of them might have heard about Eve and her situation.

"She went to her room for an early nap. But you can go see her," Ida said.

"No, that's okay. I don't want to wake her." I sat in the place my mother normally occupied. "How are you all doing?"

"Okay," two of them murmured. Another one showed me her knees that ached.

"I hope that gets better soon," I said with sincerity and then turned to Grace. "Is the constipation improved?"

She waved her thin arm around. "One week it's good, the next one it's real bad. This is a good one."

I smiled. "I'm happy to hear it."

"Do you want to see my latest pictures?" she asked, ready to thrust her phone that was surely moist into my palm.

"Another time. I just had a few minutes to run in here. But tell me this if you don't mind, Ms. Grace. What is it like being confined to a wheelchair?"

She shook her head, eyes partly closing and saddened. "It's miserable." She gave her head a slow turn toward those in her group. "These ladies, like your momma, can walk. They might have some aches while they do it, but they can get around almost anywhere."

The others in her group watched her with solemn expressions.

I clasped Grace's outstretched empty hand. "I am so sorry. I can't imagine how difficult your life must be."

She nodded and turned her face aside. "But some of those others have it much worse than me." She eyed two immobile men asleep in their wheelchairs.

My heart went out to all of them. And a question popped up. "Were any of you very young when you had to use those chairs?"

"Just one woman. She's one of the youngest people here. And she's so bitter about it she just snaps at anybody who talks to her."

I sighed. "I can understand. And I really wish the best for you, Ms. Grace." I hugged her. Sympathizing and feeling especially close to all of my mom's friends, I said, "And all of you." I hugged each one of them except the women still asleep. Their pleased smiles repaid me a fortune.

"Would you all tell Mom I stopped by?" Before anyone again questioned which twin I was, I hurried out.

My concerns about Eve multiplied since my conversation with Dave and the one I'd just had. The increased speed of my breaths while I drove toward home made me pay attention to my concerns about my twin being around. She really needed to get back to Texas.

Suppose she had decided to walk to her house? I moved through streets a little over the speed limit. I reached my street and checked to make certain she wasn't outside and nobody looked like a threat to her safety. Only two boys of about eight rode their bicycles on the road. Miss Hawthorne knelt in her yard, face covered by her brim while she planted yellow flowers.

I pulled under my carport, threw my truck in park, and rushed to the door, house key in hand. "It's me," I called, letting myself in and not wanting to scare her while praying I'd find her there and all right.

"Wow, you sound short of breath." Eve spoke from my dining room, not looking up from the drawing she pored over.

"I couldn't wait to see you again." I moved into the room.

She glanced toward the kitchen. "I didn't hear you carry any bags inside. Where did you go?"

That thought had wrapped around in my head. If I told her Dave's sister who was engaged to Stan lived in a wheelchair and sounded almost destitute, she'd likely complain about my going to meet him on the sly. Better not to tell her about that, I'd decided on my way here.

"I went by the church for a little inner peace," I said, to which she looked surprised. I really had driven somewhere near it and briefly considered going inside. "And I went to see Mom."

"How's she doing today?"

"Good." At least I hoped so. None of her friends told me otherwise.

"And you needed peace." She set down her pen. "Am I too much for you here?"

"Of course not. I love having you close, just not when you're in danger."

"I'll be fine." She lifted a charcoal pencil and added leaves to the stem she'd drawn.

"What is it?" I asked.

She stared at me. "It's a rose. Can't you tell? Is it that bad?"

"Of course I can tell what it is. What I mean is who does it represent?"

Her eyes went sad. Shoulders dropped. "No one."

"Have you done any other drawings?" I skimmed the first pages of her pad and found them blank. She didn't need to answer. Certainly she lacked inspiration at this time.

I pulled out my cell and contacted Detective Wilet. Eve looked at me when she heard me giving my name and asking for him.

The moment he got on the phone, I said, "I brought you some possible evidence and gave you information that might help guide your office toward the man trying to hurt my sister. Now what can you tell me? Are you getting close to arresting the person who attacked her?"

Eve's eyes went wide, more hopeful.

"Ms. Taylor, we do have some leads, and we're advancing on the case."

"Great." I squeezed my twin's shoulder. Maybe she was safe. "Who're you looking at? What are you finding?"

A second passed before his long exhale. "Not anything I can share with you right now. I hope it won't be long. We'll let you know."

Eve's fallen expression matched mine. She looked back at her sketch sheet and lifted a pencil.

"I'm going outside to hit on some wood," I told her.

She pushed up to her feet. "I'll come with you. It'll be fun."

"Whacking a hammer against something might get frustrations out, but you know we can't do it together." To her withered look, I said, "Go on and design more pretty things in here. Maybe when I come in and fix supper, you can go out there and smash nails."

It took a moment for her to decide and sit back down. "What kind of flower do you want me to do now?"

"As long as it's not an azalea, I'm good."

She gave me a tight-lipped half smile. As she resumed her art project, I proceeded out the door, surprised to find the wind had picked up. Rain might be nearing, but lately I seldom checked the news or forecast.

My double carport held only my truck and a wilted hydrangea plant one of my favorite lingerie customers once gave me, and I hated to throw away. From my large storage room, I pulled out a pair of plastic sawhorses and set them a couple of feet apart.

Reentering the room, I chose a couple of scrap pieces of two-by-fours and set them across each other on the sawhorse stand. Returning for the final items, I selected a mason jar of large nails and admired my treasure in a basket on the bottom shelf. It was the tattered tool belt my daddy gave me when I did some jobs with him as a teen. With the intensity of gazing upon a sacred item, I admired the stains, some of them put there by me, some by my dad. No way was I going to wash the cotton fabric. I'd gotten a seamstress from Fancy Ladies to stitch the ripped side of the pocket that held the hammer and the frayed right side of the belt. Other than that, nobody messed with this important item from my family.

It really was okay that Mom had given Eve our dad's tiger-eye ring that I had never seen on his finger. I had seen him wearing this tool belt many times before he'd passed it on to me.

I tied the belt on, adjusted tools inside it, and walked out. With no plan for creating anything, I held the tip of a nail at the juncture of the crossed wood, and smashed it in with my hammer. I smiled, knowing my power-driver tools would never provide such an outlet for my tension. I set another nail beside the first one and punctured the wood as though I was puncturing the whole problem about who was after my sister. With the next nails, I raised my hammer much higher than I needed to, imagining the forceful swing and punching down like I was hurting the man threatening her.

"What are you making, Sunny?"

The voice startled me. I hadn't noticed a person trotting out from around my truck. Seeing Miss Hawthorne also took me aback. I recognized the voice as a woman's, but when she came around my truck, she resembled a man with her stance and the brim of her wind-blown hat pressed tight against her head.

"Hi, Miss Hawthorne." It took me a second to calm from my swings. She left her yard again? I certainly wasn't going to invite her inside, where she'd see my twin. "I didn't know you were here."

"I heard you hammering and thought I'd come to see you. What are you making?"

I hadn't meant to make so much noise. Or maybe she'd already been walking this way when she heard me. I looked over my woodwork. What could I tell her it was? Total frustration? A smashed killer?

"I'm just fooling around. Sometimes I just like to swing a hammer."

She studied my creation. "That looks like a large cross. Maybe you could start selling them."

I'd be glad to if anyone wanted to pay me to get my frustrations out. "Maybe so," I said. "Were you just going for a walk?"

"No, I thought of something else you might want to know."

I took the moment to relax my right arm, noticing a slight pinch in my shoulder. Since her step-grandson told me about her making up stories, anything this woman might say would probably be statements I wouldn't believe. But maybe like some of my mom's friends who seldom went anywhere, she just needed to babble to someone. I could be kind for a little while and listen.

"Oh, really? Thanks for coming to tell me."

"It's concerning a man I believe you and your sister are troubled about. A Mr. Snelling."

"That's right. Did you know him?"

"No, but I did know his grandpa. He lived in New Orleans back when I did." She leaned close and shielded her mouth with her hand. "He was a handsome man who was supposedly involved in the mob."

"Really?" Now here was news I cared about. Possibly the info was important.

She leaned even closer so that I captured a hint of crayfish from her breath. Was I the only person not eating any now? "And that grandpa supposedly didn't wear briefs or boxers. Of course that's only gossip." Her face pulling away from mine now wore a blush on her cheeks. "Not that I've actually seen anything."

I let her news I almost believed and the part I didn't sink in. I probably shouldn't believe anything she said.

"I'm glad you came to tell me about it."

"That's no problem. I thought you might want to know." She took steps away and then turned back. "Oh, and your twin's daughter should be having her baby soon, won't she?"

"Fairly soon."

"I'd have thought she'd be in Texas with her by now."

Concern made my back tight and straight. "What makes you think she isn't?"

"I saw her in your window back there." She pointed to the front of my house. "Tell her I hope everything goes well with the baby."

She toddled away, alarm making pinches of distress grab every muscle down my back. Other people also would know Eve was here. Staying around would increase the threat to her. I rushed inside, needing to make her leave.

Chapter 23

"Miss Hawthorne saw you," I said as an accusation while dashing into the dining room where Eve sat.

"I saw her through the kitchen window when I was getting coffee." Not looking concerned, Eve tilted her head toward an empty cup on the table.

"But now people will know you're here. You need to go back to Houston."

"Sunny, one person saw me. Who's she going to tell? She never goes anywhere."

"Did you ever hear of the phone? There's also Facebook and Twitter."

The chuckle in her throat sounded deep. "You don't really think she went home and picked up her phone and dialed everyone. She doesn't seem to know anybody, except maybe whoever sells her the mulch and the flowers. And her on a computer? Come on. You told me about her ugly green bra and antique girdle."

Which I shouldn't have done. People's undergarments, or lack of them, should have been private when I made those sales. At least my sister was the only person I'd told.

"So why did she come here? I thought she just about never left her yard."

I told her everything my neighbor said about Zane Snelling's grandpa. "Of course I think she just makes up things about men without underwear."

Eve wore a naughty grin. "Don't be so sure."

"Well, I can't believe she was intimate with the man," I continued, making my houseguest's grin widen. "But maybe there's some truth to the part about his involvement in the mob."

"Who knows?" Eve lost interest in him and lifted her pen.

"I'm going to call Detective Wilet and tell him what she said," I said, walking out of the room.

"And I'll want to hear his reaction to an old man barking orders to his crime gang about who to steal from and who to kill while he's running around commando."

Wearing a frown, I went for my phone and called the detective. The person who answered put me through to his desk, where a recording in his voice told me I should leave a message. After a click, I told his voice mail the things Miss Hawthorne told me about Zane's grandpa who'd lived in New Orleans being connected to the mob, leaving out the part about what may or may not have been under his slacks. "I just thought this might help y'all some way to move closer to solving the case involving my sister. I hope you're discovering much more. As I said, this is Sunny Taylor." With finger ready to disconnect, I heard his voice.

"Wait," he said. "We already knew about his involvement in organized crime."

"You did? Well good, then it's true."

"Yes. But you need to leave the investigating to us. I know, it's your sister, but you resemble your twin so much, if you're seen snooping around, you could be mistaken for her."

"I hadn't thought about that."

"You could get badly hurt. It'd be much safer for you if you could stay in your house as much as possible until this thing is solved."

"You're kidding me."

"No, ma'am, I'm not. In fact it would be much better if you'd stay a distance away, maybe join your sister in Texas until this is over. She's still there, right?"

Lie to him? Sure, if it would save Eve. "Houston is where her heart is," I replied without needing an untruth.

"Good. Make sure she stays with her daughter. You consider going there, too."

"I will." I hurried to click off before I heaped on untruths.

Eve had her sketch going in a wide circle. "What did he say?"

"He said you need to be with your daughter. I made it sound like you're there now." She grinned, and I placed my finger under her chin, making her face tip up toward mine. "Please go. You'll be safe."

"And miserable." She backed her chin out of my grip. "I'll go when the baby's born. But don't you start doting on me. That's what they did."

"Then maybe you won't want to stay here in town."

"But I do." She pulled back the chair next to hers. "Come draw with me."

I sat but smirked. "You know I can't draw."

"It'll help calm you down. Remember how nice it was coloring with each other?" She ripped the sheet she'd been sketching on from her pad and shoved it in front of me. "You know how to draw circles. Just keep making this one smaller and smaller." She pushed a pen in my hand.

"You'll probably have me drawing something dirty." I grinned at her.

"Nope, not this time. Look, this time we'll do something we're both interested in. This will be the Meditation Path the city has talked about wanting."

Tilting my head, I realized that's what she had begun to create.

"It doesn't have to be perfect. Be like a kid drawing pictures." She gripped my hand and moved it so the point of the pen pressed on the page. "We're just starting an idea. I'll see if I can come up with how a pavilion beside it might look."

I added to the outer circle, a slow, hesitant move on my part. "You know they won't consider letting us bid on this project unless all of the mess about Zane is way behind us."

She nodded, staring at her new empty sheet, making the first marks at the bottom of the page. Her jagged lines looked like tall grass. "Right, if nobody proves that our work on the pavers where he sat didn't cause his death, no amount of sketching and coming up with low bids will help."

I didn't care that my artistic ability didn't match hers, or maybe it did and I just wasn't used to doing it. Sitting here beside my sister, glancing at her pensive face involved in what she drew, feeling her warmth and her strength, I imagined a serene veil wrapped around my shoulders. It didn't matter how crude my drawings were since we wouldn't sell from them. I was right here beside her.

What we were doing was good, healthy, much better than being outside or even in here with hammer and nails. Quiet didn't attract attention.

Making my bumpy swirl continue around the page and round and round in smaller circles, I became a girl again, content to lose myself in color and lines. Beside me, my twin's arm moved up sometimes and then drew a line down. She lifted her drawing instrument and made marks on the other side. I didn't concern myself with the efficiency of her drawing, only glad she remained intent on it as I did with mine.

After some time she glanced at my pad. "Nice pathway." She met my eyes that mirrored her pleasure.

"Thanks." I leaned closer to see what she worked on. Her drawing was almost as crude as my own. "Cute building. Reminds me of our old garage." Great memories. We had worked inside it with Dad.

She gave me a warm smile, studied her work, and nodded.

I gave her a one-armed hug. "I'm going to fix supper. You keep on with that. You're doing nice work." What she did with the sketchpad wasn't fantastic, but if we were ever able to compete for work in this town, we'd have professionals create our final drafts. For now, playing around with drawings and colors worked fine to help both of us keep more pressing concerns at bay. It was also keeping her inside.

Placing a frozen package of boneless chicken pieces under cool running water in the kitchen sink, I thought about Miss Hawthorne and shut my curtains. Drapes in the dining room were closed, just like in every other room of the house. The only way a person could see in here now without opening the door would be to set up a ladder to stare over the bottom curtains above the sink. Nobody would be so obvious as to do that. And nobody, I hoped, except Mom and my neighbor a couple of doors down, knew Eve was here.

I hummed a mindless tune, not about the holiday season, while I worked at the counter, chopping seasoning, and then at the stove. From time to time I glanced in at Eve. The telepathy we'd often shared over the years seemed to draw her attention to me looking at her during those times, and we gave each other heartfelt smiles.

"Need help?" she asked.

"At the stove? No thanks. Make me a picture."

Her grin widened. I was pleased to resemble her warm blue eyes, thick red hair, and fair complexion. The depth of her heart shown in her eyes.

I prepared a chicken and andouille sausage gumbo. When I heated the rice I'd cooked a day or so ago, I thought of when I'd borrowed noodles to get Eve to come over the first time a few days ago for shrimp creole. Had so much happened during that short time? I refused to look in on her again, figuring she'd know that concern for her remained foremost on my mind.

At the stove, I didn't hear her come into the room. A flash of her hand to my left caught my notice. She moved around, set the table, and poured our drinks.

Our jovial mood had passed. We ate in silence, except for her to mention how good the gumbo was. It was only after we set our spoons down on our bowls that, like air from a pin-ruptured balloon, our real thoughts poured out.

"Who could have done it?" she asked.

"What, all of it? The couple's deaths and the threats to you?"

Her lowered forehead hooded her eyes. "Take one at a time. Who would have killed Zane?"

I nodded. "No question, Daria did it."

She kept her gaze steady on me. "Because?"

"Zane had two lovers, Daria's sister and Lillian who wears a bikini to cut her grass."

Eve's intent stare into the space between us let me know she was mulling on that probability.

"And then Daria found out about them and learned he was leaving her, but she planned to leave him first. Maybe right after she located his fortune?"

"I believe so. And Daria told him she also had a lover, one much better than him."

"Who would be—?"

"I have no idea." I carried my plate to the sink.

Eve brought hers. "If Zane really did have a grandfather involved in organized crime, maybe that's where all the money came from." Using her elbow, she scooted me over and squirted liquid soap into running hot water. "I'll wash. You dry and put things where they belong."

I brought her used glasses and silverware. "Okay, then who murdered Daria?"

She shut off the water and looked at me. "One of those two women? The man she was seeing?"

"You think her own sister could do that?" My hands gripped my twin's forearms, my gaze going deep into her eyes.

She shook her head. Broke eye contact and turned to the sink. "But I don't know why a boyfriend would have murdered her, or for that matter, Lillian either."

I stood silent, inner vision going back. Struggling, I pulled my focus again into now. "It's difficult for us to imagine anyone wanting to kill someone, isn't it?

"Yeah."

She washed, and I buffed items dry. No one had ever been able to solve the case involving our oldest sister. A senseless drive-by shooting, police concluded.

I wouldn't stop trying until I knew Eve would remain safe. "Okay, so we told the police what we knew about Daria and Zane and those other women. And I brought Detective Wilet the nail file that might have dried glue on it, so maybe he considered checking into that and maybe not. And he took my jacket." I blew out a sigh. "Your neighbor's son Royce probably lost a lot of money to big-time gambling, and he might have lied to me about knowing the Snellings."

She stopped rinsing a pot. "What makes you think that?"

"Crayfish omelets."

She stared at me a long minute. I emptied the rest of the food into containers and gave her more pots. She slid them into the water to soak.

"What about whoever's been threatening me?"

I hesitated only a second. "Maybe one of those other people is somehow involved. Or how about Melanie? Do you know whether Jacques heard from her?"

She wiped the counter. "He said he didn't."

I considered something else. "Has he called you since he dropped you off here?"

She shook her head.

"Eve, maybe Melanie came back here alone after they drove you to Texas. She said she didn't mind all the things of value her husband gave you, but do you believe that's true?"

Scrubbing the largest pot, Eve tightened her lips. "I would mind." She sucked in a breath, released it, and stared at the next pot she attacked. "Who else could be after me?"

"There's the man who went running down my street soon after someone shot at you."

Water dripped from her hands to the floor as she faced me. "I don't know about that."

And you wouldn't want to know everything I think. "Miss Hawthorne told me she heard a pop that day, like maybe a backfiring motor. Right after that, she heard someone running on the street with a different sound from most runners. She noticed what she believed were men's black dress shoes. Oh, and black cuffed slacks."

"This is the lady who keeps telling you all the men around here are also running around commando, right?"

"Yes, I guess so. At first she even had me checking out the priests' shoes."

Eve grinned. "They the only guys you know who wear that style shoe?"

I met her eyes. "So does Dave Price."

Her head did a slight bobble. "Don't tell me you've checked?"

"I didn't mean to, but he came around to inspect your alarm when I was at your house. He knew it was me. And I looked at his shoes. Black, dress type."

"Sunny, I can't believe you'd really considered him trying to shoot me."

Words tumbled from my mouth. "His sister is engaged to Stan. She's Dave's only sibling, and he adores her, and she's immobile in a wheelchair."

Eve's mouth dropped open.

I continued. "Her boyfriend left her after an accident crippled her, and now she has little of anything left."

Deep folds entered the area between Eve's eyes. "Poor thing."

"Yes, I truly sympathize with her."

"So do I." Eve dried her hands. "How do you know all this about her?"

"Dave told me." I wasn't going to mention I'd met with him to question him at the coffee shop.

Both her hands went to her chest. "How sweet that he cares about his sister so much. Do you know if he helps her?" Now she was loving him even more.

I grabbed her hands. "Do you realize what this might mean? Even since you divorced Stan, he's given you expensive jewelry and other things of value. What if his fiancée wants those items?"

Her chin tucked near her neck when her head drew back.

"I don't want to think it either, but somebody broke into your house and then tried to kill you."

She was pulling back from me, eyes wide. "You can't be serious thinking Dave would do this."

"Eve, suppose his sister convinced him to get into your place to find the items Stan gave you and locate other valuables, including cash. We don't know her. We sympathize with her, but she could believe she deserves them since she'll be marrying Stan."

My twin's face went cold. "Don't even say that."

I stepped closer. "You know I wouldn't suggest or even think something like this unless—Sis, I need you safe."

She straightened, her chin lifted, eyes hard. "I am not the sister who died beside you. We're both grown up now. We can take care of ourselves."

My words blasted out, bypassing the hum wanting to thrum in my throat. "I know Dave's attractive, but just think of it. He knew your house didn't have an alarm. He showed up there soon after your break-in occurred. Think of the words on the wall. *Where is what's his* surely could have been him wanting to know where Stan's gifts were, and he hadn't been able to get to them farther past the locked door on your art room. He installed a system in your house afterward that worked—maybe—or maybe I *had* put in the correct code the day someone pointed a gun at you, and he went in later and changed it. Who knows what the man might be able to do since he's the one person who's now supposed to keep you safe at your house? And then there are the shoes. Miss Hawthorne says—"

But Eve wasn't staying around to listen to anymore. She whipped past me, brushing hard against my arm, stomping toward the hall.

"Where are you going?"

She didn't reply. Until five minutes later while I sat with elbows on the dining room table, hands gripping my chin. Eve stormed through the room, grabbed her sketchpad and some of her pens, and threw them in a bag. With this bag in one hand, she lifted a small suitcase with the other. "I'm going where people aren't so doubtful."

Before I could push up to my feet and confront her, she swooped past me. "No, don't," I said.

"I called a cab." The front door slammed behind her.

Chapter 24

I didn't dare rush out after her. Eve and I shouldn't be in front of my house at the same time. Few people here took a cab. I hadn't seen one in months, yet as I watched through the window, an older-model gray car marked Ray's Taxicab rolled near. Eve didn't glance back when she yanked the rear door's handle and, with her bags, slid inside.

Grabbing my phone, I punched in her number.

She glanced toward her lap, probably at her purse holding her cell phone that I kept ringing. Head raised, she set her face forward while they rolled off. I kept the taxi in sight as long as possible. At least Miss Hawthorne wasn't outside anymore since darkness had dropped in.

I left a message on Eve's cell. "Come on back, Sis. I'm sorry. I didn't know I'd make you so upset. It was just an idea, a thought about who might be after you. Come home. Let's talk."

She didn't answer me or call back. Again, she didn't when I made my second frantic call, my second petition to her. "Where are you going? Come on, you're right. It probably wasn't Dave or his sister who wanted anything from you. I really want you here. Please come back."

Since she didn't answer, by now she must have turned off her ringer. I left two more messages stating almost the same thing, pleading with her to return, and received the same silent response.

Where would she go? I dashed to my truck and went off the way the taxi did, hoping I could spot the vehicle carrying her, and cut it off. Scenes from car chases in movies no doubt made me believe I could track down the car she left in. I sped down my street that was nearly empty of cars and rushed toward the highway. Worry about Eve and someone attacking her filled my mind, making me almost miss the siren wailing behind. A glance in the rearview mirror showed a bright blue swirling light closing in on me. I pulled to the side of the street to let the cop pass.

Instead, he pulled over a few feet behind me.

I stared in the mirror, wishing away the light circling above the police car, waiting a moment for him to rush into one of the houses near us to arrest someone or discover why they called him. Using the time, I pressed in Eve's number again. Once again, she didn't answer.

The policeman stayed in his car, watching me. Time was throbbing by, I noted by the pounding in my head.

I got out and scooted to him.

The deputy was blond-haired, blue-eyed, pimpled, maybe just out of high school.

"You didn't want me, did you?" I asked.

"Yes, ma'am. Did you know you were going thirty-six in a twenty-mile speed zone?"

"No, I didn't. But I'm in a rush. I need to get somewhere." And I didn't need all these people coming outside or peeking out their windows. If they saw me here, which was highly likely with the glaring blue calling everyone's attention, they'd know Eve was also in town if she went out anywhere now, which was highly likely. I ducked my head to hide my face from spying eyes, but the light over his car made certain anyone who looked would notice my height and red hair. At least he'd shut off the siren.

"Could you please just let me go this time? I promise I'll pay closer attention to speed zones. I really am in a hurry."

"So is everyone else, ma'am. Normally they say they need to reach a bathroom. Would you step to your truck and get your registration and license and bring them to me?"

I stared at this boy, my sad eyes and drooped lips pleading for him to relent.

He did not. By the time I dug out and carried those items to him, another police car pulled up behind his.

"Thank you. You can get back in your vehicle while I check on this," the officer who'd stopped me said. Another young deputy stepped out of his squad car and moved to the window of the first one while I shuffled back to my truck. More of the people who lived near me came out on their front lawns to see the criminal caught in their neighborhood.

While I sat in my truck, mortified but mainly concerned about Eve, I checked my phone, hoping she'd returned my call, disappointed that she had not. Concern for her safety thrummed through my body, knotting my muscles, keeping my face tight.

By the time the officer trusted me enough for him to walk to my truck window to hand me a ticket, I knew I'd never catch up to my sister. I thanked the young man for giving me the piece of paper that would cost me more money that I didn't have and started my truck. Easing it out of park, I drove right under the speed limit to the highway. From there I went to the place I'd decided she might have gone—to see our mother, maybe to get some advice or comfort.

Lights shone outside the manor. I parked and rushed in. Most of the interior lighting had been dimmed. The entrance floor was shiny. A sign warned that it was wet. Only a few residents sat or wandered in the wide foyer and main visiting area. Not Mom.

I scurried down the hall leading to her room.

"Hi, Eve. Or Sunny," a trim nurse with rimless glasses stepping out of a room said.

I stopped short. "I'm Sunny." I needed to stop my tongue from asking the question stamped on my mind. *Is Eve here?*

"Your mother's already gone to bed. She wasn't feeling well, so she wanted to rest."

My apprehension spiked. "Is she sick?"

"I don't know. Maybe just a little upset stomach." She lifted a medicine bottle from her wheeled cart and glanced at the doorway to the next room.

Trying not to show my other concern, I asked, "Did Mom have any company this evening?"

"Not that I know of. But I just came on duty."

"Thanks. I'll check on her tomorrow. Or let me know if she feels worse during the night."

"I will. But I'm sure she'll be fine."

Still uncertain about leaving, I said, "I might just go take a peek at her now." The nurse couldn't argue, so I concentrated on keeping my footsteps light as I scampered toward Mom's room. Some doors were open, most were shut. My mother's door was closed tight. Maybe she was still awake. Maybe Eve sat in the recliner beside her. I eased the door open and peered in the room.

A faint light fell through the sheer curtains. The nightlight between Mom's bed and bathroom cast a brighter glow. A serene expression held my mother's face while she slept on her side, the covers pulled to her neck. Eve was not in any of the empty spaces. Making my steps extra light, I moved to Mom's bed, watched her in sleep, and touched my lips to her cool forehead, moving away right before she stirred. Still asleep, she drew the top sheet tighter up against her neck. Satisfied that she wasn't deathly ill, I swept out of her room and softly shut the door.

If I found the nurse on my way out, I would ask exactly what time she came on duty tonight. Was it minutes ago? Had enough time passed from when the cab brought my sister away and I got stopped for speeding for Eve to have come for a brief visit with our mother?

It was probably a good thing I didn't see the nurse again, I figured, making my way out. With the kind of questioning I was ready to ask, she might get suspicious. No one needed to determine Eve could be in town since word spread from here, and I had no idea who we could trust.

Aware that she might have gone to her house, I drove there, tension biting my shoulders. Maybe she thought she could hide out at home until the person after her was arrested, but her house was where she'd been attacked. I made sure to drive under the speed limit, especially once I neared our neighborhood. With drapes drawn, most houses were dark with security lights outside lit. Few cars moved on the street.

A security light hanging from the soffit in the far corner of Eve's roof offered visibility mostly away from the driveway. I sat scanning the left side of her yard and beyond to the house next door. Finding no signs of a person, I checked the right and again saw no one. I slipped out of my truck, shunning the instinct to grab a crowbar from my toolbox. I was going inside hoping to find my sister so I could convince her to come back to my place to stay. I didn't want to walk in with a weapon raised and possibly swing it down at her if she startled me.

The minute I stepped in front of my truck, a flash of light from the right called my attention. It came and disappeared, and I knew it was someone in the closest window of her snoopy neighbor's house. After I'd pulled into Eve's drive, someone there must have peeked out of that window to see who it was and then dropped the curtain.

I could probably walk over to their house and ask whether my twin had arrived here, and both of them would know. But I didn't want them to know anything about her whereabouts now. I rushed to Eve's front door, used my key, and slipped into her house that was dark except for a timed-lamp in her den.

"Eve, it's me," I yelled, not wanting to scare her. My gaze swept every area I could see. Shadows in the far reaches of her kitchen might belong to an item or person, but I couldn't stand here and find out. If the alarm was set for *Home*, Eve or someone else who knew that was needed would be in here.

Rushing to the alarm, I found it set, but not to show that anyone might move inside. Pleased to find it ticking down, I rushed back out before it blared and called Dave's office to send the police.

After locking up, I drove to my house. The only other places I figured she could have gone were to a hotel in the area or to Houston. Hotels wouldn't tell me if she checked in, and who knew what distance she might have gone anyway? Maybe the cab driver. Those with nationally known companies surely had privacy codes so they weren't allowed to tell who they drove or where they brought the person they carried. The cab she rode in must have been local.

I checked the phone book, found Ray's Taxicab listed, and called. I was content when they answered. To my dismay, the guy with the pleasant voice couldn't tell me a thing about their customers.

I pleaded, "It's urgent."

"It just took one time for a man to beat up his wife after the guy who used to work here told him where our driver brought her. Then she stayed in the hospital for weeks."

"I'm sorry. I do understand that and your hesitation about giving a man information about a woman, but I need to know about my sister."

"No, we don't give information to anyone."

In a last desperate attempt, I tried my sister's phone again, praying she would answer.

Her message box was full, but I knew she would check her phone since she'd want to know if Nicole went into labor or had problems. I shot her a text.

Please come back, Sis. I love you.

I sent the message on its way, hoping she would reply, or even better, that she would show up at my doorstep.

Waiting for her response, I stepped into the dining room. Besides blank pages, she hadn't taken the sketch I was creating or the pens I was using. I eyed her empty chair and sat in mine. On a blank page, I made wiggly lines and then crude drawings. The picture of a house like the one with a chimney that I'd created as a child began to take shape. I checked my phone. No return call. No text.

I would play a stronger card to get her back. Again, I texted.

Mom is real sick!

I sent the words off hoping they weren't really true, hoping our mother had only a slight cold, upset stomach, or other small ailment. Whether I heard from Eve about this or not, I would go back and check on Mom in the morning.

This time I kept my eyes on my cell in my hand, watching for a return text from my sister, or possibly the phone to ring. My eyes grew heavy. My body weary. I made my way to bed, keeping my phone charged on the small table beside where I slept. But sleeping was one thing I didn't do for most of the night. I waited, watched, pushed down the carol striving to come out my lips. I wasn't scared for her, I told myself. This last sister would be all right. So would our mother. How could life go on otherwise?

Chapter 25

My eyes felt swollen when they opened in the morning. I grabbed my phone. No text message from Eve and no new call. I pressed in her number. As before, a recording told me her inbox was full. I shot her a text she may have missed last night.

Mom's ill! Call me.

Holding the cell phone, I lay watching, knowing a return text would soon appear. If not, I'd hear its ring. I slid the volume control to max. Listening, I watched the screen of the device in my hand growing fuzzy, its apps blending together like one of Eve's disjointed paintings.

Pain in my neck woke me. My cheek pressed against something hard. I reached there and found my phone I'd fallen asleep on. It still showed no message. Surely Eve wasn't so angry at me for suggesting her latest boyfriend might be a killer or thief that she didn't care how our mother was doing. That attractive man might be enticing, but maybe his draw would prove lethal. I hurried to shower and dress, then grabbed a handful of dry cereal with a cup of coffee, and drove off to check on Mom.

The manor was especially active during this late morning hour. Employees rushed about, reminding me of an ant farm I'd once had in which only a few ants remained still while most jostled around as though trying to prove their missions had the most purpose. Some residents moved, none of them rushing.

My apprehension about Mom lying in bed ill waiting for an ambulance to carry her to the hospital dissipated. She sat front and center with her group, two of the ladies speaking at the same time, my mother looking from one to the other as though trying to keep up with what each was saying. Maybe she knew some trick.

"Mom," I said, happy to see her up and about.

Her face lit and eyes sparkled when she saw me. She threw her arms out, and I rushed into them. I held my mother tighter than I had in some time. When we released each other, I again felt her forehead with my lips. The soft skin was cool. I touched my palm to her even softer cheek. No sign of fever there either.

"What happened to your cheek?" she asked me.

"I slept with my phone. Not a good idea," I said with a smile.

The woman seated beside her pushed over on the sofa to give me space to sit.

I gripped my mother's hand, which was even chillier than her head. "How are you?"

"I'm fine. Just had a little indigestion last night. They told me your sister called during the night to find out how I was. Wasn't that nice of her?"

My nostrils released a long exhale. Eve could have contacted me.

"And you checked on me, too." Mom leaned the side of her head against mine.

Did she say where she is? I was ready to whisper, annoyed with Eve yet worried about her. But she wouldn't have told her location to whoever answered the phone here. She may have still been riding in the taxi, heading to Houston if my wish came true.

I hoped Mom hadn't heard about a man shooting at Eve. As much as I wanted to stay close to our mother, especially now that I'd feared for her health, I felt a need to leave before she asked anything about my twin. If I rushed off, though, the group might become suspicious. I should stay a few minutes longer.

"Well, I never sleep with my phone," Grace said from her wheelchair close to me. "Except that time I fell asleep in bed with it still in my bra. You know I don't take my underwear off under my nightgown." Her eyes swept across their circle of friends, some of them nodding like they knew.

"That must have hurt," I said, hoping to keep attention on her.

"It sure did." She shoved her hand into her cleavage, dug around a bit, and pulled out her phone. "I'll bet this boobie had a big crease underneath it just like you have on your face."

"Has your son taken many pictures for you lately?" I asked.

She pushed her lips out in a small pout. "Not many. He just got a couple of them since that Snelling man's funeral."

My heart lurched. "He brought your phone there?"

"Yes. I never went to a funeral where they had the dead person in an urn."

"Me either," two ladies said.

"Tell me about the pictures," I said, not wanting any distraction from the topic.

"Well, somebody told me they heard the funeral parlor was going to put him in an urn, so I sent my brother to that funeral with my phone to get me some pictures of it."

"Can I see them?" I reached for her phone. Ignoring its clammy feel, I got into the photo app.

"But he only got one picture. When that man's wife was walking in the church."

That might help, I thought, as I scrolled through pictures. The most recent ones were of their Chat and Nap Group. Mom's photo within it made a tight smile pull at my lips. Grace had taken pictures of some of their meals—one plate held beef stew and lima beans and chocolate cake and salad—and some photos of other residents, one man asleep in his wheelchair, some others at tables, smiling at her camera, two with *cheese* obvious on their lips.

My breaths slowed when I reached the now deceased Daria Snelling. What had happened to this woman?

"You see? That's the only one he got at that funeral, and he didn't even get the urn in the picture. The wife had already come in the church and dropped him. My brother just took this one picture and then left when everybody kept trying to get that man's ashes up." She reached for her phone, which I handed her, and flipped the screen. "But this next picture, that's a good one. An eagle in her nest that he saw in a tree near the bayou."

"That's a beauty." I pulled the phone back, returning to Daria's photo. I'd witnessed this scene. Right after Daria spilled Zane's ashes, she was straightening up, resuming her stance with the priest, seminarian, and two altar boys nearby. The one I'd thought was a priest smiled. A grin also touched the lips of the tall altar boy.

A couple of other people in church, I'd briefly noticed at that time, had also smiled, probably a reaction to what might have appeared a humorous scene if it hadn't included a dead man. Most mourners, though, had looked shocked, just like Father Prejean in this photo. Daria's lips pressed tight, her expression noncommittal.

"Would you mind if I send a couple of your pictures to my phone?" I asked my mom's friend.

"No, of course not." She leaned forward. "You want to show everybody that eagle, don't you? It's a beauty."

"It sure is. And I'd like a couple of others, especially with some of you." She smiled while I forwarded to myself Daria's picture first. And then I did as I'd said. I also grabbed copies of her eagle and Mom and some of these others. "Thank you so much." I handed the phone back to her.

"Anytime. You can check for new pictures on here later."

"Bless you." I kissed her cheek.

Mom and most of the other ladies smiled.

I leaned to my mother and gave her a hug. "Love you. I'm so glad you're doing well."

"I love you, too, Sunny. Now don't let it take me getting sick to get you back here."

"It won't." I thanked the picture lender again, told all the ladies goodbye, and rushed out. What would I do with that photo of Daria? What did it really show? Nothing I could discover for sure, but I needed any miniscule of evidence or clue I could find. I drove through streets, considering where to start. Places where Daria had been might prove worthwhile. I'd left that message on her answering machine saying I had something of her husband's that she'd want.

Where had she gone after that partial funeral?

All I knew was I'd seen her in the grocery store the next morning and by that afternoon, she was dead. She could have gone other places or been with other people after leaving the church, but I had no idea how to get that information. I knew she spoke with a man in the grocery store when her buggy looked empty. Possibly people in that store could give me answers, even though I wasn't sure what my questions would be.

Frigid air blasted me when I walked inside, followed by the odor of overripe bananas and baking French bread. Seeing the cantaloupes, I recalled that I'd also seen Jacques here and met his wife. When she wasn't around, he'd told me to tell Eve he still thought about her all the time. They both drove Eve to Texas the other day. He kept calling her to ask how she was doing and then Jacques alone brought her back. An uncomfortable rumple of apprehension wiggled along my spine.

Refocusing on what I might learn here, I couldn't recall anyone else I may have seen shopping that day. Maybe the picture from Miss Grace's phone would spark a person's memory. Somebody who worked here may have seen Daria and noticed something else about her that could be important. Sure, Detective Wilet said they spoke to workers there, but now I had a photo.

I dug my phone out of my purse and flipped through the screen till I found that photo with her in it, realizing I could be digging for one special grain of coffee out of a five-pound pack but not knowing what else to do. At least I was trying something instead of sitting home squirming.

A husky teen boy wearing the store's gray T-shirt grabbed avocados from a box and stacked them on a freestanding display. I scooted to him. "Excuse me. This is really important," I said, and he looked at me, eyes wide. "Did you happen to notice this woman? Or a man who was in the store with her the other day?"

He barely glanced at the snapshot and shook his head.

I enlarged the picture and placed the phone in his hand. "How about now? Are you sure? Look closely."

He stared at the screen and shoved it back like the thing burned his hand. "Uh-uh, I don't know her."

"I shop here fairly often. If you remember something, make sure you let me know when I come in again, okay?"

"Yeah." Turning his back on me, he shelved avocados.

I continued down every aisle that held an employee. Sometimes I found two or more of them stacking or rearranging items on shelves. One after another checked the picture of Daria and the clergy and altar boys and shook their heads. Two employees said they'd seen her shopping here some time, but probably not lately and never with anyone else they could remember.

A bearded man and short woman at the office area in front were speaking together and eyeing me as I neared the checkouts. They'd probably noticed me going up to all their employees with the phone. I would go to them with it, too, once I finished with other workers and ask the same thing, even though Detective Wilet probably already questioned them.

Before speaking with those two, I still had a few more employees to question. I kept my gaze away from the office so direct eye contact wouldn't give them a chance to wave me over to ask what I was doing.

I reached the checkout area. At the first one with a light on a pole saying it was open, I waited in line for shoppers to take care of a few items ahead of me and then showed the clerk my picture, asking the same question—have you seen this woman lately and a man with her?

The answer was always the same. No, nobody remembered seeing her.

Getting strange looks from two of the clerks who I'd seen watching me go through one checkout line after another, I eventually made my way through every one, questioning each clerk.

"What? That dude's a priest?" the final clerk asked.

I saw where his finger pointed. "He's studying to become one. I guess he shops here?"

The young man glanced behind me, where no customers had lined up. "Let me see that better." The teen took the phone and spread the photo of Daria and the others even wider. "I only saw him one time."

"Oh. Did you ever see the woman in the picture?"

He nodded. "Yeah. That tight red dress? It's the same kind my daddy's new girlfriend wears. That's really why I noticed her."

I offered a frown to show my sympathy for his plight. "What else did you notice?"

"It seemed weird that she came through the checkout with her buggy empty and didn't even seem to realize it. I asked her if she needed anything she didn't find, and then she grabbed a pack of gum."

He was telling me nothing unusual, nothing that could help my sister. "Was anyone with her?"

He shook his head. "Not that I remember. But that dude—" He shifted the picture and blew it up more, touching the seminarian's face. "He came in here—yeah, it might have been right after her—except he was wearing a baseball cap pulled kind of low over his face with some big sunglasses that seemed crazy in a store. But people do crazy things, ya know?" He shrugged. "Or maybe he had cataract surgery and needed those glasses a little while. That's what happened to my paw-paw."

I grabbed his hand to keep his attention. "Did the woman do anything else? Or was there something else that made you remember him, especially if he might have been around her?"

The clerk drew his head back, eyes narrowing. "Are you sure it's okay to tell you this stuff? Is there some kind of reward or something?"

I kept nodding. "Yes, indeed." *Your reward is in heaven.* "So what else about this man in the picture?"

He leaned toward me, arms animated. "Well, that dude threw a twenty at me, and all he had was some bread. And his twenty slipped down to the floor, and I told him wait for his change, but he was taking off, telling me to keep it and then ran outside. It was weird, man. Not that I'm complaining, ya know, keeping the change from a twenty for a loaf of bread."

I also was recalling a man in this store wearing a baseball cap and sunglasses. He'd been beyond the aisle where I stood. He'd walked on the other side of Daria. I hadn't been able to see him well when they'd gone through the checkout and then he'd taken off right behind her.

Were his pants and shoes black? I tried to recall but could not.

"Anything else?" I asked, my breath speeding.

The clerk shook his head, eyes locating the person pushing the buggy that tapped my behind.

I thanked him, hurried out, and swerved off in my truck, envisioning the implications of what might have happened. But could a man studying to become a priest carry out all of the recent violence?

Absolutely. Countless childhoods were lost to people of all occupations, including priests and surely those trying to become one. Had that happened with this person? Had the man taken two people's adulthoods—and almost a third—my sister's?

My first instinct was to call the police. Second thoughts made me wonder what I would tell him.

I learned the man who was probably a seminarian went through this store behind Daria Snelling the day after her husband's funeral and bought a loaf of bread with a twenty. He told the salesclerk to keep the change and then hurried outside. Oh, and look, he sort of grinned in this picture taken right after Zane's ashes flew. Yes, I saw a couple of other people do the same, like an automatic response to an antic. Me? My reaction was to sing "Jingle Bells."

Okay, so I didn't contact the police.

I wanted to bounce my ideas against my sister's mind and discover what she thought. Trying her cell again, I received no response except that her inbox was full, probably from all my messages.

Did I really think a man of the cloth was killing everyone? Shoulders sinking, I knew I had to tone down my detecting urge. Probably I just wanted to protect Eve so badly I was ready to believe any suggestion of who might hurt her so he'd be locked up.

Maybe a conversation with the seminarian would appease me. I might ask why he smiled after Zane's ashes flew and then surely hear that was his sudden reaction to what was an unexpected turn of events, a reaction he regretted afterward. Maybe that's what he did in the store, showed Daria how he'd grinned and then apologized. I could also check him out closer to see if I could distinguish his features and know for certain he was the man I'd seen with Daria in the store that day.

Feeling almost like a regular churchgoer, I returned to St. Gertrude's. This time I pulled up on the driveway beside the priest's house. Two cars were there, a small and a large sedan. I didn't know what kind of car either man drove.

Nobody was in the yard, so I trotted up the wooden steps to the porch and rang the doorbell. A woman wearing casual slacks and dark gray hair pulled into a knot greeted me. "No, I don't think Mr. Landers is in, but Father Prejean is. Would you like to speak with him?"

Not sure what I would tell the priest, I said, "Yes." I sat to wait only a moment before he stepped from a rear room, gave me a pleasant smile and a handshake, and invited me into his office.

Soft black leather chairs and shelves of books with worn looks and old smells filled the room. I sat with legs tense in the chair he offered, and instead of going behind his large desk, he pulled up a chair right in front of mine.

"What is it you'd like to talk to me about?" he asked with a solemn face, hands clasped.

"Oh, I didn't want you to hear my confession again or anything," I said with a shudder and sudden realization that was why he thought I'd shown up. "Actually, I'm just here to speak to your seminarian. Is he around?"

Father scooted back in his chair. "He isn't at the moment, but he should get back soon. He was supposed to be here a couple of hours ago for our confirmation class, but he probably forgot it was today. I took over for him."

"Do you know where he went?" Maybe I could go find him, surprise him out of this natural habitat.

The priest nodded. "Probably to get a haircut. Or no, he got one three days ago. Maybe he went shopping for one item or another, or to visit a parishioner. Yes, that's probably it. Did you want to wait for him or have me tell him what you want?"

"No, that's okay, Father. Thank you." I rushed out the building before he could press me for my purpose. I wouldn't tell him I wanted to see if his understudy looked like a killer.

Next, I needed to relay my information to where people with lots more resources than I did might trace an individual and hoped Detective Wilet didn't just laugh at my ideas.

Chapter 26

The detective didn't want my information. I'd called the office, learned he wasn't there, and left a message, saying it was urgent that he return my call soon.

"Do you remember that story about crying wolf?" he asked when he called ten minutes later. "And I am working on other cases."

"I know, but I'm so scared for my sister," I said in a sorrowful tone.

"I realize that." His voice revealed compassion. "But you can't jump around looking for any bit of evidence you think might point to a guilty party. You could wind up in a slander case. Or at the end of a gun barrel."

"Hmm." Those concepts were uncomfortable.

"You need to stop searching for a killer yourself." He paused as though letting that idea sink in. "You know that a killer is dangerous. He kills. If he doesn't succeed the first time, he'll often try again. And if you're in his line of sight, he won't think twice."

"But my sister—"

"This person won't hesitate to kill both of you."

I shoved out a sigh. "Okay. But you'll stay on her case, all right? See if you can find that seminarian. I could bring a phone by with his picture on it if you'd like."

"That's okay. I think we can find everything we need."

Withholding the urge to tell him to check with the priest to find out what kind of car the seminarian drove, I thanked him and hung up. He could discover that, too.

What was I thinking? I'd just stupidly told a man accustomed to detecting that a person soon to become a priest had carried out horrible things just because he smiled and then spoke to Daria and forgot to show up for a confirmation class? Eek, why did I think I could figure this all out alone?

I recalled the years I'd grown up feeling poorly about myself. But I was an adult now and shrugged away self-doubt. I had learned from reading mysteries that a murderer needed to have means, motive, and an opportunity. Zane died first. I'd known from the start that his wife had the means and opportunity. What I'd learned since then was her motive. He had been having affairs and had a large amount of money stashed. He'd planned to take it and one of his women away, Daria discovered, so she killed him. Perfect. Case solved.

Except soon afterward somebody murdered her.

I sucked in a breath. Now, *her* killer could have been... Who? And why? The means and opportunity were easy for someone getting to her, too. The killer went to her backdoor and right inside, smashed her head. That person could have used almost any hard object, I guessed, but did she open the door to that person, or had the killer broken in? The police surely checked that and wouldn't tell me, but I could go back there and check closely myself. So the person who killed her did it because...

Maybe it was one of Zane's lovers? Yes, that was it. Either Lillian or Daria's older sister knew Daria had killed him and then killed her for revenge.

Could it have been Lillian? She'd seemed a vengeful person. I recalled Daria's sister arguing with Lillian in her front yard but could never believe a woman would kill her own sister. So did that mean Lillian did it? I had no idea.

Putting that case aside, I moved on to the one most important to me. Who would want to hurt Eve? I couldn't imagine any of her three exes trying to hurt her. But then there were their wives or girlfriends or even a fiancé's brother—Eve's pseudo-boyfriend Dave Price—or possibly a neighbor or person from her line-dance class, and maybe it was a person I didn't even know.

Not figuring where else to go, I returned to her house. I hoped against hope that I might find her inside. Together we might determine what to do with new information I'd gathered.

Glancing at windows next door, I saw no sign of anyone watching me in Eve's driveway. I unlocked her door and stood in the foyer, scanning the area, listening intensified, body alert. Nothing moved. The air conditioner purred. The steady *pa-bump pa-bump* was blood pulsing in my head.

Then it happened. As I'd hoped, the burglar alarm wailed. Without checking, I knew it still hadn't been set for someone to be in the house.

I didn't need to look around every room for her or someone who might want to kill her. Dave's company would call Eve to ask for the word that would let them know she'd accidentally set it off. Would she answer her phone now? Had she cleared out some messages so that their call would go through to her?

I stood in place, letting the shrill blast slam through my body. It assaulted my eardrums. Squeezed my nerves till I felt like a twisted rubber band.

The call came. I was gripping my phone in expectation. Eve calling to tell me somebody broke into her house again? Then I could talk to her about other concerns.

"This is Downtown Alarm Systems," a woman said, to my dismay since I was Eve's first backup number. She asked if I could tell her the code word for this address.

I said, "Painting," and she thanked me. Total silence fell like a dropped curtain.

Unless I set the alarm to show someone was inside now, it would probably be counting down again and in less than two minutes, release another nerve-shattering squeal.

Was the gun still here? I dashed to the end table near the sofa and yanked open the drawer. Eve hadn't taken it. Someone could get into her house again and try to use it on her when she returned. That thought made me grab the thing and shove it in the pocket of my slacks. I rushed to the door and made it out seconds before the alarm sounded. At least I knew Dave's product still worked.

Dave, I thought, driving off. That enticing man had even attracted me. The mental image of him made me want to see him again. No, he couldn't have tried to harm Eve.

Once again, I wondered if it could it have been two separate people. One going after a certain item and painting that note on her wall and later another person going after her?

I refused to believe that option. Some man wanted something he believed she possessed.

Having a cold lethal weapon on my body frightened me. The thought of a person breaking into Eve's home and using this weapon on her scared me much more. I skimmed the area outside her house. Walking around it with heightened awareness that a gun was in my pocket made me concerned that I might need to use it. Just point and fire, she'd said. I could do that if need be, I told myself, looking for neighbors outside or peeking from their windows.

I saw no one. If Miss Hawthorne was correct, a man had run between the fences behind Eve's house to reach my street and then rushed down it as though he were a jogger. That man wore black dress shoes and black cuffed slacks. Maybe I could ask Father Prejean if the seminarian wore cuffed pants if he didn't return to their house soon. But what kind of proof could that answer provide?

Considering when Miss Hawthorne first mentioned black slacks to me, I seemed to recall she said a small green thing hanging from one cuff was what drew her attention to those cuffs above the dress shoes. I had discovered small green balls on the tips of a cypress tree near the Snelling pond. The seminarian and priest had been planting a cypress tree when I first met them.

So what did that mean? The green item my neighbor noticed may have been a blade of grass or piece of thread.

Discouraged, I sat on one of my sister's patio chairs to think. Yes, Eve had come walking from her neighbor's house on the left that day, and a man wearing a knit hat pulled down over his face had stood there on the right and shot at her. I sang a little about roasting chestnuts, reliving those moments, and thought about Crystal dying in front of me years ago. My song grew in intensity while shivers vibrated inside, and I pulled the image back, making my insight return to today. Here and now was where a threat to my living sister existed. But why? What did that person want?

As if being pulled by a string, my eyes turned to Eve's fountain and the splashing where an angel poured chlorinated water. No live angel in the current scene and not in events happening around us.

This angel was pure white, newly painted by Eve after she'd drained her pond and attacked the whole thing with her paintbrush. The angel kept dumping water that sounded like a fast waterfall. It splashed when it hit the surface of the water in the base and some of it bounced off the large molded goldfish. When one of them swayed under where the angel poured, the fish's nose tipped down and then lifted. Splashes made another one fall over on its side. Immediately, it righted itself.

I picked up two of the plastic fish. Closer inspection let me see what I'd believed. On each one, the seam ran down the center of its back. The seams continued all around, both sides the manufacturer had glued together to make them look uniform. All of the fish looked the same.

I scrambled to my truck. Forcing myself to stay within range of the speed limits, I left my neighborhood and raced along Felicity Bayou to the Snelling home.

If I was correct, I would find answers that would prevent another murder.

Chapter 27

As I expected, no vehicle was at the quiet Snelling house when I pulled in. Shoulders tight, I stepped around the left of the building to the backyard, where I was met by a setting so serene it could have been on the cover of Cajun holiday cards.

The swamp with scrub bushes and vines made a perfect backdrop for the serene area stretched before it. A musky odor from the swamp pinched my nostrils. Yes, what I imagined could have occurred here. Daria could have followed Zane right after overhearing his phone call with Lillian and shoved him so that he tripped on the cypress knees and hit his head on the tree, which knocked him out so he fell in.

I sat on the bench Zane had sat on. It topped the pavers Eve laid over the space we both had dug. I didn't know why Daria died but would inspect the doorframe for signs of forced entry.

Except how would that help me know why anyone would want to harm Eve?

Grass in the yard was growing tall. Clovers and weeds with small yellow flowers could use a cutting. Nothing besides this seating area with a couple of cypress trees would be in the way of a grass cutter since the yard was otherwise empty. That small stack of extra pavers sat beside the backdoor.

My gaze focused on the pond. The water looked peaceful. How could such a peaceful place pose a threat to anyone? Unless a person in it were knocked out or couldn't swim.

Some sections were probably deep. The water appeared murky, undoubtedly because recent strong winds stirred it up, pulling in more of the surrounding dirt. Strings of brown-green algae stretched out from the side. I concentrated on the pair of geese floating out there. A breeze pushed on my back while I eyed those decoys, watching them shift. Zane wasn't a hunter. He hadn't set them out there to attract geese. Neither had he done it for decoration. Nothing else decorated their yard. Except for these pavers and this bench. The bench he'd wanted to sit on alone so he could drink beer?

No—to view his treasure! Those floating birds.

Excitement made a painful grab at my throat. Watching the molded geese turn, I slid on my glasses and stepped to the edge of the pond to see them better. The two were a few feet from shore. Like the goldfish, a central seam glued both of their sides together. Individual feathers appeared to jut out a little from their bodies.

I walked to the right of the pond, watching them. They turned even more with the stronger gust that fluttered the bottom of my shirt. A square appeared to have been cut and glued on the side of one bird. I couldn't tell whether the same thing had been done to the other one. Those geese might provide a large piece of the puzzle of why two people were murdered and almost another one. I needed to keep that third murder from taking place.

I had no idea how deep the water was, but I could swim. With this pond not as clear as a swimming pool, I preferred not to. I moved even more to the right, closer to the house, where the dirt sloped.

Removing my shoes, I stepped out into the water. The coolness surprised me. Dirt under my feet gave way a little and felt pleasant, almost like sand. Not wanting to let my feet sink farther, I stepped quicker. And stubbed my toe.

The water wasn't clear enough to see through, so I reached down and lifted a paver. Why was one here?

My sight swerved toward the stack near the door. Just inside that door, had this been the weapon that smashed Daria's head?

Tossing it to shore, I felt around with my feet for more pavers but discovered only mushy dirt. Those white floating objects had brought me here. I stepped farther out to them. The ground under my feet gave way, and the water deepened.

Taking a minute to adjust, I swam a modified breaststroke, striving to keep my anticipation in check. A retriever must feel like this while it swam for a shot bird, I thought, keeping the geese in view.

I reached the first one. Grabbing the bulky decoy, I lifted it from the water, surprised that it weighed more than I'd expected. Using a modified scissor kick to keep me afloat, I inspected the bird. Yes, some type of adhesive that didn't look altered held both sides together. A connected rope hung below it. I pulled the rope higher and found a small anchor at its end. Of course that was what held the bird in place, yet let it shift on the water's surface.

This decoy might answer a pressing question, yet I thought not.

I let its anchor sink down and let the bird go so it floated again. Kicking my feet under water, I moved to the one farthest from shore.

The second decoy resembled the first one—almost. It bore the same shape and molded feathers and eyes and central seam, but one thing was different. Instead of all the feathers on both sides running from the central seam to the bottom, a section about two inches square had been cut and separately glued.

The job on it had been done well so that it would be barely noticed— unless someone like me would be searching for it.

A thin rope with a small anchor also held this decoy in place on the water. The weight and bulkiness of both geese would create problems for me to try to swim with them together, so I would take one and then get the other.

I grabbed the one with the side cut first. Lifting its string and anchor, I tucked all of this under my left arm, gripping the anchor with that hand. With my right arm, I swam a slow stroke toward shore, my heart racing in anticipation of what this might mean.

I reached the shallow area where I could stand. Doing that made carrying this bulky item through water much easier.

"Yes!" a male voice shouted.

He was behind me. I'd been so busy with the geese and water that I hadn't been checking the shore.

Intense quiet pressed against my eardrums. Until I heard *click*.

Did he cock a pistol? Some unknown person shot and killed Crystal. *This* person tried to kill Eve.

"Sunny!" Dave Price called. *Oh, Dave, I didn't want it to be you.*

Angry and scared, I felt "Jingle Bells" rush from my throat as I shivered and turned, pulling the gun from my pocket, not knowing if it would fire when wet but needing to try. I shot at the person on shore, who satisfied me because it wasn't Dave, and felt the sting of a bullet strike my left shoulder.

The backs of my eyes burned from tears trying to rush out ever since I'd watched Crystal die, but I forced them inside, pouring out my fury on the man facing me. I kept firing the gun until my view of the world dimmed, grew unclear, and went out.

Chapter 28

My eyelids fluttered. A siren screamed from the vehicle transporting me and made me wake up. My arm ached too much. So did my head. I squeezed my eyelids together and forced the agonizing world away.

The next time I opened my eyes a slit, the bed I lay on felt softer. I was no longer moving. The tube in my mouth felt like a hose, and a thick bandage kept my shoulder in place. Needles and tubes were connected to me. My hand—the one without a needle taped to it—felt warm. A hand held mine.

I slid my gaze up from that hand to find the rugged face of Dave Price. He smiled and tightened his grip on my fingers. "She's awake," he said.

Indeed I was, and pleasantly surprised to find him with me. I smiled back at him.

"Good job, Sis. God, I'm so glad you're safe."

Seeing Eve on my other side squeezed opposing reactions inside me. I tugged my hand away from Dave's and smiled at her, happy to see her but not this minute. Right now he was with me. Or had he come with her?

I'd heard him calling my name near the pond. "Where were you?" I asked Dave, although I'd soon want to know the same thing about her.

"I was going to see about a job down the highway past the Snelling home when I noticed your truck in their driveway. I wondered why you were there, so I turned around and went back to find out. I was concerned about you."

"Going there alone was stupid," Eve told me.

"I couldn't find you to come with me."

Her lower lip pushed out. "I am so sorry. After that happened while Dave waited for police and an ambulance, he tried my number and found my messages full, so he texted me and said you'd been shot."

"Where were you?" I asked.

"Being silly, staying at the hotel in town." It was the only one. They wouldn't have let me know whether she was there.

Dave touched my arm. "Eve told me you had an argument that caused her to leave your house and not tell you where she was staying. Although I can't imagine what you two would argue about."

You. I kept the word hidden inside my mouth.

"I parked in front of the Snellings' place," Dave told me, "and walked to the back, calling your name. That was probably about the same time the seminarian yelled something and shot at you."

Eve bent down and hugged me. "I am so glad you're safe."

"Me, too." I embraced the love she was sharing. Her soft cheek against mine made me feel at peace, as though I were floating.

I'd drifted off, I later learned. I learned many things in bits and pieces, some from Eve, a little from Dave, much of the information from Detective Wilet, who came to visit and question me and fill me in.

The man who'd been a seminarian would need crutches in prison for a long time. Good. I'd been firing wildly but got him in the knee. He had parked down the road and had been searching around the Snelling house, trying to find a way inside when he heard my truck. Then he hid on the other side of the house and watched me bring what held the treasure to him, he thought. But Dave was hurrying near when he heard the gunshots. He knocked out the seminarian and rushed into the water and plucked me out.

Motives and events that transpired to get so many people involved began to take shape. Landers, the seminarian, confessed he had begun having an affair with Daria while assigned to a church in New Orleans, a city she'd often visited. She had told him she wanted to leave Zane and would as soon as she found the cache of illegal money he'd received from his grandpa.

So Miss Hawthorne was right about Zane's gangster elder, although I wouldn't want to know whether he really went around commando.

Daria had killed Zane during their argument once she ran out of their house after him. His conceit about his prowess with women better than she was made Daria determine she'd dump his ashes so people could walk on him and grind his ashes into the church's carpet. She'd brought that nail file, the seminarian confessed, and worked to pry the glue loose from the minute she had the urn in her hand. And she ripped the plastic bag inside.

He met her at the grocery store the next day when I saw them, but she hadn't wanted him to stay around her in a public place, so she'd rushed away. He followed to her house, confronting her at the backdoor where they couldn't be seen. He wanted his share of Zane's cache that she'd promised would simplify their lives.

Daria ordered him away, saying she wasn't sure where the money was but would find it and tell him. He figured she would take the fortune and run. He had already ruined his future by fooling around with her.

Spotting the extra pavers Eve had stacked near the door, he grabbed one and smashed Daria's head with it. She went down inside her kitchen door. He panicked and spied the blinking light on the answering machine on the counter. Maybe someone saying they were coming right over. He punched the playback button.

It was my message telling Daria I was the tall redhead from the funeral, not bothering to say there were two of us, and I had something important of her husband's. She should call me.

Of course she never did. But the seminarian was in so much trouble already and needed a lot of money to get a distance away. He figured Daria's caller had the stash from Zane's grandpa. He had once visited a parishioner down Eve's street, noticed Eve at her mailbox, and thought she was that redheaded caller. He broke into her house through the sliding door but couldn't get beyond it. Furious, he smashed her paintings and wrote on the wall.

As days passed, he'd grown more desperate. He returned to her house with a gun and tools to get past her studio. Of course Eve was in the backyard. He'd been ready to shoot her, but I was inside the glass door and scared him away, making his gunshot miss her when she dropped to the ground.

It seemed Zane's grandfather had hoarded numerous large bills he'd gathered illegally, five hundred dollar bills and ten thousand dollar gold certificates, no longer printed but still legal tender and worth many more times their original value.

Zane hid this inside the goose he then floated in the middle of his pond. The seminarian said Zane had told Daria of a stash, maybe at first planning to share it with her and leave town. Second thoughts most likely came once he continued affairs with other women. He probably hadn't decided when he would leave Daria and needed to make arrangements about where to live, and with whom, so the law wouldn't become suspicious.

"In the meantime, he'd enjoy sitting alone in the area you and I prepared for him and watching his fortune float right in front of his wife's nose," Eve said. "And he drank scotch, not beer, as he'd told me."

The detective said Daria's older sister had let Zane rest at her house whenever he worked in the town where she'd lived. One thing led to another, she'd told police, and Zane swore to her he no longer loved Daria. That had been easy for her to believe, especially since Daria had always been the spoiled sister.

I could relate. I loved my twin, but had sometimes felt a pinch jealous and hadn't minded a few of the times Eve didn't seem totally happy.

But what about these new feelings I'd been experiencing? Every time Dave came around, which he did often to check on me, I wanted him to stay close. My whole body turned warm, with an inner tugging toward him.

I was released from the hospital, and he came to see me at my house, where I insisted I stay while Eve returned to hers. We sisters needed to work on getting our lives back to normal.

"I'm really sorry I pretended to be Eve when I first met you," I told Dave while we sat alone near each other on my sofa.

The right corner of his lips tilted up. "I knew you weren't Eve. I'd met her once, and she came on a little strong, a trait I don't normally admire in a woman." He leaned his face closer to mine so that his breath feathered my lips. "I prefer one who isn't so bold."

I wanted to be that woman for him. An instinct tugged inside, making me want to move closer, to snuggle my body against his.

But he was my sister's. Eve wanted him. And she found him first.

Dave's grin widened. "I also knew you weren't her that first day at her house because of the striking gold flecks in your blue eyes."

Striking? Gold? I was flattered, struggling with temptation.

"I also knew you two were playing me. When Eve phoned you in her house to ask if you were all right while you sat next to me on her sofa, I could hear every word she said."

"Oh." I felt my cheeks growing pink. "I guess I should have moved away from you sooner."

He chuckled a good-hearted laugh. I laughed with him. My laugh didn't feel so sincere. Maybe a smile or a laugh now and then was all I would ever share with this man.

Eve visited Mom, giving her more accurate news than she might have heard otherwise. She promised Mom for me that I would be in to see her soon once I healed up a little better. She also told Grace her pictures had helped police solve a mystery.

"Grace keeps bragging about that to everyone who visits the retirement home," Eve told me.

People kept calling Eve and me, rescheduling jobs they'd canceled. Word got around quickly about all that transpired with the Snellings and seminarian and me and my twin. New customers wanted us to work for them. We made lists, needing to put people off until my shoulder and achy joints improved.

Detective Wilet returned my silk jacket bearing some of Zane's ashes. I knew what I would do with them.

Chapter 29

I contacted Lillian, the one woman I felt had truly still loved this man, and extended my sympathy.

But he'd been playing different women, pretending he loved each one of them. Zane Snelling died because his wife discovered all she had about his romances. Lillian didn't want any of his ashes.

Eve drove me where I wanted to go. Beside the pond in the backyard of the Snelling residence, I removed my jacket. I'd once thought Zane was a great guy and had wanted to find a proper place to bury him.

"Turns out he was hot stuff. He needs to cool off." I turned my pocket inside out, rubbing out all of the ashes I could into the water. Still, a few remained caught in threads along the seam.

I tied my jacket into a big knot and threw it out as far as I could. We watched the thing bubble up and sink.

"I'm good," I told Eve.

She hugged me. "I just want you to be happy." Her eyes were intense with sincerity.

I was a stronger person now. We both were. Yes, this was the time.

"I want to tell you something," I said. "I believe you may have been right when you spoke in the manor the other day. I think what I do need is a gratifying romantic relationship."

"Yes! Oh, Sunny!" Hands clasped together, Eve looked thrilled.

I dreaded popping her happy bubble, but I must. I needed to tell her the truth. She wouldn't be at all pleased with the man I hoped to share that warm encounter with.

Her brows lifted, eyes as wide as I'd ever seen them while she watched my lips, waiting for them to express more about my anticipated romance.

Her phone rang. She'd obviously gotten rid of some extra messages.

"That's okay," she told me, glancing at her purse hanging on her arm. "Come on, Sis, tell me more. I can't wait to hear about this."

I opened my mouth to do that, but she yanked her phone out of her purse.

"Wait, it's Randy. I need to check this call." Her eyes spread even widener while she listened. Her face that showed total joy minutes ago now expressed pure ecstasy. Her lips squeezed together and quivered.

"What?" I asked.

"It's a boy!"

It took seconds for me to swallow and let her words drop inside me. "My sister's a grandma." A tear of happiness rolled down my cheek.

I wrapped my arms around Eve. She was still living. And soon both of us would rush to snuggle the unseen child we already loved. He was the main male she and I would be talking about for quite some time.

One day, though, I would need to tell her about the other one.

Meet the Author

From the bayou country of South Louisiana, June Shaw previously sold a series of humorous mysteries to Five Star, Harlequin, and Untreed Reads. Publishers Weekly praised her debut, Relative Danger, which became a finalist for the David Award for Best Mystery of the Year. A hybrid author who has published other works, she has represented her state on the board of Mystery Writers of America's Southwest Chapter for many years and continued to serve as the Published Author Liaison for Romance Writers of America's Southern Louisiana chapter. She gains inspiration for her work from her faith, family, and friends, including the many readers who urge her on. For more info please visit juneshaw.com.